Replacement

DATE DUE

L

E

PRINTED IN U.S.A.

One
LAST TIME

NEW YORK TIMES BESTSELLING AUTHOR
CORINNE MICHAELS

Editor:
Ashley Williams, AW Editing

Proofreading:
Kara Hildebrand, Janice Owen & Virginia Carey

Cover Design:
Sommer Stein, Perfect Pear Creative

Cover photo © Perrywinkle Photography

DEDICATION

To women who stay when they should leave . . .

You deserve to be loved.

You deserve to be happy.

You deserve to be free.

CHAPTER ONE

KRISTIN

"JUST LEAVE THEN!" I scream at my husband as he tells me, once again, how worthless I am. I've had it. Years I've stayed by his side, but I won't do this anymore. No one should feel this empty and unloved.

"I'm not leaving this house, Kristin. If you want this to be over, then pack your shit and get the hell out of my house."

I stare at the man I've loved since I was twenty-two. The father of my children. The person I thought I'd grow old beside. The man before me is a mirage of that man. Scott has changed so much in the last fourteen years that he's unrecognizable. Now, he's just someone that I used to love.

The man I knew would never throw me away so easily. He would've done anything to make it work.

"This isn't just your house, Scott. I'm your wife!"

He shakes his head with a smirk. "I'm the one who pays for it. How will you afford your designer lifestyle without a job?"

Designer lifestyle? I can't remember the last time I bought

myself anything. Mostly because I'd rather not listen to how stupid I am.

"I'll get a job and do what I need to. I'm not moving out because of that."

He rubs the bridge of his nose. "So, now you'll work, but not the last ten years?"

"You wanted me to stay home with Aubrey and Finn! *You* told me to quit my job, you don't get to throw it back in my face!" I slam my hand on the table.

It's like *Groundhog Day* with us. The same fight, over and over, with nothing ever reconciling. I have a master's in communications, and it's the one thing neither of us does well.

Scott demanded I quit my job as a reporter when we found out I was pregnant with Finn. I was always traveling, covering breaking stories, and he felt I wouldn't be able to devote enough time to being a mom.

At first, it made sense. I always wanted to be the kind of mother who baked cookies or sent the kids off to school with a kiss on the cheek and their lunches made. My mom was that way, and I have the fondest memories because of it. I think she might have been part alien because, most days, I'm lucky if my kids wear clothes that match and have enough money in their lunch accounts.

My life is nothing like I thought it'd be. Instead of baking, I'm running around trying to keep the house clean so he isn't angry. I spend an hour at the gym so Scott doesn't tell me how I've let myself go. Between trying to look like the perfect wife and mother and actually being one, I'm drowning.

And Scott is holding my head under as I gasp for air.

Scott grips the edge of the table and stares at me. "I'm always the bad guy here. I *made* you leave your job. I *made* you have kids. I *made* you be the miserable woman you are. I'm the one who made you cold and bitter, right? I did it all. So fucking go!"

Tears spring up in my eyes as he slashes my heart apart. "I'm that expendable to you?"

Scott's eyes fill with rage. "You're the one who wants to leave, Kristin. It's you standing there, all high and mighty and telling *me* to leave. God forbid, I want a wife who actually likes me. When was the last time you actually wanted to have sex with me? When have you given me what I need, huh?"

Once again, we move to the next part of the argument. "It's hard to want someone who makes you feel like shit."

"And how do I do that, Kris? By telling you the truth about your issues?"

My issues. It's always my issues, even when we talk about his. It's me who causes his reactions. Scott has no accountability for anything that happens in our life. It's always bounced to someone else. I'm so damn tired of being the reason for everything wrong in his life, of feeling small.

"Sure, Scott. That's it."

There's no point in arguing. I've tried so many times, and nothing I say matters.

Our kids are with my parents, and this was supposed to be a weekend for us to reconnect. My mother knew we were at the breaking point, and I wanted to try one more time. I thought that if we could spend some time together, just us, we'd find a way.

It seems I was a fool once again.

"I'm so tired of having to fix everything in this marriage," Scott says as he paces around the room. "You keep saying you want to make me happy, but then you do everything wrong. It's exhausting repeating myself."

Yeah, it's exhausting, all right.

I feel myself start to drift to that place in my head to protect myself. There's only so much I can take before I'm completely shattered. "Stop," I beg.

"When will you learn, Kristin? If you gave a little more effort, I wouldn't be so disappointed."

I do nothing right. Nothing. I don't dress the way he thinks I should, raise the kids the way his mother did, look the way I did when he fell in love with me, and Lord knows, I don't please him in any way.

"I guess I'll never learn," I say to pacify him.

"I guess not." He crosses his arms over his chest and stares at me.

My husband was once a good man. He doted on me and told me I was the most beautiful woman he'd ever beheld. Everything about us seemed to just fit. Two years after we were married . . . it changed. No longer was I perfect for him. Instead, I was difficult and needy. It was a snowball that kept growing bigger the farther it rolled. I thought I could make him happy, so I tried harder and failed more.

He wanted a baby. If I could give him a child, we'd be fine. I truly believed that, but each month I got my period, he'd remind me how I couldn't even give him a baby.

The day I found out I was pregnant with Finn, things changed. The man I love came back to me. But after Aubrey, I was back to being worthless.

That snowball has rolled me over and left me lifeless.

"It never changes," he huffs. "I'm done trying!"

So am I. I'm tired of being tired. I'm over having my heart

trampled for nothing. He'll never love me. I've got nothing left to give.

"How did we get here?" My voice cracks as the pain takes hold. "How has this become our life? I used to love you so much it hurt to breathe, and now? Now, it just hurts. I can't do this anymore. I can't spend every night with us at each other's throats. It's too hard."

"If you'd just try to do more—"

"If I'd just? Are you kidding me? All I do is try! All I do is give you what you want, but it's never enough!" My God. How can this be all on me? I can't possibly be that bad. I do try. I try and try, and it never changes.

Scott runs his hands down his face. "You used to be."

"Right." A tear falls. "I used to be a lot of things, and so did you."

My heart squeezes and everything inside me hurts. I look at Scott, wanting one reason to fight. If I could find some glimmer of hope that we could figure out a way, I'd garner the strength to go on.

His eyes meet mine, and I know there's nothing left to fight for.

There's no hope left, and I break. A strangled sound escapes my lips at the loss I feel deep in my bones.

He moves quickly, gathering me into his arms, and I sob. I clutch him, needing to hold on because I feel so alone.

"Don't cry, baby. I hate when you cry. This isn't what I want for us, Kris."

Maybe I was wrong. Maybe he does care. "I don't want to fight anymore."

Scott takes my head in his hands and his eyes are soft. "Then do better."

This is what he does to me. He breaks me down and then does something sweet to make me think it was in my head. I'm so fucked up because of it.

He doesn't want *me*. He wants some version of this woman, and I can't be that. I'm tired of trying to be that because it isn't possible. The reality is . . . he doesn't love me anymore, and I won't live like this.

I pull back, needing space because I'll fall right back into our pattern.

I hate that two people who would've done anything for each other are so far apart they can't even see each other anymore. Our relationship is a series of battles, all of which I've lost.

"This isn't okay." I sniff. "The way you treat me. The things you say about me . . . it's not okay, Scott."

His eyes close, and a tear falls down my cheek. We both know this is the end, but I don't know how to take the first step.

Anger is easy to hold on to. It's the loss of all hope that is killing me inside.

"I'm not going to apologize for the truth. I think you should pack and leave."

I don't want to lose my husband, but I won't be this woman anymore.

I take a step back, wipe the moisture from my cheek, and nod. "I hoped . . ." I'm not sure what I hoped for. Maybe it was for him to love me enough, but he never did.

His brown eyes pierce through me. "I'm tired of being miserable and neglected."

Hurt and anger flood through me. He's such an asshole. He thinks *he's* neglected? Unreal. I erect the walls around my battered heart so nothing else he'll say will hurt me. "Okay then. I'm sorry you feel that way. Where do we go from here?" I ask matter-of-factly.

"I want a divorce."

Four words.

Four words are all it takes to destroy my seemingly perfect life.

"And what do we tell the kids?" I choke on the words. Scott may be a shitty husband, but he's always been a great father.

This is what hurts deeper than anything he's done to me. The fact that we'll disrupt our children's lives with this is almost more than I can take.

Those two little angels are what have kept us trying this long. Finn and Aubrey don't deserve the home they're living in now, though. The constant fighting, the angry words, finding their father on the couch night after night. It isn't healthy or fair to anyone.

Aubrey is who I worry about. She adores her father, and this will destroy her. Every little girl's first love is her father, and I hate that she'll know what it's like to lose him in a small way.

Scott grips the back of his neck and drops his head. "I don't know."

When his eyes lift, I see the glimmering of unshed tears. A tiny glimpse of the man I once knew returns. I know he's in there, and I wish he'd come back. I take a step forward. My heart is pulled in so many different directions. Wanting to save him, wanting to love him, and wanting to leave.

Then I remember that he's done. He's said the words that he can't ever take back. In all the years we've been battling this, we've never said the d-word. I thought if one of us ever did that I would fall to pieces. In my head, the scene was of me crying and begging him to love me, him assuring me that he did, and then we'd find a way. I hadn't realized that even in the sadness, there would be a swell of relief. I've been in purgatory for so long. I'm ready to live my life again.

"Well." I suck in a breath. "I think the first thing we do is decide who leaves, and then we should make a plan to talk to the kids."

Scott and I sit at the table, and for the first time all night, we act like adults. There's no screaming or name-calling. We work to create a list of things that need to be handled and who will tackle each task. We don't have much debt, which is thanks to the inheritance my grandfather left me, so that is handled quickly. We both agree to tell the kids together and try to keep things civil. The last two items are the ones that will be where, hopefully, this whole grown-up act doesn't fall apart.

The house and the kids.

He's going to have to kill me before he gets the kids. I won't give them up.

"We've put these off, but we should make the choices," Scott says with his hands clasped.

"The house." I place the pen on the table.

This is the one I'm willing to concede if I have to. I can live with my parents or ask my best friend, Heather, to stay at her place since it's empty. There are options for me, but I can't live without my babies.

"I'd like to stay here. You can't pay the mortgage, and I can't afford rent and the mortgage," Scott requests.

"What about the kids?" I switch because, really, that's all that matters.

He sighs. "I won't do that to you."

"You won't what?"

I pray he's telling me he won't try to take them. They're all I have.

He runs his fingers through his hair. "As much as I want them, I can't do it. I travel too much, and we both know Finn will never leave you. However, I want them on weekends and stuff like that. I love them, too."

"Thank you," I say with gratitude.

We both agree that he'll remain in the house, but we'll split some of the furniture to keep the kids as comfortable as possible. I'm not sure how this will work, but at least we're in agreement for the most part.

I climb into bed and the cold sheets cause me to shiver. My hand slides across to where my husband should be, but it's empty. Scott won't be there anymore. The events of the day come crashing around me.

It's really over. My husband and I are divorcing.

I clutch the pillow and bury my face, trying to muffle the sounds of my uncontrollable crying. I never knew a heart could hurt so much, but I'm in agony. I love him, but it's over. We couldn't make things work, and I've failed. I gasp for breath as the tears soak my pillow.

"Kristin?" His deep voice fills the room.

"Please don't," I plead. I don't want him to see me this way.

Scott moves forward anyway and then crouches beside me. Even in the dark, I see the pain in his eyes. "Don't cry, baby."

That breaks me. I cry harder than before, and he pulls me into his arms. He holds me to his chest, and I struggle to gain control. There's just no stopping the tears. I cry for the years we had, the years we've lost, and the years we'll never have. I would've stayed if he told me he wanted to try. I know it's stupid, but giving up on him feels like defeat.

After a while, I start to relax. My heart still aches, but I'm not sobbing. Scott rubs my back, and I sniffle. "I'll be okay."

He leans back and cups my face. "Are you sure?"

"I'm just sad."

"I'm not happy about this, either, Kris."

That's the worst part, we both love each other, but we can't fix what's broken. "I know."

His forehead rests on mine, and we both sit here. Scott's thumb moves across my cheek as he tilts my head up. "I loved you, Kristin." His voice is husky. "You were the most beautiful woman in the world."

My heart races as something shifts between us. "Scott," I whisper. I'm not sure if I'm asking him to stop or to keep going. How do you stop loving someone? How do you push away the only man you've ever loved?

He's still my husband.

The air in the room is charged as we breathe each other in. Scott's other hand glides to my neck before sliding down my chest. My body tingles as he grazes my breast.

"Tell me to stop, and I will," he murmurs against my lips. "One more time, Kris. I need this. I need to feel you."

Confliction stirs, but I'm so raw I can't say the words no matter how much I want to. I've been lonely, and I want to be loved for once.

Just as our lips brush, Scott plunges forward. He guides me to my back as I welcome his weight above me. His mouth melts against mine, and I kiss him like none of the events of the day happened. He moans into my mouth while I cling to him. I need him to make me feel alive.

It's been so long. Too long to count since we've made love. How many nights did I pray he'd come to me, love me, but he hadn't.

My hands tangle in his dark brown hair, holding his lips to mine. I force myself to pretend we're still madly in love and life is perfect.

But we aren't perfect.

This is a fantasy that will end in tragedy if I get lost in the illusion.

Those four words ring in my head, reminding me why I was crying to begin with.

I can't do this to myself.

One more time won't do anything to stop what's coming. He doesn't love me anymore.

I disappoint him.

I fail him.

I'm not good enough.

"I can't," I say as I push his shoulders. "I can't do this, Scott."

He rolls off me and onto his back and covers his face. "You can't?"

"If it's over, then we have to act like it. You can't want to divorce me but then make love to me. It's too confusing." I sit up and adjust my clothes back.

Scott gets to his feet and walks to the door. He pauses and looks back at me. "It's fine. It's not like it's ever that good anyway."

He closes the door, and I curl up, clutching my knees to my chest as I cry as quietly as I can manage.

CHAPTER TWO

KRISTIN

~ Six Months Later ~

"FINN, move that box into your new room," I instruct him when I find him sitting on the couch with his headphones on.

"I'm watching a video," he snaps back.

"I don't care. You have to help," I say as Heather, Danielle, and Nicole carry boxes inside.

Heather places a box on the floor and rubs Finn's head. "Hey, can you help Eli with the table?"

He looks at his "aunt" and smiles. "Sure thing."

One day, I'll remember why I wanted children. I smile at my best friend who is standing in what used to be her home. There's not a day in my life that I don't thank God for my broken ankle in seventh grade that forced Heather into my life. She's saving my ass right now by giving the kids and a me place to live—rent-free.

"Thanks a lot, Finn! I'm not putting up with this attitude of yours," I yell at the back of his head.

Finn glares at me and crosses his arms. "I didn't ask to move."

"Let him be, honey." Heather squeezes my hand. "We're here to help."

I close my eyes and count to five. I know this has been hard for the kids, but Finn has been unbearable. Aubrey isn't a walk in the park, but at least she's mainly stuck to tears, which can be comforted.

"I wish this were easier," I muse.

"I'm sure, but they'll adjust." She smiles reassuringly.

If anyone knows about adjusting, it's Heather. Her life has been one thing after another, and she's still standing.

We both make our way into my bedroom and start unloading clothes.

"Was Scott still his ever-lovely self on the phone earlier?"

She caught that. I guess being a cop for as long as she has been makes her the most observant of us all.

My husband—soon to be ex-husband—has made my life absolute hell during the last month. He's gone back and forth on everything we agreed upon. I had hoped we'd have a smooth separation and then an amicable divorce. I should've known better.

Nothing with Scott is ever easy, but when you add money in, forget it.

He's threatened everything under the sun to keep from having to pay for anything.

"He now wants to discuss more of a joint custody agreement so that he doesn't have to pay any child support. He says he's paid his dues, and if I want to push him, he'll go for full custody."

"Such a fucking prick," she grumbles as she places shirts in the dresser.

"Yup."

"So, he's threatening you?"

I sigh and place the hanger on the rack. "Not threatening as much as making this difficult. We got the divorce papers, and they are completely ridiculous. Nothing we had agreed on is there. I mean, basically, he wants me to walk away from the marriage without a penny and pay him."

He's out of his freaking mind if he thinks that's going to happen. I've suffered through his constant bullshit, and I tried to make things civil. If he wants a fight, then I'll fight.

"I really wish you'd find a reason for me to legally shoot him."

I laugh, wishing I could as well. "He's not worth it."

She leans her hip on the dresser. "No, he's not, but you are."

Am I? I don't feel like I'm worth a damn right now. I just landed a job, thanks to Heather. I only have a roof over my head, thanks to Heather. The minimal furniture here is because of Nicole being an interior designer—I swear she takes stuff from the houses she stages, and my form of child-care is Danielle.

Really, what am I worth?

My friends are worth their weight in gold, but I'm the rust that needs scraping.

"I don't feel like—"

"One of you two!" Nicole yells with strained effort.

"Shit," we both say in unison and rush out. Nic isn't exactly the most graceful of the four of us, and she sure as hell doesn't do manual labor.

When we get into the living room, I rush over and take the top box, which is in front of her face, and restrain my giggle.

"Jesus Christ, it's hotter than Satan's ass out there," Nicole groans as she fumbles with the other box in her hand. "Why do we live in Tampa again?"

"You know what Satan's ass feels like?" Heather asks.

Nicole puts the box down, flips her off, and plops into the chair. "Fan me," she demands.

"I'll get right on that." I laugh.

Danielle exits the kitchen with a glass of ice water. "I've got the cabinets organized."

I smile at the people who have never let me fall. These girls are the only reason I'm functioning right now. All three of them showed up at the house when I texted Danielle the day after Scott and I decided on the divorce. They hugged me as I cried, made me laugh, and forced me to drink wine until I passed out.

Today, they're sweating their asses off and helping me haul boxes and furniture.

Nicole snorts. "I'm sure Kris will redo them all. We know you're not exactly known for your organizational skills."

Danielle slaps the back of her head. "Shut up. You're the one sitting on your ass."

Here we go again.

Heather and I share a knowing look. One of us has to intervene before it ends in a catfight.

I throw my arm around Danielle and squeeze. "I'm sure it's perfect."

"Mommy." Aubrey comes over. "I miss my old room. It was purple."

"I'm sure Aunt Heather will let us paint it." I take her tiny hands in mine and squat so I can look her in the eyes. "You could pick any color you want."

I don't even look to Heather for approval since I already have it. From the first conversation, she's told me I can do anything I want to make this house mine. Plus, I think she's happy to have another excuse not to sell the place. For the last two years, she's been living with her boyfriend Eli, who happens to be an uber-famous singer and actor. His house is the most ridiculous place I've ever seen on Harbour Island, but she's always loved this house. Not that I'm complaining— she's saving my butt from having to move back in with my parents.

It's crazy how they met and became a couple. Who knew that a girls' night out where four friends went to pay homage to their favorite childhood boy band, Four Blocks Down, would result in a love like that? Not me, that's for damn sure.

"I bet we could get Eli to help us," Heather says conspiratorially. "He loves to paint!"

"What does Eli like to do?" His deep voice fills the room, but I can't see his face past all the boxes he's carrying.

Aubrey squeals when she hears his voice and runs back to her room.

I laugh at the sight of this superstar carrying boxes for his girlfriend's best friend. Sometimes, this feels like a cosmic joke the world is playing on me.

Heather heads over and removes a few boxes from his stack. "Babe, it usually helps to see where you're going," she chides.

He looks at the rest of us all sitting or standing around, and he smirks. "I see how it is . . . the men do all the work and you guys supervise?"

It sounds about right.

"At least you're learning, big guy." Nicole lays her head back and closes her eyes.

"Why do you guys like her again?" he asks.

"We're not sure." I shrug. "We've tried to get rid of her, but she's like a bad case of chickenpox. For each one you scratch, another one pops up and is even itchier. We stopped scratching finally."

We're the four most unlikely friends, but we work. Our group is unique, in that while we are all close, we're also close in different ways. Heather is who I call when I need someone to cry to. She's the most sympathetic person out of the three of them. Danielle is who I call for relationship or parenting advice, and Nicole is who I call when I want to forget the night before. She's a nut.

I always thought Danni was my person, but when I told her about the separation, she pulled back a little. At first, I thought it was because we would both commiserate over our shitty marriages and now hers is better, but then she offered to watch the kids for me when I have to work, so maybe I'm imagining it.

"Watch it, Eli," Nicole warns. "You're not officially a member of this tribe. We can still vote your ass off the island."

Eli grins and pulls Heather's back to his chest. His arms wrap around her middle, and I fight the pang of jealousy that arises. "Is that right, baby?"

Heather rolls her eyes and looks over her shoulder. "I'm pretty sure you're staying. It's still debatable, though."

"Can you at least wait a few weeks?"

She shrugs. "I guess so."

He laughs and kisses her. I turn away, wishing it didn't hurt.

Scott used to look at me that way. We were playful, loving, and he made my heart skip a beat. He was my knight in shining armor, and I was the princess he rescued, but the fairy tale is over. There is no happily ever after.

We finish getting everything unloaded, and with as much shit as I give Nicole, the girl is busting her ass to get this place decorated. I now understand why she's one of the top interior designers in Tampa. The house actually looks like a home.

In a few hours, we are able to get the main living areas pretty much done. Nicole directs where the guys should move the furniture, and she manages to mesh what I was able to take from my old house with what she brought.

Scott refused to let me take anything except the bedroom furniture. He said he didn't want to be reminded of what we once shared. I don't even know what he means, but it was one less thing I had to buy.

"I'm beat," I say as I collapse onto the couch. Nicole is the only one still here.

"Me, too."

I rest my hand on her leg and wait for her to look at me. "Thank you. I couldn't have done this without you."

Nicole covers my hand with hers. "It's what we do."

It really is. Whenever disaster strikes in any of our lives, we don't hesitate to jump to aid whoever is in trouble.

"I'd like it if we didn't have to do this again," I remark.

"If you'd all just stay single like me, you wouldn't have to worry about it."

I just laugh. There aren't many people I know who are built like she is. She lives by her own set of rules, which is something I've always admired. No matter what people think about her, she does what she wants. I'm the opposite.

I was expected to get married by twenty-five, so I did. My mother believed you spent the first three years of your marriage building a strong foundation, so we waited to have kids. Then, a mother stays home and raises her babies.

Someone left out the part about what I am expected to do when the foundation has cracks and ends up crumbling.

"I liked being married. I can remember waiting for him to come home because I missed him all day," I tell her.

She shifts and props her head on her hand. "It's been years of him mistreating you, Kris. I kept my mouth shut because I didn't think you'd hear me anyway, but it was uncomfortable to watch. You and Heather are the best ones of the four of us. You guys have these big ass hearts, but you've let men trample them."

"Scott isn't like Matt," I defend a little. Matt was a piece of shit for what he did to Heather. They were married barely a year before he walked out on her. Scott and I were together for almost seventeen years between dating to now. "He wasn't always bad. That's what makes it so hard."

She sighs. "No, but he wasn't great, either. You can't tell me he wasn't emotionally abusive."

"Stop," I request. I don't want to talk about it or be reminded of how much I hate myself for accepting it.

"I'm not judging you." Nicole grabs my hand. "I'm really not. I get it, he was your husband, but watching you drift away was hard." A tear descends across my cheek, and Nicole pulls me into her arms. "I'm not happy this is how it turned out. We all hoped he'd get his head out of his ass and fix his shit."

"I did, too." I lean back and nod. I know she isn't judging me, just as I never judge my girls for things they choose.

"You're going to get through this," Nicole promises.

I know she's right. She has to be. There is no other choice. I have two kids who need me. Motherhood is filled with doing things for the sake of the children, even if you don't want to do it. I'd love to lie in bed and eat nothing but junk food until my emotions are sated, but I can't. Besides, I'm not sure if I'm sad about losing him or sad that I wasn't able to see past the hope I clung to.

"Thanks to you guys, I will be. He's an asshole, and I'm ready to move on."

"That's it!" Nicole slaps my leg. "Asshole be gone."

She rests her head on the back of the couch and yawns.

"You look beat. Do you want to stay the night?" I ask.

"Listen," she grabs her glass of wine. "I know you guys think I'm kinky, but I like men in my threesomes, not vaginas. I'd do you, but . . . I'd need more wine."

I burst out laughing and slap her arm. "You're such an idiot."

"I made you laugh."

"That you did."

Nicole covers herself with the throw blanket behind her and we laugh like old times. She tells me all about the new contracts she's working on. Of course, she tells me about the new guy she's sleeping with, too. I don't know how she does it, but good for her. She's happy, even if her love life is ridiculous. As she talks, I let myself forget that I'm spending the first night in my new house single and alone.

CHAPTER THREE

KRISTIN

"LET'S GO!" I yell to the kids as I stand at the door.

"I can't find my shoes!" Aubrey yells back, and I groan.

It's my first day back to work, and I'm going to be late. Finn finally comes out with his headphones on and the phone glued to his hand. He doesn't acknowledge me, but I don't care this time. He's moving to the car, which is all that matters.

I look at my watch and tap my foot. "Aubrey! Come on, honey! Just put anything on your feet! I don't care if they match."

She comes running, and her blonde hair is already falling out of her ponytail, but I don't have time to fix it. "Sorry, Mommy."

"It's fine, baby. Mommy can't be late, so let's move it, okay?" I usher her out and lock the door behind me.

Once everyone is in their seat and buckled, we head to the babysitter—also known as Aunt Danielle. I can't afford to pay someone since my starting pay at Celebaholic isn't great, but having Eli make a call on my behalf definitely helped in getting a little more than what they originally offered.

I'm not sure how comfortable I am covering Eli and his friends, but . . . it's a job.

One that I know I'm going to suck at. I can't remember the last adult television show I watched, and I've never even seen *A Thin Blue Line*, which is something Eli finds hilarious since he was the star. Following celebrities was the last thing I cared about with everything going on in my life. I'm not even sure who is popular now . . . I wonder if people still like Josh Hartnett? He was my ultimate crush.

While my friends like Nicole were soaking up the gossip, I was focused on the PTA, the community book club, and Scott's work functions. But, after spending the last two months scouring for something and coming up short, I can't be picky. If I had any other choice for a job, I'd take it, but the hours are perfect for a single mom. I can work from home at least three days a week, which means I can still do the things that I've come to love doing for my kids.

My lawyer told me it's actually perfect in case Scott changes his tune and suddenly wants custody. I'll be home with them for the most part, earning a salary, and have the flexibility that no judge could argue with. This job tosses any reservations he has about me out the window. I have to succeed.

Plus, my lawyer has basically said if I want to ensure I maintain custody of the kids, I need to show a stable income.

"Are we going to Dad's this weekend?" Finn asks as I make the drive to Danni's house.

"Yes." I glance at him in the rearview mirror.

He shakes his head and pops his earbuds back in. Clearly,

he isn't getting any better with adjusting to our new living arrangements. I'm not sure what to say at this point because nothing seems to make a difference.

Aubrey gives me a sweet smile and then looks out the window. It's hard to believe how old they're getting. Finn is ten and Aubrey just turned six, but they are both too young to have their worlds flipped. They've been handling things well, though. The last month we were in the house was tough, but now that we're in our new home, the normalcy will come.

We reach Danielle's house with a little time to spare, but she's already waiting for us.

"Hey," I say when she opens the door.

Danni looks at me and laughs. I can't blame her, my keys are in my teeth, the bag holding Aubrey's toys is half-open and everything is spilling out, and my shirt is only half-tucked in. I'm the definition of a hot mess.

"Give me the bag, Kris."

I hand it over and try to right myself. "Bad morning."

"It's your first day back to work in a long ass time. You've got this."

Right now, I don't feel like I've got this. I'm not sure I have anything handled.

I hug both the kids, Finn is more of a pat on the shoulder as he moves away, and do my best to fix my shirt.

"Does the outfit say forty-year-old divorcee with her life in the crapper or seasoned reporter ready to take on the world?"

Danielle taps her lips. "I'll go with the second one."

"Good. I need to get downtown. Thank you for this. Seriously." I kiss her cheek. "I love you."

"Love you, too!" Danni calls as I'm scampering down her walkway to the car.

I have twenty minutes to get to the office. I added another fifteen minutes on top of that, because I hate being late. It's my biggest pet peeve, which is why we lie to Heather and tell her to meet a half hour before we actually mean.

The drive isn't awful, but traffic is a little heavier than it was a half hour ago. Thanks to my planning, I'm still early. I park the car and check my makeup, which is light and fresh. My hair is pulled back into a ponytail, and I actually still have both my earrings in.

Whether I'm ready for this or not, I'm going to look the part.

My phone pings with a text.

> **HEATHER**
> Kick ass today!

> Thank Eli again for me.

> **HEATHER**
> He was happy to do it. Plus, at least we know you're not going to make up some crazy shit like I'm pregnant and that's why he's dating me.

Oh, God. I hope I never have to write anything about Eli. But he's famous, which means I may have no choice.

Damn it.

> I already regret this.

> **HEATHER**
> Don't. You're going to do amazing.

> I covered politics before! How the hell am I going to write about gossip now?

My head falls back against the headrest, and I close my eyes. Who am I kidding? I'm going to get fired.

The phone rings, and I don't even have to look to know it's her.

"Do not pep talk me," I warn before Heather can get a word out.

"Well, don't be so damn pessimistic! You're the one who always had rainbows shooting out of her ass. Now you're all doom and gloom."

I grip the steering wheel. "That was before my husband served me with divorce papers three months ago."

"Welcome to the club, bitch."

"I never wanted a membership," I say with a hint of hostility.

"I know you can't see it now, but trust me, you'll thank your lucky stars later. When you meet a man who loves you through all the shit, it won't seem like the worst thing in the world. You've just got to get through this part," Heather tells me with so much hope in her voice that it stuns me.

Her divorce wasn't easy, I get that, but we have two children involved. There's a home filled with the life we shared, child support, alimony, debt, and so much more. Since moving out of the house, he's attempting to be cordial, but our lawyers are the ones communicating about the ugly stuff.

It's almost like Scott lives for finding ways to make my life hell since he found out how much he'd pay in child support.

"Regardless, I'm not there yet," I sigh.

"Today you're starting your new life, Kristin. You get to be anyone you want when you walk through that door. Be fearless."

"I don't know what I'd do without you." I smile, knowing she's right.

Fearless is the last thing I am, but I can fake it. Can't I?

Heather laughs. "You'd be lost. Now go in there and show them who's boss."

I exit the car and head into the small office building.

"Hi." I smile at the woman sitting the front. "I'm Kristin McGee. I have a meeting with Erica."

My nerves are high, but I do my best to keep it together. Erica and I spoke at great length on the phone, but we didn't actually meet before she offered me the job. All she needed was Eli Walsh's endorsement.

She nods, looking at her screen. "Yes, you're the new girl. I'm Pam."

We exchange pleasantries as she walks me to a desk in the back corner. I place my things down, and then she leads me to what should be an office, but I don't think I can call it that. There are two partitions, which I guess are supposed to be walls, posters tacked in random places, papers all over the desk, and clothes all over the chairs.

What the hell have I gotten myself into?

"You must be Kristin!" A short woman at least half my age jumps up. "It's great to meet you."

"You, too." I plaster a fake smile on and shake her hand.

"Excuse the mess," she says with a smile as she looks around sheepishly. "We moved to this office last week, and it's been a transition, to say the least."

I shake my head, dismissing her worries. "I just moved myself, I get it."

Erica pulls her hair into a messy bun, and I realize how

overdressed I am. She's barefoot and wearing a pair of workout shorts and a T-shirt that says: Y'all Need Jesus.

I'm not sure if I'm excited about the possible dress code or scared.

"Please, sit." She motions for the chair.

"Thanks," I say as I move the shirt to the other chair.

"So, you're *seriously* friends with Eli Walsh?"

This is going to be so awkward. "Yes. Heather, his girl-friend, is one of my best friends."

She leans back with a grin. "That's amazing. FBD is defi-nitely one of the hottest Tampa stories. Even though we have readers across the country, we started as a local blog, and Tampa is still our base. Eli and Randy are the area's golden boys, so we need to keep our followers fed."

It doesn't surprise me. I've seen firsthand how crazy people go over the band. They've been around since we were kids and haven't lost their fans. Eli and his brother Randy grew up in Tampa, which makes the people here a little more nuts about the Walsh brothers. I can't say anything because I was one of them until I got to know Eli. Now, it's kind of sad how much of his life people think they have a right to know about.

The worst is how they treat Heather. Thankfully, she couldn't give a shit less.

"I want to be clear that I won't actually be writing about Eli. I won't do that to him or my friend." It's the same thing I told her during our phone interview, but there's no harm in reiterating it.

Erica leans forward with her arms on the desk. "Of course not. I completely understand that. However, you do have access to the celebrities in his life, which is one of the reasons Eli suggested you'd be a great fit here."

Perfect. I don't have to write about him, but his friends are fair game.

Maybe I can't do this. I'm not comfortable with being that lurking friend always thinking of a story.

Then I think about what my lawyer said about Scott and the kids. I can't go to court saying that I took a job and then quit the first day. It definitely won't bode well for my character should Scott actually try to fight me about custody.

Eli is the one who suggested this, so he must be okay with it.

I shift, straightening my back. I may not want to do this, but I will. I'll do the best damn job possible. "Do you have anything you'd like me to start with?"

"Actually . . ." Erica's smile is mischievous. "I got a tip that I want you to follow . . ."

And so it begins.

CHAPTER FOUR

KRISTIN

SITTING at my dining room table, I chew on the inside of my cheek, wondering how the hell I approach this. I know if I ask, Heather won't tell me no, but I'm starting to feel like a shitty friend.

She's done so much for me already, I won't ask for more favors. I just need to be creative.

I think back to when I was a reporter and didn't have connections. Being resourceful was paramount. The file Erica gave me, the one filled with information about Noah Frazier, sits on my table. He'll be in Tampa on Friday to visit Eli for the weekend, which means I'm supposed to have a story for the blog on Monday.

Considering I know nothing about Noah, I need to get busy trying to find an in.

I open it and read the info laid out like a police record.

NAME: NOAH JOSEPH FRAZIER
BORN: NOVEMBER 3, 1977 (SCORPIO)

I smile when I realize we share a birthday.

LOCATION: CURRENTLY LIVES IN NEW YORK CITY.
BORN IN NEWTON, IL.
MOVED TO LA AT EIGHTEEN.
EYE COLOR: GREEN
HAIR: DARK BROWN
HEIGHT: 6FT (ALTHOUGH I THINK HE'S AN INCH SHORTER)
WEIGHT: WHO CARES? HE'S HOT.

The next line makes me chuckle. Who the hell comes up with these forms for stalking celebrities?

RELATIONSHIP STATUS: SINGLE AS FUCK.
BODY TYPE: ATHLETIC. STRONG JAWLINE AND HAS A BANGING ASS.

I almost spit my coffee. It literally says "banging ass."

There's loads of information about his career, food likes, and pretty much anything I could ever want to know. It isn't until I turn the page that my jaw drops.

Holy shit.

He's freaking hot. Like *really* hot.

Maybe this job won't suck as much as I thought it would.

I open my laptop and click on the browser so I can search his images. Noah is photographed with Eli quite a bit, most of the shots are them on the set of *A Thin Blue Line*, but then there are a few of them out at various bars. He looks damn freaking good in a police uniform. I rest my chin on my hand as I click through the images. The next photo is of his back, and in it, he's squatting a little and his gun is drawn . . . I now fully understand the banging ass comment.

My scrolling continues through delicious photos of Noah, and I sigh.

I keep clicking and then stop when I come to a photo from the Emmy Awards.

Holy mother of God.

He's in a black tux that fits him perfectly. Even with all the material he's wearing, I can see the angles of his body. Broad shoulders, trim waist, and strong arms are visible in the shot. His dark brown hair is parted to the side and pushed back into a sleek, polished look. The photographer captured him in the middle of a laugh, and his green eyes are bright and full of life.

I could stare at this all day. If my job is looking at him, I may never quit.

My phone rings, and I jump.

Shit. It's Scott.

"Hi." I close the laptop, feeling a *little* guilty that I was drooling over another man while I'm legally married to this man.

"Hey." My heart thumps at the sound of his voice. We haven't spoken since I moved out two weeks ago, and hearing it now hurts. "I was verifying the kids are staying with me this weekend."

"That's the plan," I say as I run my finger along the mug. "I can drop them off after work on Friday."

He clears his throat. "I can get them."

"Okay, I was offering since I'll be in West Chase. And per the temporary agreement, I either drop them off or pick them up. This seemed to be the perfect compromise. I have to go into the office on Friday, which means the kids will be at Danielle's. I have a ton of paperwork to fill out."

Scott goes quiet and a knot forms in the pit of my stomach. "I'd rather us have a meeting place in the middle. The lawyer suggested having a neutral place. For the kids . . . and for us. That way, we're not in each other's business. I'd rather you stay away from my home."

My hand stops moving and I grip the mug. His home? It's *his* home now. He had to say it like that? I've known this was going to be difficult, but no one warns you about the pain during it all. It's about lawyers, money, and keeping things separate. Civility is a struggle when you're dealing with a selfish asshole.

I do my best to hold back the tears that threaten to form. It's so much easier said than done. He's still the guy I always wanted to love me.

"That's really not convenient for me, Scott. I can't drive out there on Sunday."

He huffs. "I'm not trying to be a dick, *Kris*."

It just comes natural to him.

"We agreed that one of us would drop them off and the other would pick them up. When you sent your requests the other day, that is what I signed off on." I can be a bitch, too. I won't let him walk all over me.

My lawyer called me Wednesday night to let me know we got our court date and to go over Scott's requests during the separation. I agreed to some, this being one of them, but he's out of his damn mind if I'm going to drive them to *and* from his visits let alone meet in some random place. They're his kids, too. He can be the one inconvenienced if he wants to change shit around. I was the one who had to deal with him until the kids were out of school and then uproot my home and the kids because he wanted to stay in the house, which I still think is totally ridiculous. Why the hell does he need a four-bedroom house?

"My lawyer believes this is the right choice."

He and his lawyer put all of this crap in the letter, and now he's acting as if none of it works for him. Too damn bad. It didn't work for me to move, but I did it. Time to grow the fuck up. I'm being nice by offering to take them to *his house* so he doesn't have to drive out to Carrollwood when he works clear on the other side of Tampa.

I huff. "I'm happy for you and the lawyer, but I didn't agree to these terms. You can't decide something and just expect me to do it. I've been more than accommodating so far. I'm offering to drop them off Friday and then you can bring them back to me Sunday by the agreed time, which is exactly what you wanted and exactly what I agreed to when your lawyer delivered the terms."

Driving to a central location makes absolutely no sense. I'm not doing it.

"I have to work on Monday," he complains. "You'll need to meet me at the neutral location in the morning instead of at night. I can have Jillian meet you if the time doesn't work."

He has to be kidding me. He must be out of his ever-loving mind if he thinks I'm dropping the kids off with his *assistant*. Especially considering I've never liked the bitch. She's always been nasty to me and up his ass.

"I'm not meeting you—or your damn assistant—and per your stupid agreement, you have them until six. I have plans on Sunday."

Stalking Noah Frazier and getting my blog post together, but I don't tell him that.

"Plans?" He laughs. "Give me a break, you don't have a life. I have a big meeting. For once, don't be a bitch."

I'll show him a bitch.

"I'm sorry to hear that." My words are laced with sarcasm. I'm not sorry about anything. "However, that's not my problem. I will drop them off on Friday at the house, and I expect that you'll drop them off at my home on Sunday after six. That's what we agreed upon *in writing*."

"When did you become so fucking difficult? Can you do anything helpful?"

Such an asshole. "I'd love to chat about that, Scott, but I'm busy right now. If you have an issue with the arrangements, take it up with my lawyer. I'll drop the kids off Friday after work at your place. Thanks for calling." I disconnect the call, and my head falls back as I groan.

I don't feel like doing anything but passing out. This single parenting thing is exhausting. I get up and head toward the bedrooms.

Carefully, I open Aubrey's door and move to her bed. She looks so little when she's sleeping. I brush back her hair, kiss her forehead, and sit on the edge of her bed. Last night was hard on her. She cried for Scott for almost an hour, and I couldn't calm her. In my arms, she begged to go home and stay with Daddy. I'm not sure how many nights of that I can take before it breaks me.

She nestles into the pillow, clutching the blanket she's slept with since she was an infant. "Sleep tight, my beautiful girl," I whisper and kiss her again.

I make my way to Finn's room and smile. He's the craziest

sleeper in the world. I find him with his head hanging off the bed, his one foot is on the wall, and the other foot is on the pillow. I'll never understand how he wiggles himself into the positions he does, but no matter what we did, it was the same each night.

My poor sweet boy is so out of control. I've always been close to him, but lately, he hates me. I don't know if he assumes that us moving out was my choice or if he thinks it's something else. I grab his legs and spin him back into a normal position.

"Mom?" He rubs his eyes, and I brush his hair back.

"Go back to sleep, honey."

Finn sits up and wraps his arms around me. "I'm sorry I'm being mean."

"You don't have to be sorry," I murmur while pulling him to my chest. "I know you're just working out your feelings."

He pulls back and tears fill his beautiful brown eyes that mirror Scott's. "Why doesn't Daddy love us?"

I take his chin in my hand. "He loves you very much. Don't you ever question that."

"Then he wouldn't make us leave."

Oh, Finn. I wish it were that easy. I'm not sure how to explain this to him, but he's a smart kid. He's always had this innate ability to sense when someone is lying, so I shake my head, wanting to choose my words extremely carefully.

"Sometimes, moms and dads can't make things work." A tear falls down his puffy cheek and slices my heart apart. "Sometimes, no matter how hard we try, we can't fix it. It's not because of love, honey. I love your daddy very much, and I know he cares deeply about me. It's just . . . ." I sigh. "It's just better if we don't live together anymore."

All of that is the truth. Well, as much of the truth as my ten-year-old needs. I will never bash their father. No matter what happens, I'll protect the hearts of them toward him. He's their father and a man I loved for a long time, and I want them to love him.

"At least you won't be sad anymore," Finn notes as he wipes his nose with his arm.

Boys.

"What do you mean?"

He lies back on his pillow, and I cover him with the blankets. "You were so scared at night. Daddy was always yelling at you, and then you'd cry." Finn lets out a yawn.

My chest tightens as I clutch my throat. I thought we were doing a good job hiding things. Scott and I would never say anything in front of the kids, and I worked hard to hide my pain. Seems I sucked at that, too.

"I love you, Finn." I touch his cheek, but he's already out.

Now to cry myself to sleep another night in my lonely bed.

ERICA CALLED me this morning to inform me that "the Arc has moored in Tampa." I'm assuming that is her not-so-subtle way of saying Noah is here, but who the hell knows with that girl.

She's absolutely certifiably crazy.

For real.

She's unglued. Erica believes the government is performing an experiment on humans, and we're in some sort of Hunger Games reality series. I'm not sure what district she's in, but I'm hoping we aren't in the same one. We'll all die.

She also lives at home with her parents, who still pay her

bills while she works to find her cause in life. What does that even mean? Her cause? Shouldn't it be purpose?

I wish I were making this shit up.

I text Heather, praying this stupid plan of mine will work.

> Hey! You busy?

HEATHER:

I'm working now, but I get off in an hour.
What's up?

She's never going to buy this, but my bullshit ability is at zero with my life being in the crapper.

> I was thinking we could all go out tonight . . .
> I could really use the distraction. I'm
> dropping the kids off at Scott's in a few.

HEATHER

Oh! Of course! Eli's friend from New York is in town, but you're welcome to come over if you want! We can drink by the pool and have a slumber party. Especially after being around Asshole.

> Yeah, Asshole will definitely hamper my
> mood. I could use some Heather time.

I hate myself. I'm the worst friend ever.

Guilt gnaws at me for misleading my friend at all.

I pace the living room with my phone in my hand. I won't be this person. Heather doesn't deserve me being this way.

> Okay, I lied. I mean, not totally, but my intentions weren't the best. I have to put a blog post up on Monday or I'm going to get fired by my twit of a boss. She told me to write about Noah. Don't hate me! You can tell me to go to hell now. Don't worry, I hate myself enough for the both of us.

My phone rings, and it goes clattering to the floor. Why does she always call instead of texting? I'm quick to pick it back up and hit the green button.

"Hello?" I say with trepidation.

"You're such an idiot! A complete and total idiot! If you needed to meet Noah, I would've brought him gift-wrapped to you. Dork." Heather laughs, and I hear her partner, Brody, in the background. "All you had to do was ask."

She doesn't get the hatred I have for doing this. "I don't want to ask you! I'm supposed to be a journalist or whatever the hell they call this shit. It's my job to get the dirt on Eli's freaking friends."

Heather sighs. "Eli knows this, and he got you the job because he knows you're a good person, Kris."

I don't feel like a good person. I feel like a user.

"I owe that man. You should give him sex as a thank you." I smile.

"Oh, I will. Lots and lots of hot, sweaty sex. The kind that people write about."

Brody grumbles loud enough for me to hear it and then makes a gagging sound. "Good. But please don't tell me about it. I'm going to be sex-less for a while. It's already been more than eleven months. Last thing I want to hear about is your fantastic sex with a guy who was on the cover of Men's Health last month. Could he have at least one flaw?"

"Tell me about it. I keep waiting for him to grow love handles. When he does, I'm going to poke at them daily."

I laugh as I imagine her teasing Eli. It really is not fair. However, he works hard. I've never seen anyone be so regimented about their diet. While we gorge ourselves on nachos with guacamole and queso, Eli eats hardboiled eggs and boiled chicken.

I'll take the love handles if it means I don't have to give up guacamole.

"Thank you for not being mad at me." I chew on my thumbnail.

Heather releases a deep sigh. "You're going to have to get over this, Kristin. Come over tonight at eight, and we'll hang out, okay?"

"Okay. Shit! What do I wear?"

The only famous people I've ever been around are the guys from Four Blocks Down. The first time we met them all, I almost died. Now, Shaun, PJ, Eli, and Randy have been sort of inducted into our little group, so it isn't so bad.

Still, my pulse was going so crazy when Shaun kissed my hand that I almost fainted.

Meeting someone for a work reason . . . I'm not sure what the protocol is. Do I dress up?

"Noah is really sweet, Kris. We're going to drink by the pool, so just be you."

"I'm—"

The radio blares, cutting us off. "Shots fired. I have to go. Love you." Heather hangs up before I can respond.

I absolutely hate when she's on shift. When she first joined the police force, I was a nervous wreck. She was required to text me each night after she made it home safe. There was no way I could sleep if she didn't. I know I'm weird, but it was scary as hell knowing she could be shot.

She finally had enough and told me to take a sleeping pill or get a therapist.

Every now and then, I'm reminded how dangerous her job is.

Instead of freaking out—about Heather's safety or my meeting Noah—I grab my stuff and head out of the office.

This will be the first time I see Scott since I moved out. I'm part nauseated and part terrified. Our last phone conversation was not good, and the text I got this morning told me to meet him at the house.

Time to find out if that meant the house or his unknown neutral spot in Tampa.

CHAPTER FIVE

KRISTIN

"MOMMY!" Aubrey comes flying out the door with a huge grin. "I missed you today!"

"I missed you, too!" I clutch my little girl and rock back and forth.

The thing I love about my job is the time I still get with the kids. I was able to work from home two days this week, and the more I learn about the inner workings of Celebaholic, the more days I can be remote. My actual position may not be what I want, but the hours are kind of awesome.

I urge Aubrey back and smile. "Did you have a good day with Aunt Danni?"

She nods and then whispers in my ear. "She gave us ice cream."

"She did?" I act shocked.

"She said not to tell you."

I giggle. "Then we better not tell her you did."

"Did you tell your mom about our secret?" Danielle asks with a fake angry look on her face.

Aubrey's hands go behind her back, and she shrugs. "Maybe."

Danni makes a huge huffing sound and crosses her arms. "Aubrey Nicole McGee, you're going to get me in trouble."

"Should we let her off the hook?" I ask Aubrey.

"Yup!"

Danielle laughs and pulls her into her arms, kissing her cheeks while she giggles. Danielle is Aubrey's godmother, and the two of them are trouble together.

Finn walks out with his backpack on and the phone, which I now think has actually attached itself to his hand, in his view. "S'up, Mom?"

"S'up?" I repeat. "S'up with you, dude?"

That gets his attention. "You're so not cool."

"Oh, I'm the coolest mom ever. I'm so cool that you wish you could be my friend."

Finn shakes his head and smiles. I can't help but light up a little. He's been so depressed that it's good to see a glimmer of the boy I know.

"Aunt Heather is cool . . . you're not," he says playfully.

I can't deny that Heather being with a television star gains her cool points with the kids, but I miss the days when they thought I was the best.

"Well, get your butt in my car before this non-cool mom starts singing and dancing with Aunt Danni." I raise my brow, challenging him. Finn knows we'll do it. I have no problem embarrassing him.

He practically sprints toward the door, and a piece of my heart stitches back together. The kids will have their challenges with all of this, but I could use more smiles.

I get Aubrey buckled in and then meet Danielle at the front of the car. "You doing okay?"

"I'm surviving."

She grips my arm and gives a sad smile. "I want you to know I love you and that I'm proud of you—we all are."

People have no idea how lucky I am to have my girls. There is no way I could survive without them. I know we all share the same feelings, which makes it that much more special. I would do pretty much anything for the three of them.

"Proud?" I ask.

"Yeah, honey. You left him when Lord knows you should've left years ago. I'm proud of you for doing what you have to. It's been weird because he calls Peter all the time, and . . . I just felt very in the middle."

Peter is really Scott's only friend. I haven't even considered that Danielle would be hearing the other side of it. No wonder she's been kind of weird.

"I'm sorry."

She shakes her head quickly. "No. You have nothing to be sorry for. It was stupid, and Peter knows everything now. You don't have anything to worry about."

"I wish that were the case." I smile and then glance back at the car, keeping my voice low. "You know who gave me a hard time about this weekend, and I'm waiting . . ."

Danielle grips her neck and sighs heavily. "He's going to do it because he thinks he can. He's pushed you around for so long that he doesn't know how to handle this new, badass and pissed off woman. Don't be a doormat ever again—not with him or anyone else."

"I'm not." There's no mistaking the conviction in my tone.

He can try, but I've had it. This was my first test, and instead of caving to him, I stood my ground. Our time in that house, while we waited for the kids to finish school, was very . . . eye-opening. I saw him for who he is, and the rose-colored glasses shattered. He's a giant dick and not the good kind.

"Good. I'll see you Monday?" she asks.

"Bright and early." I give her a hug and promise to call if I need anything.

Off to my date with the Devil.

The kids fill me in on their day, and Aubrey is going a mile a minute. The ride to my house—old house—is a few blocks, but I drive extremely slowly. I want to delay this as much as possible. Knowing that I'm going to see the home I once loved has my stomach doing somersaults.

We pull into the driveway, and I fight back my discomfort. The kids need to see me as a pillar of strength.

Scott opens the red door and heads down the walkway. He's wearing his black suit pants I had pressed last month, the blue shirt I bought, and his smile is effortless. I could almost believe he's happy to see me.

But when I exit the car, his smile shifts to a look of disappointment. I realize he's still the same miserable person, but I've changed and no longer care if he's happy.

I walk toward him, wanting to be polite. "Hi."

"Hi."

Silence.

We stand in front of the home where we shared our lives and can't even look at each other.

"Are the kids ready?" Scott asks.

Okay then. "Yes, they're—"

"Daddy!" Aubrey screams as she spots him, cutting off this

extremely uncomfortable exchange. "Daddy! Daddy!"

"Princess!" Scott calls back and rushes to her side door. He has her in his arms immediately.

She squeezes him and kisses his cheek. "I missed you so much, Daddy! So much!"

I move to the trunk so I can grab their bags.

"I missed you more. You got so big! Hi, Finn! How are you, buddy?"

Finn doesn't respond. He just puts the headphones back over his ears.

"I never want to leave you, Daddy." Aubrey giggles and wraps her little arms around him again.

My heart breaks, leaving nothing but tiny bits remaining. I can't stop the tears this time. I shift to put my back to them and wipe away the moisture before anyone sees. I hate this so much.

I draw in a deep breath and pull my shoulders back. Time to be the bigger person again. I carry the bags to the sidewalk before heading to Finn's side.

"Come on, dude. It's time to go see your dad."

"I'd rather stay with you." He glares at his father and then his eyes turn pleading. "Please, Mom."

Please, God, help me through this.

I touch the side of his face, mustering every last bit of strength I have. "You should spend some time with Daddy. He probably missed you, and I'm sure he hasn't been able to get to the next level in Overwatch."

My eyes meet Scott's, and I see appreciation for the first time.

Scott clears his throat, drawing Finn's attention. "I've been trying, but you know I can't capture the objective without my sidekick."

Finn's chin drops, and he unbuckles his seatbelt. "Fine, it's not that hard anyway."

"Why don't you guys head inside so I can talk to your mom. I got some new stuff for your rooms." Scott gestures to the front door, but before the kids can run inside, I stop them.

"Come give me hugs."

The kids each wrap their arms around me, and I hold them tight. This is going to be the hardest thing I do. Dropping them off every other weekend will never be something I look forward to. I love these kids and would keep them with me every day.

"Bye, Mom!"

"Bye, guys!"

They run off, leaving me with Scott. Hopefully, this time he can actually say more than a few words to me.

I rock back on my heels and slip my hands deep into my pockets. "So?"

"So, where do you want to meet on Sunday?"

He isn't seriously asking me that, is he? Not after the whole fight on the phone. There is no way he can possibly believe I'm going to come get them. No. I don't believe it.

"Excuse me?" I keep my voice calm.

"I figure we can meet at the McDonald's between our houses." Scott cracks his neck.

He's fucking for real.

"For the last time, I'm not meeting you, Scott. You will bring Finn and Aubrey to *my* house at the time we agreed on through the lawyers."

His eyes turn hard, and he makes a low growling noise in his throat.

Good. Be pissed. I don't give a shit. This is absolutely ridiculous considering it was *his* stupid agreement.

"I don't see why you can't just meet me!" He bellows. "Fucking hell, it's like you never change!"

I'm not going to stand here and allow him to yell at me. It's why I'm living in my best friend's house to begin with.

"You're living in the house because you asked to stay, even though it was more of a goddamn upheaval on our kids, but you didn't care. I moved us out without any help from you. You don't want a wife anymore, so I'm not going to act like one." I rip open my car door and get in, my chest heaving in anger as I jam the key into the ignition. The old Kristin would've met him because she wanted him to be happy.

The new Kristin doesn't give a shit how he feels.

Scott stares at me in disbelief as I back the car up. I'm done making everyone else happy. It's time for me to enjoy life a little.

———

I HEAD BACK to my place to try to assemble an outfit for tonight.

Forty minutes later, I've dug through all the boxes of clothes I've yet to unpack and am wearing a simple black two-piece bathing suit under my cute floral-print romper. I throw my dark brown hair into a messy bun and call it a day.

There's no way I'm going to stay out late tonight, I want to wallow in my self-pity. But once again, I must do something I don't want to . . . work.

If I can get myself in the mindset that this might actually be semi-enjoyable, I'll be golden.

HEATHER

Where are you?

I'm still sitting on the edge of the bed giving myself the world's worst motivational speech ever.

I'm leaving the house now.

Or as soon as I can get my lazy ass up.

HEATHER

Okay! I can't wait to see you. I'm making margaritas! Olé!

Oh, boy. This is going to be entertaining. Heather is the best drunk ever. She can't hold her liquor and usually does something epic . . . like landing in bed with a rock star. I force myself to get up and go.

Twenty minutes later, I'm at Heather and Eli's house.

I can do this. I can go in there, do what I need to do, and get home where I can shovel my face with crap food and watch movies that only depress me more.

I knock on the door, and Heather opens it with a huge smile on her face. "Kristin!" Her arms wrap around my neck, and I go falling forward.

"Holy shit! How much did you drink already?" I laugh as we both steady ourselves.

She releases me with a laugh. "I only had one, but Noah makes these *really* strong."

If this is her after one . . . we're in so much trouble. "Pace yourself, honey."

Heather rolls her eyes and pulls me into the house. "Start

drinking. You need to forget your worries, and I have my friends Jim, Jack, and Johnny all here ready for you. Or we can hang out with Jose."

My brows raise, and she thrusts a glass into my hand. "Who are you, and what have you done with my best friend?"

Her gaze drops to the floor, and when she looks up, a tear forms. "It's two years today . . . since I lost her."

She doesn't have to say another word. I pull her into my arms and rub her back. "Oh, Heather. I'm sorry."

It's hard to believe that she lost her sister two years ago. It feels like it's been so much longer. There's nothing to say to ease her pain, but I wish I could. Stephanie was more than a sister to Heather. She was like a daughter.

"I'm okay," she says as she pulls back.

"Today is a shitty day all around." I shrug.

"Scott?"

"Yup." Then, because there isn't anything she can do to make it better, I shrug again. "You know . . . exes."

"All too well, my friend." Heather laughs and takes a sip of her drink. "Now, drink so I can bring you out back. Eli and Noah are both in the pool. Shirtless."

Maybe a little alcohol will make me not such an awkward turtle. I follow her advice and take a gulp, shuddering as the alcohol hits me. "Holy hell!"

She wasn't kidding about the drinks being strong. I don't know that I can taste the mix. It's basically straight tequila. I take another gulp and look out the back window.

The back wall of the house has the best views, though. The sun is setting, giving the sky a pink and yellow hue, but that isn't what my eyes are fixed on.

Standing on the edge of the pool is the most gorgeous male

specimen I've ever seen. The photo of Noah Frazier is absolutely nothing compared to the living version. He's taller than I imagined with a wide frame and tanned skin. His hair is wet, appearing almost black, and little drops of water fall from the tips, sliding down his perfect body. I watch the rivulets slide from his chest and then lower as they follow the ridges of his six-pack.

I grip the counter to stop from falling over. "Oh my God," I say, barely breathing the words.

Heather's head twists, and when she looks back at me, her grin is wide. "Yeah, God definitely made them."

"I can't go out there," I stammer. "I'll never be able to speak."

There is not a chance in hell I won't make a total fool of myself.

"You have to!" Heather grips my hand. "He's expecting a reporter friend to interview him."

My stomach drops. No, no, no, she didn't.

"You told him?" I scream the question.

She laughs and drains her glass. "Of course we did. Trust me, it's better he knows. We explained you're one of my best friends and that you wanted to talk for a bit. Eli said he was more than happy to do the interview for you."

Jesus. I'm going to kill her.

I grab my drink and throw it back. My throat burns, and I cough as the warmth starts to flow through my veins.

"Easy!" She warns while slapping my back.

"This is going to be so embarrassing," I whine.

Heather laughs as she pours another drink. "Yup. Yup it is, but oh so entertaining."

Maybe I can duck back out and no one will ever know.

There's nothing saying I have to do this. My boss is, like, twelve, I'm sure I can come up with something plausible. Celebrities aren't known for being reliable.

Ugh.

I need this job, though.

Before I can make a move either way, the glass door slides open and Noah walks through the threshold.

My legs start to quiver as his eyes meet mine. All I can think about is how I'd like to climb him like a tree and shake his coconuts. I thought he was hot in the photo, then he was better through the window, but up close, he's otherworldly.

"Hi." Noah's throaty voice floats around me. "You must be Kristin."

Instead of speaking, I stand here with my mouth hanging open. Some small sounds that could be words escape, but they aren't coherent.

Kill me now.

"Noah, this is my best friend, Kristin. Who we told you about." Heather elbows me.

"Yes. Me. Hi. Kristin. I. You. Hi."

Smooth. Someone should video this because I'm sure it's highly entertaining.

"Right." Noah flashes a blinding smile. "I hear you're a reporter?"

Okay, Kristin, you have to speak in more than one-word increments or grunting noises.

I grab Heather's glass she just poured and hope it'll act as a talisman. "Yes, for a small blog, but I'm that. A reporter. For a blog. I write."

And a bumbling idiot.

Noah's green eyes are filled with humor. He moves a little

closer and places his hand on top of mine. "Eli filled me in a little. I'm happy I came."

I'm pretty sure I just came. At least we're all coming.

"Me, too."

His lips turn up as his eyes rake my body. "See you out there." He winks and walks back out.

My ovaries have officially disintegrated.

I turn back to Heather, who bursts out into a fit of laughter. "Oh, that was epic. You all said I was starstruck when I met Eli? You should've seen that!" Heather continues to laugh at my expense. "Yes. Me. Um. Blog. Er—" She mocks.

"Shut up." I laugh—because, really, what else can I do—and bump her hip before moving around the bar and grabbing a glass. "Now, pour me a shot before I drink straight from the bottle."

There's only one way to get through tonight.

Alcohol.

Lots of Alcohol.

CHAPTER SIX

NOAH

I'VE BEEN AROUND beautiful people for a long time, but Eli failed to mention Tampa seems to grow their own breed of hot chicks. Fucking hell, that girl is gorgeous.

Her deep blue eyes are hypnotizing, her dark hair is the most beautiful shade of chocolate brown, and those plump lips have my balls tightening.

"Did you meet Kristin?" Eli asks when I walk over with the beers from the wet bar.

"Could've warned me she's hot as fuck." I laugh as I take a seat.

He smirks. "All of Heather's friends are hot."

"Good to know. What's her deal?"

I'm hoping Eli reads between the lines of what I'm asking. If I'm going to spend some time hanging around Tampa, it would be nice to maybe have some company.

Eli studies me and sighs. "I wouldn't get any ideas, Noah. She's had it rough, and I'm not sure you'd have a chance in hell. Plus, Heather will have your nuts in a jar if you played any kind of games. And she just got out of a pretty fucked-up marriage. Kristin isn't a girl I'd chase if I were you."

"Right." I look through the window and catch a glimpse of her smile. The way her whole face looks brighter before she throws her head back and laughs without any reservations.

Eli clears his throat. "Don't be stupid, Noah."

I give him a look that causes him to laugh. "Maybe casual is what she's looking for."

"I'm warning you." Eli's eyes are serious. "She's not a girl you fuck around with. She's got two kids, a piece-of-shit husband, who is going to make her life hell through their divorce, and if you hurt her . . . I'll beat the shit out of you before Heather has a chance to."

The threat doesn't go unheard, but I'm not sure I'll be able to stay away from her. Instead of saying that to him, I take a swig of my drink and keep my eyes forward. The last girl I had this strong of a pull toward was my high school girlfriend. I loved Tanya with everything I was, and if she were still alive, she and I would be married. I know that in the depths of my soul. She was taken too soon, leaving me unable to move on.

"Shots!" Heather yells as she and Kristin bounce out of the house, halting our conversation.

"Oh, for fuck's sake," Eli grumbles. "Baby, you know you can't hold your liquor."

Heather laughs and curls up on his lap. "Kristin and I did four already!"

Kristin sits on the lounge chair next to me and sips her margarita. "You're such a lightweight, Heather."

"Whatever, Eli likes what happens when I drink." She runs her finger from his lips down to his chest. "Don't you, honey?"

He laughs and looks at me. "This is going to be a very interesting night."

I look over at Kristin and can't help but agree. "It seems so."

The girls continue to drink and do shots through the next hour, but then Eli takes the bottle back into the house, cutting them off. Now they're dancing—sloppily. Kristin tries to move her body seductively against her friend, but they keep giggling and almost falling over.

"I should stop this, but I'm having trouble forcing myself," Eli mutters before taking a swig.

"You stop it, I'll kill you," I warn.

"That's my soon-to-be fiancé you're watching."

"No," I reply, keeping my eyes on the brunette. "I'm not."

Heather moves behind Kristin, giving me a clear view of Kristin's body. Her hands are on her hips, swaying back and forth.

Kristin pulls her lip in between her teeth as she drops low while watching me.

Fuck me.

Every muscle in my body wants to go to her, grip those hips, and have her touch me. Eli's words ring in my head, keeping me exactly where I am, just staring at her.

I'm going to need a cold shower.

They dance for a few minutes, laughing and falling over, and Eli and I both shake our heads. Girls are a fucking odd breed. You'd never see guys do this crap, but when a chick does it . . . it's hot as hell. Kristin's eyes lift to me and she gives me a coy smile.

She's really fucking beautiful.

Heather's arms wrap around Kristin's neck and they sway together. Both giggle as they whisper something.

"Want to share with the group?" Eli asks.

"Nope. Girl talk," Heather replies.

Kristin sticks her tongue out at him and spins her around. "Yeah, girls are talking. No penis input allowed."

Eli snorts. "I'll be inputting something later."

"I'm so tired," Heather complains as she rests her arms on Kristin's shoulder. "I need to lie down."

Eli stands with a groan. "Come on, baby. Let's get you to bed."

"I'm not tired yet," Kristin juts her bottom lip out.

"I'll watch her," I say without a second thought.

Eli sighs. "Remember what I said."

"You know me. I'm not *that* guy." I'm not a dirtbag. I would never fuck around with a girl who is this drunk, but more than that, I wouldn't betray our friendship. Friends and acting don't go hand in hand most times, so I wouldn't do a damn thing to screw up my and Eli's camaraderie.

He nods, grabs Heather, and carries her inside.

"Want to dance?" Kristin asks hesitantly.

Very fucking much, but it would be a bad idea. "Why don't you come sit?" I suggest.

She huffs dramatically, which makes me smile. She's so goddamn adorable. "Fine. Party pooper."

"Did you call me a party pooper?"

"Yup! Every party has a pooper, and that's what you are."

I'm not sure I've ever been called that. I move over to the couch area where she stands. "You know, this isn't even a party. It's just two people."

Kristin places her hands on her hips and sticks her tongue out. "Party pooper."

I seriously hope she remembers this in the morning. "What would make me more fun then?"

She taps her lips and looks around before her legs seem to give out. I catch her in my arms, and her hands rest on my bare chest. Those blue eyes stare at me with desire swimming in them. It's good to know I'm not the only one feeling this. My dick reacts, and I try to think of anything but the feel of her skin. Neither of us makes a move, I hold her, and she lets me.

Kristin's fingers slide back and forth on my shoulder. "You're so pretty," she slurs. "I wish I was pretty like you."

"You're breathtaking," I reply.

Maybe I don't want her to remember.

Maybe I want her to forget this whole thing because I shouldn't have her in my arms still. I should've let her go, but my arms won't move.

Her soft fingers move over my pec, and I'm doing everything I can to stop my cock from going rock hard, but her floral scent is too much.

"Kristin . . ." I rasp her name.

She pushes her hips forward, feeling my erection, and her eyes widen. "I-I—" She takes a step back. "We should . . . umm . . . do it."

Now it's my turn to be shocked. "Do it?" I'm not sure she means what I mean. Even if she did, there's no way I'm touching her tonight. I'd like her to remember everything when I have her.

"Yes. The interview," she clarifies.

"Now?"

"I'm a good worker," Kristin says and starts to walk,

holding on to the chairs as she goes. "Professional through and through."

"Why don't we wait until you're sober?"

She spins around and laughs. "I'm not drunk, you are."

"Pretty sure you're toasted, sweetheart."

"Why do you have two noses?" Kristin's head tilts to the side as one of her eyes closes.

This is the most fun I've had in a long time. I'll play along. When she resumes her walk, I follow her, wondering what the hell she's doing as she moves around the backyard.

"Is that part of the interview?

"What interview?" Kristin stops walking. "Oh! Yes. You should sit."

I don't argue. I sit in the chair, hoping she'll do the same.

"First question, what is your next job?"

I shrug. "Not sure yet. I'm deciding what to do next."

Since we wrapped on filming the series finale of *A Thin Blue Line* six months ago, I have way too much time on my hands. I've had a few casting calls but haven't decided if I'm going to take a new job right now.

My agent wishes I'd move quicker, but I'm single, rich, and want to enjoy my life for a bit.

Kristin huffs. "Are you hot?"

"I'd like to think so." I smile.

Her eyes bulge, and her cheeks turn bright red. "I didn't mean it like that! I mean like, hot, outside hot. I'm *so* hot."

"I agree." I'm hot, she's hot . . . I'd like if we were both sweaty hot together, but I'll have to settle for drunk innuendoes.

She's still standing and takes a step back. "Are you flirting with me?"

"Maybe."

"You shouldn't flirt with me."

I know this, but it's too fun watching her react. "Okay, I'll stop."

"Okay, because you're totally hot, and I really want to kiss you, but that would be bad, right? I shouldn't want to kiss you. You're drunk, and I'm drunk, and that would be wrong. I don't do wrong things. I'm a good girl who follows the rules." She rambles almost as if she's forgotten I'm here. "Plus, I have to write about how sexy you are, which would be *tooooootally* awkward if we kissed. However, your lips are lickable. I would lick 'em."

I grip the armrests to get up, and Kristin takes another step back. "Careful," I warn as she gets close to the edge of the pool. "Come sit."

"My husband . . . well, ex-husband-to-be"—she sighs while shaking her head—"says I'm not a great kisser anyway. Not that I ever did much right for him. I was really good in bed in college. I had a guy tell me I was the best lay ever."

"Kristin," I warn as she goes back further while rambling about things I'd like not to think about since I just got my cock under control.

She rolls her eyes and throws her hands in the air. "How do you go from the best ever to nothing? It has to be him, right?"

"You're going to fall in the pool." I try for a more direct warning this time.

"It must be because I'm totally a good—" Her eyes meet mine, and I watch her fall backward with a squeal.

Damn it. I rush over as she comes up for air.

"Shit, shit, shit!"

"Give me your hand." I smile as she grumbles.

"I'm all wet," Kristin notes.

"That's what happens when you fall in." I hold both hands out and she swims to the edge of the pool to grab them.

"My clothes, too! I'm so getting fired."

Kristin places her fingers in my palm, and I start to pull her up. However, she falls back, and I lose my footing, causing me to go headfirst into the pool with her. I get to the surface quickly, only to find her giggling uncontrollably.

"You fell in, too!"

"You pulled me in," I say as I splash her.

She leaps into my arms, and my heart races. "I'm sorry."

"It was worth it." She wraps her arms around my neck and her legs around my torso. There is no way in hell I'll stop her this time. I don't give a shit about right and wrong or friend-ships. I want her. I want to kiss her.

Kristin's eyes stay on mine, her breathing accelerates. My hands are splayed against her back and then her eyes close. The urge to close the distance between us and kiss her is strong, but I don't. Instead, I let her lead it. If she kisses me, I can't be at fault, right?

Sure. We'll go with that. It isn't as if I'm the sober one and know better . . .

Her lips come closer, closer, until her head lolls to the side and falls onto my shoulder.

Okay, that was unexpected.

"Hey," I say softly, but she doesn't respond. I can honestly say this is a first.

Her legs go limp around me, and she lets out a loud snore against my ear. "All right," I say as I lift her in my arms. "You're asleep. In the pool." I push her hair back, and she sighs as I pull her legs up into my arms and hold her against my chest. We get to the stairs, where she becomes dead weight as I climb out of the water. Her arms and head hang down, but I know she's breathing thanks to the loud sound escaping her mouth.

I carry her to the chair and place her there.

Now what?

Eli's house is fucking massive, there's no way I can carry her up those damn stairs without falling. I'm not in my twenties anymore. Hell, I'm pushing forty.

Still, I can't leave her here soaking wet and passed out drunk.

Thankfully, it's hot as hell in Tampa, so I don't have to worry about her freezing to death. I'm not sure what the protocol is here, but I don't think she should sleep in her clothes. The idea of undressing her doesn't exactly seem right, either.

I'm an actor, a damn good one, and I can put myself in a role. Sure. I'm her gay best friend and don't give a shit about finding whatever is underneath these clothes. I'm not attracted to her in the least. That's my role.

I'm a goddamn idiot.

Sliding down the strap of her outfit, I focus on anything but the way her skin feels against my fingers. I don't concentrate on the humming noise that she lets out when I repeat the motion on the other side. Hell, I don't even register the uptick in her breathing when I graze the top of her breast to pull the one-piece whatever the hell this outfit is down her body.

My eyes look to the wall as I remove it from her long, toned legs, praying to God she's got something on underneath. If she's naked, I'm fucking done.

When I look back, I'm grateful she has a bikini on. "Noah," she moans.

"I'm just getting you out of the wet clothes. It's okay."

"Okay," Kristin rolls over as I get it off her feet. "You're so hot."

Kristin is back to snoring and pulls her legs up. I grab two towels off the table to cover her with. Her tiny fingers grip the edge of the towel as she tucks it under her chin.

I push back the hair from her face, and her eyes open just a little. "I'll stay out here with you," I say, not even sure if she's awake.

"Camping is fun."

My lips form a smile as I rub my thumb against her cheek. "Yeah, camping sure is."

I head inside to change and grab a few blankets. I have no idea if it gets cold during the night, but I'd rather not take a chance. When I come back outside, I place one over her and then settle into the chair next to her.

I may have to stick around Tampa a bit longer than I thought.

CHAPTER SEVEN

KRISTIN

WHO THE HELL turned on the lights? I roll over, hoping to block out the insane brightness that penetrates my eyelids and shriek when I hit the hard ground.

Ouch.

"You okay?" A deep raspy voice asks and my eyes pop open, only to slam shut again.

Shit. Where the hell am I?

I lift one lid and look around. Why am I outside? My eye finds the source of the voice, and I jump. Noah is staring at me and has a huge grin on his lips. His hair is pushed to the side, and he's sitting in the chair next to mine with his knee up, sipping from a coffee cup.

How in the hell is the man *this* perfect in the morning?

The morning? Wait, it's the morning. And last night, I was . . .

Oh dear God in Heaven, please tell me I didn't do anything stupid. Then I remember the tequila shots. Dancing. Swimming . . . maybe?

Another memory, or maybe a dream, comes forward. His eyes. I was so close to him, thinking about how much I wanted to get lost in his eyes. Imagining his lips against mine and wondering if he thought I was special. My entire body was alive for the first time in forever. I can almost recall the way his fingers were digging into my back, but there's no way that was real.

Noah clears his throat, and I look up. "How are you feeling?"

"Oh, I'm not sure there are words to describe it," I say and clutch my head.

"Here." He shifts to grab another mug and then hands it to me. "You probably need that."

I lift my arm and the blanket falls, exposing my bare skin. How the hell did I lose my clothes? This just keeps getting worse. My hands tremble as I check to be sure I have my bathing suit on, and then I release a sigh of relief. At least I'm not naked.

Time to get some answers about what the hell happened last night. "I remember wearing my romper yesterday. Any idea when that came off?" I ask as I take the cup.

Noah smiles, and my heart skips. He's really unbelievably good looking.

"I took it off."

I spit my coffee across the chair. "You what?" I yell.

He laughs as I wipe the liquid from my chin, place the cup on the ground, and wrap the blanket around me. I don't think I could actually embarrass myself any more at this point.

"You were drunk." He moves his legs over the side so he can turn to face me. "I mean, really drunk."

"So you took my clothes off? You thought that was okay?"

I'm pissed now. I get that Mr. Hollywood big shot gets what he wants, but taking my damn clothes off is not okay. I'm sorry, but I clearly wasn't in my right mind. "Who the hell do you think you are?"

Noah rubs his forehead as I wait for an answer. "You fell in the pool, Kristin. You were passed out and snoring as I carried you out."

"No," I gasp. "I what?"

The pool. The way I wanted to kiss him, it wasn't a dream. It was real.

"I didn't think you'd want to fall asleep in your soaking wet clothes."

Realization slaps me upside the head. I was a drunken idiot and he got stuck caring for me. I pull the blanket over my head and wonder if I can disappear inside here. "I am *so* sorry," I say without showing my face.

Noah's deep laughter grows closer. I feel his fingers touch my arm a second before he pulls the blanket so he can see me. "I didn't mind."

"You didn't?" I ask.

No one can convince me that I wasn't a hot mess. I'm in my bathing suit, on the patio, and have a killer hangover. All signs point to a very mortifying night. One that I was supposed to be working on learning about Noah.

How stupid can I be?

His green eyes soften, and he keeps his hand on me. "No. I really didn't."

My pulse quickens as we stare at each other. This can't be happening to me. There is no way that the emotions Noah is stirring in me are real. I'm married still. I've just left my husband, and yet, right now, I'm thinking of how much I liked

Noah touching me. I'm wondering, if I leaned up a little, would it feel good to kiss him?

It has to be the remnants of the alcohol. There's no other explanation.

Noah shifts, breaking the connection.

"Thank you for making sure I didn't drown." I attempt to laugh, but it sounds off.

Noah's voice turns playful. "I enjoyed camping, too."

What? I don't camp. Who the hell—

"Oh, God!" I close my eyes and try to form some way to get out of this without needing an identity change. Nope. There's no other option. "I'm going to crawl in a hole and die now," I mutter.

"I especially liked the interview," Noah adds on. "I will say, though, as a reporter, you didn't ask the important questions."

This is why I don't like to drink. I can only imagine the crap that came out of my mouth. I already know I clung to him like a barnacle on the hull of a ship, why not make it worse?

"Please, make it stop." I grip the sides of my head, praying it'll explode to relieve the pressure.

His hand touches my back and slowly rubs. "Kristin?"

"Yes?" I don't look up.

"Look at me," Noah demands.

I lift my head, and he leans closer. "I know you probably regret last night, but I don't. Not one minute. It also means we'll have to spend the day together so you can really get your story. Funny who has the dirt on who now, huh?"

Noah stands, his tall frame blocking the sun for a second before I watch him walk inside.

I don't know what to think. Everything inside my head is

bouncing around, causing shooting pains as it moves. Thinking hurts.

Drinking sucks.

Heather is dead to me.

I lie back and start to laugh. This would be my life. I would be the one who has a job to do, can't talk around him because he's that freaking hot, and gets drunk. However, I don't even do that half-assed. Nope, I go balls to the wall and get so hammered I fall into a pool and pass out right in front of the guy I'm supposed to be getting the scoop on.

Oh, how the article has changed now.

The one thing I've noticed in my hazy mind is that he didn't look at me as if I was a drunken idiot when I woke up from God knows what I did last night. In fact, his gaze was full of tenderness. Noah didn't make fun of me or make me feel stupid, which is what I expected. It would have been like any other time I made an error and had it flung back in my face.

Doesn't change the fact that I made a total ass of myself.

The door slides open, and I expect to see Noah returning with his glowing tan and perfect hair, but it's Heather. She looks exactly how I feel. Black streaks are smeared on her face, her hair is in a messy bun, and she's sporting her sunglasses.

"How you doing?" I ask before I sit up, grab my mug, and gulp my coffee.

"Dude, how much did we drink?" She flops into the chair Noah vacated and rolls to her side.

"Way more than we should."

Heather pulls her shades down and peeks over the rim. "What the hell happened to you? Are you naked?"

I wrap the blanket a little tighter. "No, but according to Noah, it was an interesting night."

"Did you get your interview?"

I glare at her. "Nope. I was so hammered that I fell in the pool . . . with my clothes on. I think I tried to kiss him, but I could be drunk dreaming that part. I know I attempted an interview and remember saying something about . . ." I drop my head in my hands.

I did not do that. No, I couldn't have said all that.

"About?" She prods with a hint of enjoyment in her voice.

"Being a good lay," I mutter each word tentatively.

Heather bursts out laughing. She holds her stomach as she goes on and on. "You didn't! Oh, God. You would, Kris. I love you, but you're such a spaz-ass."

"I would've been professional if my best friend hadn't gotten me sloshed."

Then I recall the way I couldn't even look at him when he walked into the kitchen. I was practically drooling on myself as I sputtered out one-word responses. That is what caused me to take a stupid shot. I figured if I could get myself under control, I could manage it. Apparently, I was seriously mistaken.

"I wasn't holding a liquor bottle to your head. You did that all on your own." She pushes her glasses back up.

"Thanks for reminding me," I grumble. "I can salvage this."

She snorts and takes the coffee from me. "How?"

"I haven't figured that part out."

There is an advantage to this, I know a little more about him. Noah is a sweet guy. Considering he didn't leave me out here cold and wet all night, I could also add on caretaker as well. I can work with that. If he were an asshole, he'd have left me to fend for myself. The memories come in small, random bursts. His smile, his laugh, the feel of his big, hard ... I gasp.

"What?" Heather asks, sitting up and looking around.

"It's fine. I just remembered something," I say quickly.

"Please tell me you didn't do anything with him." She gives me a pointed stare.

I shake my head. "Nothing happened."

"Not that it would be a bad thing," Heather clarifies. "Noah is a good guy, and ... you know how I feel about Scott. Plus, rebound sex is the best sex."

I groan, taking my coffee back. "Yes, I know how you all feel about my worthless husband."

I've never said anything to my friends, but it was incredibly difficult knowing what they thought of him. They were right about a lot, I can admit that much, but I hated it. Having to bring him places, where he wasn't truly welcome and hoping they'd be nice, was almost too much at times.

When the people you love hate the person you choose, it's like being torn in half.

Scott complained about my friends constantly and tried to drive a wedge between us.

Thankfully, he was never able to sever the bond we share.

"You know I would've put up with him for the rest of my life if he made you happy, right?" Heather says as she grips my hand.

"I know."

"There is no man who will ever break us."

I smile and sigh. "Four chicks?"

"Four chicks who can never pick the dicks," Heather finishes the joke.

We always joked as kids that no dick would come between

the chicks. I'd say the joke held up better than we could've ever imagined. Friends for over twenty years who were still as close as we were in high school.

I laugh as an anvil slams against my skull. "I should get home," I practically cry as I press my temples.

I want to sleep.

And drink ten gallons of water to rid myself of this hangover.

"Are you going to register for the marathon today?"

My head falls to the side and I give her a blank look. "I'm not running a marathon today. I'm not moving from this chair if I can avoid it."

"Kris, it's not today," she complains. "It's in a few weeks and you promised this would be our thing. That we'd run in Steph's honor."

"Can't our thing be napping?" I think that's a much better thing to have. "I'm sure Stephanie would've supported this."

In fact, that's my plan for today since I'm kid-less for the first time.

Heather rolls her eyes. "I promise not to call Nicole if that'll help persuade you. Lord knows if she hears about you falling in the pool and sleeping on the lawn chair, she's going to have ammo for a year."

She wouldn't dare. "You better not tell her."

"You better not bail on me."

I shake my head, regretting it instantly. I need to get out of here before she convinces me to do some other random shit. "You were my favorite. Now, not so much."

She laughs. "I'll live with the guilt."

"I'll remind you more often."

"I look forward to it," Heather replies as I get to my feet.

I toss the damp towel on her as I pass by, and she laughs. "I hate you," I say with sarcasm.

"I love you, too. Say goodbye to Noah!"

I internally groan as I enter the house. If there's a God, he'll let me get out of this house without running into Noah. My feet hit the ice-cold tile floor, and I remember just how unclothed I am. However, I'm not going back out for the damn romper. It's Florida and bathing suits should be part of the acceptable daily wardrobe.

The coast is clear as I start to move toward the front door. I get to the handle and am about to turn it when my hopes of getting away undetected vanish.

"Running away, are you?" Noah's raspy voice stops me.

Damn it. I clearly have no luck.

My head thumps against the door, and I close my eyes. "You caught me."

His low chuckle rumbles through the foyer. "I wanted to make our date."

Umm. "Date?"

"You owe me," Noah says as he descends the stairs.

My head drops a little to the left, and my hand finds my hip. "Oh, I owe you now?"

"I did fall head over heels for you . . . into a pool."

His lips turn into a cocky grin, and I can't help but laugh. "Yes, you did."

"I think that at least buys me dinner." Noah's shoulders rise and fall, and he is standing so close that I have to tilt my head back.

I study his eyes, the way the shamrock color swirls with a seafoam color in the center. Noah moves a little closer, making me lean back so I'm pressed against the cool wood. I itch to touch him again, to remember the way his skin feels beneath my fingers, but I won't.

"Well?" he asks, leaning in so there's almost no space between us.

Dinner with him is a bad idea.

My lips part, and I speak. "You owe me an interview."

That was not what I was going to say.

"Is that a yes?"

There are two choices. I'm so stupid and know exactly which one I'll take.

"Fine. Dinner—for work only." I tack on the last part, hoping to save myself a little dignity.

Noah's chest touches mine, just a brush of his body against mine, and then he steps back, leaving me freezing. "I'll see you tonight at eight."

"For work," I clarify again.

"Sure, sweetheart. Work it is."

I may have just fallen in love with my job.

CHAPTER EIGHT

KRISTIN

"YES, MOM, I KNOW." I try to contain my frustration as I tidy the house. She's been yammering in my ear for the last ten minutes about how hard it is to maintain a marriage.

"Then you should know that a divorce is ten times harder," she admonishes.

I understand that my parents have the marriage of the century, but my father is a unicorn. He loves my mother so much that it's almost painful to be around. I tried to pretend that I had even a sliver of that, but I didn't.

"You know what's really hard? Being with a man who puts me down all the time. Loving someone who doesn't love me back. More than anything, it's hard when I know I can't fix it because I'm never going to be good enough." I pull in a heavy breath and fight back any tears.

"Oh, Kris."

"I need you on my side, Mom."

"I'm always on your side. Always. I just don't want to see you do something rash." Her voice cracks.

My mother and father have been there for me every step of the way. They are the kind of parents who should've had twenty kids instead of only me. There is no woman in the world who deserved to be a mom more than mine, but she couldn't. She almost died having me, and Daddy refused to try again no matter how much she begged. I know she wants what's best for me, but now that I've had time away from Scott, I see how bad it was.

"It's not rash. It's been a long time coming, and honestly . . ." I sigh as I plop onto my bed. "I should've left years ago."

Mom goes quiet and then clears her throat. "I should've done more earlier."

"What?"

"I kept making excuses for the things he said." Her tone is dejected. "I would tell your father how much I worried, but then I would rationalize it away."

"I did the same thing," I admit. For years, I would find one reason or another to allow his behavior to continue. Then, after a while, I accepted it as normal and what I was worth.

It wasn't until Nicole made a comment about a year ago that I finally took notice of how wrong things really were. She asked me about what I would have said if it were Aubrey who was married to a man like Scott.

For the first time, I saw it from an outsider's eyes.

And I didn't like a damn thing about it.

"I'm sorry, Kris," my mother says.

"It's Scott who needs to apologize . . . not you."

We talk a little more about my job and how my first weekend has been without the kids home. I miss them terribly. Being in my home without them is weird, and I keep listening for Aubrey's sweet laughter or Finn yelling at the video game.

"I want you to know how much admiration I have for you," she says after I tell her I need to get ready for tonight.

"Why?"

"Because you're doing something about your life. You could've taken the easy road and stayed with him, but you chose yourself and your kids, and I'm proud of you." Her words mean more to me than she'll ever know.

This has been the hardest thing I've ever done. Some days, I'm not sure I'll survive, but I haven't died yet.

"Thank you, Mom. I love you."

"I love you, too."

After not finding anything in my closet and unpacking two more boxes, I finally settle on a turquoise slip dress. I haven't worn this in forever, but thankfully, it fits perfectly. My hair is smooth, hanging past my shoulder blades, and has enough Marula oil in it to keep it controlled without it looking heavy.

Considering the freak show I looked like when I left Heather's, anything is an improvement.

I grab my phone to call Aubrey and see a text.

> **HEATHER**
> I gave Noah your address since he said you were meeting but didn't know where you lived . . .

Oh!

> **HEATHER**
> A date? Are you sure you're ready for this?

It's not a date. It's work.

She's never going to buy this.

HEATHER

I'm not judging if it is. I worry about you, that's all. Just promise me you won't drink yourself stupid so you can say more than one word.

I need new friends.

Have I told you lately that I hate you?

HEATHER

Yup. Just making sure it was still the same. Don't do anything I wouldn't do.

You're telling me to sleep with him?

HEATHER

No! I guess I'm not the pillar of good choices anymore.

Nicole. I blame Nicole.

I smile and put my phone down. Now that I know he's coming here, I start to panic a little.

He's wealthy, gorgeous, and probably has some huge house while I'm living rent-free in my best friend's place.

On the other hand, why do I care? This isn't a date. I don't have feelings for Noah. He's just some guy I'm supposed to write about. No reason to care what he thinks of me.

None at all.

Who the hell am I kidding? I'm a bad liar and as parts of last night come back to me, I don't know how I'm going to look at the man with a straight face.

Nervous energy pulses through me as I move around the house. I place a few photos on the end table, arrange and then rearrange the table decorations, and then I head to the couch to wait.

After a whole three seconds, I can't stand the sitting and jump up. As I'm heading to once again fix the table, the doorbell chimes.

Okay, this isn't a date, it's a work function.

At this point, I should just hope I don't pee myself, which is pretty much the bottom of the barrel for me.

I take two deep breaths and open the door. Noah's face is right there as he leans against the frame. His emerald eyes are deeper than before thanks to the green shirt he's wearing. His dark brown hair is pushed back from his face, and I can't breathe.

He flashes one of his luminous smiles, and I think I actually hit the bottom of that barrel.

"Hi." His voice washes over me.

I stare, and my legs go all mushy. I lean my head on the edge and smile back. "Hi."

"I brought these for you."

Noah hands me a large bouquet of calla lilies. "They're beautiful."

And I want to make sweet, sweet love to you.

I need a therapist.

I look at the flowers, which are an array of pink and white, and am grateful for something to distract myself with.

"Not half as beautiful as you are," Noah says, bringing my attention slowly back to him.

My cheeks burn, and I swoon. I've never swooned before, but I rise up on my toes, sigh, and drop back down. Like a freaking teenage girl with her first crush.

If I could slap myself right now, I would. Instead, I

straighten my back and vow to get a handle on my shit.
"Thank you again. I'll just put these in water if you want to
come in."

"Sounds good."

Noah enters the house, and I head to the kitchen, realizing
too late that Danni organized the place and I have no bloody
idea where my vases ended up. I end up grabbing the first cup
I find and put the flowers in my makeshift version of a vase.

"So this is Heather's old home?" he asks from the other
room.

"Yup. I spent countless nights here as a kid so it kind of
feels like home to me," I reply as I look around the cabinets for
anything better than Aubrey's pink Barbie cup. I search high
and low, but there is nothing to be found.

Anxious, I close the drawer quickly, catching my finger.
"Shit!"

"You all right in there?"

No, I'm the walking definition of a hot mess. "Yeah, everything's great!" I call out and roll my eyes. I should assume this
is how the rest of my evening will go.

Not wanting to keep him waiting or show my ass, even
more, I grab the cup and place it in the center of the table.

Classy is my middle name. My mother would have a coro-
nary if she saw this.

"Sorry," I say as I turn to find him watching me. "Ready?"

Maybe I can distract him and he won't notice? I move over
a smidge to block his view and lean against the edge of the
table.

"You in a rush? I figured we could talk a little, get to know
each other." Noah's voice is deep and smooth.

Couldn't he sound like a girl? Anything to make him a little less appealing. I don't feel like that's asking too much. I need to find anything to keep me from embarrassing myself.

He moves toward me as I study him. Looking for that thing . . . he has to have one. I search his face, finding nothing but beautiful green eyes and a come-fuck-me smile. My gaze roams lower, already knowing this is a bad idea but unable to stop myself. His shoulders are broad and the angle tapers into a triangle. I remember how my legs fit perfectly around his waist and wish I could forget the way my hands moved against the muscles on his arms.

"Kristin?" Noah breaks me out of my trance.

"Oh! Umm," I stammer. "Yeah, no. We should . . . you know . . . go."

Real freaking smooth, Kristin.

Noah chuckles. "Did you hear me?"

Crap.

"Sorry, I must still be a little hungover." Or a little smitten and unable to focus.

He pushes back a strand of my hair that fell forward and tucks it behind my ear. "Well, you look beautiful."

My fingers grip the edge of the table, tightening at his compliment. "Thank you." I look at my toes, hoping to hide the blush on my cheeks. I can't remember the last time I was this nervous around a man.

I don't know if it's because I'm free from Scott, but it's strange and unnerving. This shouldn't be how I'm reacting to him. He's an assignment, and as a journalist—which I'm calling myself even though in actuality I'm writing for a gossip blog—I should be professional. Noah brings the doe-eyed girl in me out.

Noah's finger moves to my chin, and he lifts it up. The

intensity in his eyes causes butterflies in my stomach to flutter. Has a man ever looked at me like this? I don't think so. There's so much desire there that I could drown in it.

I've already drowned once before. In fact, I'm still treading water now.

"Noah," I shake my head. "I . . . I have to pee." He takes a step back, and I could quite possibly die of mortification. "I mean, I have to see . . . something."

He laughs, and I slap myself mentally—twice. "No problem. I'll move so you can . . . see something."

"Can we just go since I clearly am hell bent on making all of our interactions awkward? I *really* need this interview, and I'd like for us to do it before I scare you off."

Noah's lips turn up, and he lifts his chin. "You want us to do it, huh?"

I release a heavy sigh while looking at the ceiling. "Shoot me now."

"I'm just giving you a hard time." He nudges me.

"I guess I deserve it after you babysat my drunk ass all night."

Noah slowly nods. "This is true."

I push his chest lightly and giggle. "You're not supposed to agree."

"You said it," he defends.

"I give up."

Noah wraps his arm around my shoulders, pulling me against his side. "I'm kidding. It was my honor to make sure you didn't drown in the pool."

Our eyes meet, and something electric flows between us. It's different from last night, more intense if that's even possible. My heart races as his fingers tense, and we stare at each other.

The phone rings, and he slowly drops his arm from around me.

"I should get that," I croak before clearing my throat.

"Right."

I grab the phone and see Scott's number. That's one way to kill a mood.

"Hello," I answer, keeping my back to Noah.

"Mommy!"

"Hi, baby." I smile hearing Aubrey's voice over the line.

I turn, look at the sexy celebrity standing in my house, and cover the receiver. "It's my daughter. I'll be just a second."

Noah nods.

"Do you miss me?" she asks.

"Of course, I miss you. Are you having fun with Daddy?"

Aubrey lets out a heavy sigh, and I picture her little face. "I guess."

"You guess?"

"Daddy is working, and Finn is being mean."

"I'm sorry, Aub. Maybe you can ask Daddy to do something fun?" I suggest. Scott has never had the kids on his own. I was always there, handling everything and keeping them entertained.

She goes silent for a second. "I guess."

"Is something wrong, honey?"

I hate hearing her like this. She's my bubbly, happy kid. Aubrey is always the one who brings people's spirits up. Her heart is huge, and her smile is contagious.

"No, I miss you. Daddy doesn't tuck me in like you do, and he doesn't cook."

I do my best to explain that he and I are different and comfort her at the same time. This is the part of divorce I wanted to avoid. Having my children struggle is all I worry about. They don't deserve this, but it's unavoidable. That doesn't mean I still don't hate it.

"I'll see you tomorrow," I remind her.

"I'm going to hug you!" Her sweet little voice proclaims.

"You bet you will!"

We hang up, and I release a heavy sigh.

"Everything okay?" Noah asks.

"Yeah." I smile. "Mom life."

"Not that I have a clue what that means, but it sounds like your kid loves you very much."

Still smiling, I walk over to the table to grab their picture. "These are my babies." Noah grips the photo frame, and I stand beside him. "That's Finn, he's ten, and that's Aubrey, she turned six a month ago. This is the first time they've been with their father alone for the night, which sounds crazy, but they've always been with me or my parents."

Noah's eyes fill with a sadness that mirrors my voice. I don't think I ever allowed myself a chance to think about it until now. I have no idea what they'll eat, do, think about, dream of. My parents would come to our house if we wanted to go out, and Scott never wanted to go away just the two of us so they've only spent a night at my parents, but I went to get them before they woke up. I've been there each morning, and now I'll have every other weekend without them.

His hand touches my cheek, and I realize a tear fell. "You're not crazy to miss your kids, Kristin."

"I'm sorry. I'm the most unprofessional reporter ever." I wipe the other side of my face, take the photo, and put it back.

"You're not." He smiles, but I don't believe him.

"You're lying."

"Maybe a little."

I laugh and shake my head. "Okay, interview and no alcohol or crying, deal?"

Noah extends his hand. "Deal."

CHAPTER NINE

NOAH

"SO, WHAT'S GOOD AROUND HERE?" I ask as we climb into the car. I meant to ask Eli, but he was too busy lecturing me on why this dinner shouldn't happen. Then Heather chimed in.

I assured them both this was mainly a business dinner, which was partially true. Heather's narrowed eyes told me she knew that as well. Kristin needs her interview, we clearly didn't do that last night, and time is expiring on her deadline.

I'm being a nice guy, that's all. It has absolutely nothing to do with the fact that I still smell her shampoo in my nose, feel her skin against mine, and want to hear her laugh.

Kristin tucks her brown hair behind her ear and tilts her head. "Well, we're not New York City, that's for sure, but I love Whiskey Joe's. It's low-key, and since it's off-season, you won't get hounded."

There's nothing more appealing than the idea of privacy with Kristin, but I remember to keep myself in check since this is business. "Sounds great."

"I haven't been there in so long, I love the food and it's right on the beach."

Her excitement has me wishing we were already there. Dinner and a moonlit stroll on the beach with her might satisfy my need to be around her. I want to know what it is about her that has me twisted inside.

"Why haven't you gone?"

She turns her head to look at me with a sad smile. "Life."

I get it more than she knows. Some of my favorite things I've quit doing because my days are reading lines, traveling, press bullshit, and personal trainers. The last few months have been the first chance I've gotten to take any time to do things I enjoy. "Life can sure get in the way."

"Life can be a bitch."

I laugh. "Yeah . . . it can."

She releases a heavy sigh, and I can almost feel the weight on her shoulders. I remember the way my mother would do the same. "Tell me more about your kids," I prompt.

Kristin instantly perks up and smiles. "Well, Finn is difficult, but he's my spirit animal. I swear, that kid is so much like me it's a little scary."

"Scary? From what I know, you're pretty awesome."

"Oh, yeah!" Kristin giggles. "I'm a whole lot of awesome when I'm drunk or passed out. Life goals right there."

I want to reach over and take her hand because, even in her laughter, I hear the pain. There's something inside me that wants to comfort her, but I don't. I have to keep my lines clear. "We all need to relax a little."

"I clearly need to find a way to balance that."

I shake my head. "One night of letting go doesn't make you reckless. So, what does Finn like to do?"

She shrugs and turns herself a little to face me. "Finn is very mechanical. I watch him take things apart and put them back together. He's definitely a literal kind of person, who thinks directions are meant to be followed. Aubrey is a free spirit. That girl is going to be big trouble when she's older."

As she speaks, I think about the fact that I have none of these things. Money, fame, and nice things aren't fulfilling. Once upon a time, I wanted a life like hers. Kids and a family were the only things on my mind, but that evaporated quickly. If only things hadn't happened the way they did that night.

My heart begins to pound so hard in my chest I swear I could bruise. It's been so long since I've allowed myself a moment to think about her.

Think about all the plans we had and how they were torn away.

"Noah?" Kristin touches my arm. "Are you all right?"

"Sorry," I say quickly. "You were telling me about Aubrey?" I think that's her name.

Kristin's hand drops, and I feel the loss. Fuck. What is it with this girl? It can't just be that she's gorgeous. I've seen plenty of hot chicks and have been fine. If I could place it, I could figure out how to deal with it.

"We don't have to talk about my kids," she offers.

"I'm not complaining. If you'd rather talk about something else . . ."

"I don't want to bore you."

The thing is, I never get to do this anymore. Normal conversations don't exist in my world. People are either asking me a million questions or trying to get something from me. "I have a feeling I'll do a lot of talking about myself once we get our date going."

"Working. Dinner." Kristin glances at me with the mom look.

"Sure. Our working dinner." My voice is patronizing. "How about you tell me about Heather and your friends? Eli's stories are . . . entertaining."

Kristin bursts out with laughter. "Oh, I can only imagine! My friends are definitely interesting."

She fills me in on how they met in high school and the way they've kept their friendship intact through the years. It's insane to me that they've been able to keep in touch the way they have. My best friend from high school only hits me up when he wants cash.

"You're closest with Heather, though?" I question because their dynamic baffles me.

"Umm." She bites her thumbnail. "I don't know how to answer that. We're all close in different ways. Heather and Nicole are really close and Danielle has been my person mostly. Since my separation, it's weird . . ."

"Why?"

Why the fuck do I care so damn much?

"Danielle and her husband have been having issues for a while. If I had to guess, it scares her that Scott and I couldn't find a way. Then her husband and my . . . well, ex-husband-to-be are close friends. It's put a strain on our friendship a little."

Scott. Even his name is stupid. He's clearly a fucking moron for letting her go or saying she was anything but beautiful. I shouldn't ask her, but I'm dying to know. "Why did you guys . . . end things?"

Kristin's eyes fill with sadness, and I hate that I put it there.

Heather kept calling him Asshole as if it were his name,

just Asshole. I'm assuming he's a fucking tool, and I'm waiting for confirmation.

"Our working dinner is taking a turn . . ."

I smile. "I'm just wondering why, if you're the best lay of some guy's lifetime, your husband could walk away. You know sex is key to a healthy relationship. I figure either you're lying about the good in bed part or your ex is the issue."

Kristin covers her face with her hand. "It had nothing to do with that, and I'd totally be fine with you forgetting everything I've ever said since we met."

"Doubtful."

There's nothing about last night I'm likely to forget.

She shifts in her seat. "You know, I've always wondered why someone hasn't invented a magic pill that can make you forget things you don't want to remember? Or give you the ability to eat any food you want and not gain weight. With all the smart people in the world, how has this not happened?"

I glance over at her and laugh. "I have no idea."

"These are real-life issues. Oh!" Her voice shifts to excitement. "I love this song!"

Kristin turns up the radio and starts to hum softly. For a moment, it's as if she forgets I'm here and belts out the lyrics. I'm stopped at the red light, and I can't keep my eyes off her. She looks free, happy, and lost in the song. She sings louder and bobs her head.

The one thing Heather kept repeating is how broken Kristin is. I've yet to see that in her. All I see is someone who makes my heart race. I watch her letting go to the music, hoping the light never changes. I could stare at her like this all night. The song hits the chorus and as the note escapes, her eyes fly open, and she covers her mouth.

"You have a beautiful voice," I say, wanting her to keep going.

She scoffs and then laughs at herself. "I'm such a dork. I can't even."

"You're adorable." I go for honesty because I doubt she'll believe it anyway.

The light changes and I can't see her reaction, but the sound of her groan causes me to grin. I like that I keep her slightly off-kilter.

"Why do I continue to embarrass myself with you? It's like I forget to be normal."

I pull into the parking lot of the restaurant, if I can call it that, and place my hand on her leg. "I like that you feel comfortable enough around me to sing. Not many people are that secure. They act like they think I want them to be."

Kristin's blue eyes meet mine. "I'm not usually like this," she admits. "I'm the uptight one out of my friends."

"Don't be anyone else but who you are, Kristin. There's nothing sexier than a woman who's confident. Trust me."

She clears her throat, and I watch the walls go up. "Ready to eat?"

I'll let her win this one, but the game is far from over. "Sure."

CHAPTER TEN

KRISTIN

DINNER IS nothing like the beginning of our night or the damn car ride where I felt like pretending to be auditioning for *The Voice*. Thankfully, he hasn't mentioned anything about either incident, and we've moved on to strictly interview conversation. Noah is in actor mode, and I've fallen into the reporter role. It is as if a switch has been flipped for both of us as soon as I pull out my notebook, which is fine by me.

"And what about any possible love interests?" I ask as I continue down my list. Noah is quiet long enough that I look up. "Noah?"

He wipes the ketchup off his chin and leans back. "I wasn't prepared for that one."

"Oh?" I question. "I figured that's probably the most common question you get asked."

Noah is definitely one of the most eligible bachelors in Holly-wood. He's attractive, smart, sexy, rich ... did I mention sexy?

I'm surprised that isn't the leading question on every

reporter's mind. I've left it for later because I felt like I've already done enough damage as it was. Might as well leave the juicy gossip questions until the end when I can run out and grab a cab if I have to.

"It is," he clarifies. "I guess I wasn't sure we were going to go there. I don't want to lie to you, but at the same time, I'm not sure I should answer."

"So, does that mean there is someone?" I try not to feel any sense of disappointment and fail miserably. A small part of me wants there to be no other woman. A larger part of me wants to not feel that way. I have no claim on him. I'm still married for fuck's sake. Yet, I can't help it.

Noah's hand glides across the table, coming to a rest close enough to me that I could touch him. "It means I shouldn't tell you, Kristin."

My heart flutters at the way he says my name. "But you're going to anyway?" I smile.

"I'll say this part on the record, but only if you agree to go off the record after."

I nod.

"I need you to say we'll be off the record when I tap my fingers."

"Okay, we'll be off the record when you tap your fingers."

I'm going to have an exclusive for my first interview. Oh, my could-be-my-child boss will be happy.

"There's someone I have feelings for." Noah grins.

"Care to comment more?" I urge.

"No." He taps his fingers and falls silent.

Well, that sucks. I needed more to make it really juicy.

"Okay, we're off the record." I turn my recorder off and put the pen down. I hate that he's going to say something, and I can't write about it.

"I'm looking at her." Noah pulls his hand back, grabs his beer, and smiles before taking a drink.

My lips part and I don't say a word. Me? He's crazy. I'm the awkward friend of his friend's girlfriend who got drunk and passed out. I'm the nut job who pulled him into a pool, and he got stuck dealing with. I'm the unprofessional crazy lady he had to go out of the way to have dinner with because I failed the first time we met.

He must be joking. Maybe this is some kind of celebrity hazing experiment.

Screw with the new journalist.

That has to be it. Because I am a frumpy old housewife who couldn't keep her husband satisfied.

"Did Heather put you up to this? Or Eli, because I called him old the other day?"

"No."

I lean back as the air pushes from my lungs. "You don't even know me. Other than I'm clearly a mess."

Noah pushes his sleeves up and rests his arms on the table. "I know that even after Eli and Heather tried to warn me off, I couldn't wait to pick you up for our date."

"Working. Dinner."

Maybe he has a memory condition and he doesn't realize who I am.

"Semantics." He smirks.

Oh, Jesus. Heather's texts now make sense. She knew he was interested or whatever. Why he would even consider wanting to get to know me is baffling.

"Noah, you don't know me. Trust me, I'm the last person

you would ever want to think about. I'm going through what I can only assume will be a nasty divorce. I'm a single mom, who clearly can't hold her liquor, and my job is to write gossip about you. Oh, and I can't sing for shit."

I figure it's best to lay it all out.

I am the last person he should ever want to date.

Noah smirks before running his hand through his thick, dark hair. "Well, when you put it that way . . ."

A short laugh escapes me, and I look at my hands. "With the never-ending line of actresses dying to get with you, it's crazy that you even blink twice at a hot mess like me. I'm no one special."

"Hey." He waits for me to look up from my hands before he continues, "We're all messes. If you think anyone in Hollywood has it together, you're wrong. I haven't had a girlfriend in almost fifteen years, and I'm not asking you to date me. Heather already threatened to castrate me if I tried."

There's my best friend I know and love.

"But I won't lie, I'm attracted to you, and if all we'll ever be is friends . . . I'm okay with that."

His words wash over me, and I'm not sure how to respond. It's clear that I'm attracted to him, but then again, any sane woman would be. He's Adonis . . . on crack.

And he's one drug I'd like to be addicted to.

Instead of saying any of that, I lean forward, mimicking his position. "We can't really be friends, can we? It's my job to write stories about your life."

He shrugs. "It means you'll be around a lot. Lots of time to win you over."

Okay, that's going to be a problem I didn't even consider.

"More like realizing you need a therapist more than I do."

Noah leans closer. "Maybe, or you'll see I'm just a normal guy."

I laugh. "Yes, normal. Because most guys are on the cover of *People* and *GQ*?"

"In my world."

"Yes, but I'm not from your world. I live in a world filled with bills, kids, an asshole ex, and a boss who thinks adding an emoji on every article gives it *pizazz*."

He smiles while shaking his head. "She sounds interesting."

"You have no idea." I sigh. "She's making a meditation room so that we can find our center when we feel stressed. According to her, my aura is messed up, and she wants to cleanse it. Whatever the hell that means."

Noah extends his hand across the table and touches my wrist. "I'm not asking for—"

"Kristin? Is that you?" I look up to see Scott's assistant, Jillian standing there. Her eyes move from me to Noah, and I quickly pull my hand back.

"Hi, Jill. Long time no see." I stand and give her a hug. "This is Noah Frazier. I'm writing an article on him for my new job. Noah, this is Jillian Cruger, she's my husb—ex-husband's assistant."

Her cheeks flush, and she giggles. "Of course. Nice to meet you. I'm a huge fan."

Noah shakes her hand and gives her a smile I haven't seen before. It's forced and almost looks fake. "Thank you. It's great to meet you."

She looks back to me and touches my arm. "I'm so sorry to hear about the divorce. Scott told me a few months ago, and I was so sad for you guys. I thought about calling you, but that would be really awkward."

"Yes, awkward would be a good word."

It must be awkward for a woman to come face to face with the wife of the man she's been vying to sleep with.

Scott may have treated me like shit, but Jillian walks on water. I'd listen to him constantly praising how she anticipates his needs and ensures his life is in order since I constantly missed things. In his eyes, the woman is perfect. I don't think for one second she's sad. Now she doesn't have to hide that she wants to sleep with him, if she isn't already.

"I just mean with all our history."

"Yeah, it's been tough, but the kids and I are moving on and are happy."

Jillian nods. "I'm glad. He's holding up well. I'm taking care of everything and making sure the weekends he has the kids are clear. I'll keep him in line."

Oh, I bet she will.

"Thanks, I'm sure the kids will appreciate their father's secretary making sure to pencil them into his schedule," I say and look back to Noah. "I'd love to catch up, but I should get back to my meeting."

"Yes, of course, sorry to have taken so much of your time. My friends and I are heading to another bar . . ." She looks at Noah with a coy smile. "Anyway, I should get back, but maybe I'll see you around?"

"Sure." I plaster a smile on. "It was great seeing you."

Lie.

"Oh, I'm sure we'll see each other again." Jillian fake hugs me again, waves to Noah, and walks off.

I watch her head back to the table, where she points to us

and giggles. Her friends all move around, trying to get a peek at us.

"How do you handle that?" I ask Noah, looking back over my shoulder at them.

"The stares?"

"It's invasive."

Noah grips the back of his neck. "Are we back on the record?"

Crap, the interview.

"No, I would never . . ."

"Let me say this, and then we'll get back to the interview." Noah reaches as if he wants to touch me, but then rethinks it and picks up his drink instead. "The stares are part of my life. I accepted it when I went into acting and live with it because, if they're not staring, then I'm irrelevant. But more important, you're ten times more beautiful than she is." He lifts his chin toward Jillian's table.

Confusion fills me with his statement. It came out of nowhere. "What?"

"I saw the way you looked at her, and I'm telling you if your husband ever touched her, he downgraded. You're by far the most beautiful woman I've ever seen, and he's a fool. Now, we're back on the record." He grabs the recorder and turns it back on.

"I-I—" I don't know what to say. "You . . ."

Noah slips back into work mode. I see the difference in his eyes, but I can't find my own bearings. He was able to see in just a moment what I thought and felt, then he said something that would comfort me. Who is this guy? Surely he can't be this perfect.

He probably has a small dick.

If my drunken memory is correct, I already know he doesn't.

Still, he has to be overcompensating for something.

"You're sure you want to go for a walk?" Noah asks again.

"Yeah, I haven't been here in forever."

I could use the fresh air. We finished dinner, and my mind keeps spinning back to what he said about being interested. I pull my shoes off and grip them in one hand as we head toward the water.

"I've noticed that most people who live by the beach barely ever go," he notes.

"One word: tourists."

He nods. "Makes sense, but then why live here?"

My laugh is a mixture of wonder and sadness. "I don't know. It's like I want the option of going to the beach on the off chance that people aren't here."

There's also the fact that my entire life is here. However, I can't remember the last time I took the kids to the ocean. Finn used to love it, and Aubrey was little the last time we came, but they have this right in their town, and they don't get to enjoy it.

"Like now?" he asks.

"Exactly."

The sun is setting, painting the sky in beautiful orange hues, and the little beach area is empty. Noah and I walk along the shoreline, allowing the water to cover our feet. He tells me a little about the upcoming audition he has and how his agent is pushing him.

I listen, not for the story, but because he's sharing pieces of himself. Noah's hand brushes the back of mine as our arms swing. Each time our skin touches, a thrill runs through me, and after the third time, a part of my brain tells me this isn't an accident.

Sure enough, his hand captures mine. My breath hitches, but I don't pull back. I stare at our entwined hands and try to slow my racing heart.

Noah stops walking, pulling me to do so as well.

"Dance with me," he requests.

"What?"

He takes a step closer, tugging gently so I'm only inches from him. His voice is deep and seductive. "I've always wanted to dance on a beach at sunset. Will you dance with me?"

I should say no.

"Yes."

Or I can go the opposite.

Noah doesn't wait, his arms slip around me as if they are meant to be there and my hands rest on his chest. We sway to the sound of the ocean, and my pulse races. I don't know what it is, but there's something happening between us. It scares me more than I want to admit, and still, I'm not pulling away.

I'm leaning a little closer.

We move as the sun dips lower and the pink sky darkens more. Noah's hands splay across my back, and I stare into his eyes. I want to say so many things, but I'm afraid to speak.

His hand moves to my cheek as he pushes a lock of my hair away from my face. "I don't know what it is about you." His voice breaks the silence.

Needing to shift the moment from intense, I take a step back and laugh. "It's because of the best sex comment. That's all; I promise it'll pass."

Noah chuckles, pulls me to his side, and then releases me. "We'll see. No guy would pass up the chance to see if it's true."

He nudges me as we start walking back toward the car. "I know of one," I say under my breath so low I know he can't hear me.

CHAPTER ELEVEN

NOAH

I FUCKING suck at this backing off thing.

Eli and Heather are going to kill me, but I'll go down a happy man. Everything about this woman is intoxicating. She has no idea how beautiful she is, and when she laughs, her blue eyes brighten and make me want to drop to my knees. There's no reason I can find as to why I feel this way about her, yet here I am, making the wrong choices.

Telling her shit I swore I wouldn't.

Doing things I promised my friends I wouldn't even attempt.

The way she smiles without any reservations, sings as if no one is listening, and danced with me without hesitation have all combined to make me well and truly fucked. I couldn't walk away now if I wanted to.

The car ride has been quiet. Kristin seems lost in herself, and I don't want to push her. I think through all the stupid shit I let fly out of my mouth, hoping I didn't sound like a lunatic.

"You okay?" I ask as we pull into her driveway.

"Yeah, sorry, just piecing together the article in my head."
She smiles.

"I hope I gave enough for the interview."

"You did. I think it'll be great."

I nod once and exit the car. I know this isn't a date, but my mother would kick my ass all the way back to the farm if I didn't treat a woman with respect and open her door. The few steps I take, I remind myself to back off.

After a deep breath, I pull the door open and help her out. She wobbles a little, catching herself in my arms. I pull her against me, holding her a bit closer than strictly necessary. Kristin's eyes lift, and there's no denying the desire floating in them. I can feel her pulse racing, but I lock myself down.

"Noah," she says my name with a sigh.

"Tell me you don't feel anything." I give her a chance out of this. I'll let her go if she says the words. "Tell me to stop coming around and that you're not interested."

"I can't . . ."

My hand slides up her back, molding her body to mine. "I want to kiss you."

She shakes her head, but her fingers move against my chest and find their way to the back of my neck. "We shouldn't."

"No, we shouldn't," I agree. "But if you don't stop me, I'm going to."

Kristin's fingers play with the hair at my nape.

My restraint is slipping.

"Three." I start to count.

"Two."

Kristin moves a little closer to my mouth, and I'm done.

Our lips meet, and I lean her back against the car, pinning

her so she can't escape. I kiss her as if it could be the last kiss we ever share. My hands move higher so I can cup her neck. When she sighs, I take the opening and slide my tongue inside. Kristin kisses me back, meeting me in every way. She wants me just as much as I want her.

Each time her tongue reaches mine, she makes a sound that goes straight to my dick. As much as I wish I could've kissed her last night, I'm damn glad she can't blame this on alcohol. My hands move down her body, loving every curve and dip.

Her fingers roam back to my chest, and her body tenses before she pushes me back.

"That . . ." She struggles to catch her breath. "That was . . ."

"Fantastic." I finish for her.

"Yes. It was, but that shouldn't have happened. Damn it. What is wrong with me?"

I take her face in my hands. "Nothing is wrong with you."

Kristin's eyes fill with regret. "Oh my God. I'm so sorry. I shouldn't have done that."

"You didn't do anything." This is all my fault. I'm the one who kissed her when I know all the shit she is going through. "It's me who should be sorry."

Kristin looks at the ground. "No, you shouldn't. I wanted you to kiss me. I wanted to kiss you, and I want a lot more, but I can't . . ."

My finger hooks under her chin, and I force her to look at me. "Because?"

I know all the reasons, but I need to be reminded so I don't kiss her again.

"I'm writing an article on you and your love life."

Is she serious? She thinks I give a fuck about that? She can write whatever she wants, they all do anyway. If that's her big reason, she has a whole new fight on her hands. One I'll win.

"It doesn't matter."

"I can't do this." Kristin slips out from between the car and me and starts to walk off.

I rush after her, not wanting this to be how our night ends. "I'm sorry," I say as I grab her arm. "I didn't mean to push you."

She lets out a deep breath. "You didn't do anything wrong. It's been a really long time since I've felt anything like this, and it's confusing and exciting and scary as hell. The truth is, we would never work." Kristin's hand rests on my chest. "I'm not ready, and I promise you don't want to even dip your toes into my crazy life."

If she only knew that I'd dive in headfirst.

I release her arm, knowing that I have to take a step back. Heather's words of warning ring in my head about the piece of shit her husband is and all the damage he's done to her that she doesn't even see.

"Can we be friends?" I ask, because I have a feeling it's the only way she'll agree to see me again.

"Really?" There is a cute little hint of surprise in her voice. "You want to be friends? I'm starting to question your sanity."

"Are you not ready to be friends? I figured we crossed over to that when I didn't let you drown."

She looks at the sky and mutters. "I'm never going to live that down, am I?"

"Probably not. Plus, it's my insurance policy if you write some crap about me that isn't true. It's all about leverage."

"Good to know." She slaps my arm. "I'm pretty sure my reporting that you stripped an unconscious drunk girl wouldn't bode well for your reputation, either."

I lean in, inhaling the scent of her citrus perfume. "That's not how I remember it."

"Well, Mr. Frazier, we'll just have to keep our aces in our pockets, now won't we?"

I rock back with a grin. "I guess we will. I look forward to reading the article."

Kristin grins. "I appreciate the exclusive, and tonight. I'm really sor—"

"Don't say it." I lift my hand. "It's me who needs to apologize. Can we start over?"

She nods. "I'd like that."

I reach into my pocket and pull out two sticks of gum. I hand her one. "No magic pill, but I have gum that helps you forget."

Kristin's smile is wide as she accepts my offering. "Magic gum, huh?"

"I hear it helps when you want to erase the past and start over."

I'm being the cheesiest fucking guy ever, but it's working.

"Well, then." She unwraps the stick and pops it into her mouth, and I do the same. "Working yet?"

I am an actor, time to do what I know. "I'm Noah Frazier, Eli's friend." I extend my hand.

"Nice to meet you, Noah," she says as she shakes. "I'm Kristin McGee, Heather has told me so much about you. I'm hoping to talk sometime soon for an article I'm writing."

"I look forward to seeing you for an interview."

"Me, too." Kristin pulls her bottom lip between her teeth as she ducks her head.

I cover her hand with my other one. "Have a great night, Ms. McGee."

She removes her hand and touches my arm. "Good night, Noah. I had a great time."

"I look forward to more." I wink and turn toward the car.

I remember what my drama teacher said about always leaving them wanting more, and that's exactly what I plan to do with her.

CHAPTER TWELVE

KRISTIN

I LEAN AGAINST THE WALL, wondering what the hell just happened.

Noah kissed me. I mean, *really* kissed me.

And I kissed him back.

Damn that was a good kiss.

A kiss that should never have happened. I don't know what came over me, but I couldn't stop myself. I needed to kiss him more than I cared about self-preservation. I barely know the man, but it's as if we've been friends forever.

There's this thing . . . this stupid thing that is going to fuck everything up if I let it happen again.

It won't. I won't let it because I'm in no place to bring another set of issues into my chaotic life. Jesus, how dumb can I be? I'm in the process of finalizing a divorce, a single mom, and I'm assigned to write about him.

After I'm sure I won't look like a giraffe learning to walk after the kiss of a lifetime, I find my way into the kitchen to pour a much-needed glass of wine. My deadline is Monday morning, and I'm way too keyed up to sleep, so I change into my comfy clothes and turn on my laptop.

The Word doc comes to life, I press play on the recorder, let my fingers hover over the keyboard, and start to get a rough draft going.

I mentally giggle about the title, knowing he'll get the inside joke.

Stripping Down to the Truth About Noah Frazier by Kristin McGee

NOAH FRAZIER, one of the leading men on *A Thin Blue Line*, which aired its series finale in late April, is undoubtedly a fan favorite. His character, the charming, broken-hearted, and endearing Officer Writt has been winning hearts for seven seasons. After we, here at Celebaholic, got a chance for an exclusive interview, we aren't surprised why. He's funny, sweet, and sexy as hell, but what sets Mr. Frazier apart is his down-to-earth attitude.

During our talk, we learned a little about his aspirations for the future, but more importantly, we asked if there's a special someone he's after. That seems to be the burning question on every single, and many married, women's minds.

Sitting in a local pub in Tampa, Noah spent a few hours chatting and giving me the answers we've been dying to know.

I put the tape on and start transcribing.

CELEBAHOLIC: Thank you so much for meeting with me. I can't

tell you how much of a fan I am and what an honor it is that
you agreed to do an interview.

NOAH FRAZIER: Thank you for inviting me. I'm happy to be
here.

CELEBAHOLIC: Are you enjoying your break from acting?

NOAH FRAZIER: I actually am. I've been spending time visiting
family and friends, trying to find the role that really fits me.

CELEBAHOLIC: Do you have any prospects for future projects?

NOAH FRAZIER: There have been two scripts I've been excited
about. We'll see, though. I'm enjoying being in Florida
right now.

Noah's voice is low, and knowing what I know, I hear the
double meaning. I write the responses regarding his work,
what it was like to be nominated for an Emmy, and how his
ultimate goal is to become a producer.

Then I get to what readers really want—the dirt.

CELEBAHOLIC: You're in town visiting Eli Walsh, correct?

NOAH FRAZIER: I am. Eli and I became close friends while
working on *A Thin Blue Line*.

CELEBAHOLIC: I'm sure you two get into a lot of trouble.

NOAH FRAZIER: Well, only when tequila is involved. Usually,
we're pretty boring, other times trouble falls in our laps or
pulls us in.

I can't help the smile that forms. I can see his grin clear as
day as he said that part. The way his green eyes were full of
mischief.

CELEBAHOLIC: I can only imagine. We know the world cried a little when Eli was no longer available, any possible love interests?

NOAH FRAZIER: There's someone I have feelings for.

CELEBAHOLIC: Care to comment more?

NOAH FRAZIER: No. She knows who she is.

CELEBAHOLIC: Well, she must be flattered.

NOAH FRAZIER: With any luck, she'll be more than that. I'm hoping for interested.

My heart starts to race, and my throat goes dry. I'm the girl he's talking about. I'm the girl that Noah Frazier has his sights set on, and I know what it feels like to be in his arms, touch his body. My lips tingle as I remember the way his mouth moved with mine, the mint taste on his tongue, and I have no idea what to do about any of that except stay away. Noah has no idea how damaged my heart is, and there isn't a chance in hell that he'll stick around if he catches a glimpse of it.

I lean back, close the laptop, and drain the remnants of my wine, already knowing there's no way I can finish the article now. I have Noah on the brain. It's been so long since anyone has looked at me like he does. Like I'm worth a damn. A man who has no business chasing a regular girl like me thinks I'm special.

No. I don't believe it.

He can't possibly want me for more than just a quick lay. I'm definitely not that kind of girl. I need more, I always have. The last thing I want is to be good, but not good enough for more.

I head to the bathroom to wash my face and get ready for

bed. "What was I thinking?" I say aloud as I stare at my reflection. "You're simple, frustrating, and couldn't get things right, Kristin. You failed at keeping Scott happy. You're worthless, just like he told you over and over." Tears start to fall as Scott's words fill my head. "You let yourself go. You *used* to be so pretty. Not tonight, I don't feel like working that hard to get you to the end."

There's no way a man like Noah is going to stick around. I'd be a fool to think otherwise.

LAST NIGHT WAS the worst night I've had since I left Scott. I cried myself to sleep, hearing fifteen years' worth of put-downs.

Doubt is irrational and doesn't care that the voice inside my head is from years of being with an unhappy man. I can tell myself that Scott used his insecurities on me so he felt better, but in the end, I'm not always strong enough to believe it.

Last night was one of them.

Now, in the mid-morning light, I know I was crazy to allow Scott to have that kind of power over me. His words are noise, and I'm going to drown it out with the positivity that lives inside me. Negativity is so much easier to believe, but I'm done with living in that hell.

I have a few hours before he's due to drop the kids off, and I frantically start to clean just to prove him wrong. I'm a good mother, I can keep a tidy home, and I'm pretty.

A knock on the door startles me.

"Kristin, you home?" Danielle's voice comes from the other side.

"Hey." I smile as I pull it open.

She lifts a cup of coffee in her hand, and I want to kiss her. "You are the best friend a girl could have."

Danni laughs and enters the house. "This place looks great, hun. You've done a great job of making it look different and yours."

"You think?"

She nods. "I do."

"Thanks." I motion to the couch, and we both take a seat. "I'm trying."

Danielle looks at her own cup and then back to me.

"You okay?" I ask.

"Scott told Peter something, and I went back and forth because Peter asked me not to repeat it, but fucking hell, you're my best friend. I don't care that they're friends. It's me and you against the world, right?"

My stomach clenches thinking this must be bad if Danielle is here at ten in the morning on a Sunday. Peter must have thought it was bad enough to repeat it as well.

"You're scaring me a little." I try to laugh but it sounds weird.

"Scott called Peter and told him that he has proof you've been having an affair."

Okay, now I laugh. "What? An affair?" I shake my head at the idiocy. "How could I have time to have an affair when I was too busy being a shitty wife to him?"

She closes her eyes. "I guess last night—"

"Oh, for fuck's sake!" I get to my feet. "I was working! I had an interview. Noah is who I'm covering right now, and we had dinner for my article. Unbelievable." I start to ramble because he's ridiculous. "How does a dinner equal an affair?"

Danni puts her hands up. "Don't shoot the messenger. I just know he's going to be a prick and try to use this."

Use this? Good God, he's unreal. Then it hits me, the only person he could've heard this from is Jillian. "So, his assistant sees me not even twenty-four hours ago and calls him on a Sunday to let him know that I was out to dinner. She's a very dedicated employee." I spit the last word.

"I want you to be prepared, Kristin. He's the guy who doesn't want the cookie but doesn't want anyone else to have it, either. I worry about you. I worry that he's going to fuck with you if he suspects things. Peter and I got in a huge fight this morning when he told me. I went off about how Scott shouldn't have a say in your life when he's the one who asked for the divorce."

I take her hand in mine and squeeze. She has no idea how much I appreciate her friendship. Peter and her relationship has been strenuous, and they've finally found a way to work through it. The fact that she's fighting her husband for me is unfair.

"Please don't do that. Don't let your marriage get tangled in my divorce."

She gives a sad smile. "We're fine. He understands now that I hit him over the head with the truth. Peter and I think Scott is using him right now. He calls to get information that Peter doesn't have, and he's seeing it now. Then he told Peter that he was clearly under the web of lies you've been twisting to make us all think you're the victim."

"He is such a narcissist!" I groan. "How was I making a web of lies? What lies, Danni? That he probably cheated on me

God knows how many times? Whatever, he wants a fight, I'm more than prepared for one."

Scott could make me think I was crazy for thinking what he was doing was wrong. It was as if my questioning things meant I was delusional. I don't know how he does it, but he can twist anything so that it's someone else's fault, spin a lie into a truth. I never saw it until I got out, but now that I have, it's crystal fucking clear.

Danielle releases a loud breath through her nose, and I know this next part won't be good. "You know Peter refused to take his case, but he wanted me to warn you that if Scott claims you were unfaithful during the marriage, it can affect custody, alimony, and child support."

I'm not playing this game with him. "I was never unfaithful."

"I know."

"If he accuses me of this, I swear . . ." I trail off, not even sure what I'll do. My lawyer is good, but I'm sure she's no match for whatever he could afford.

I'm so fucked if he does this. Peter works for a top criminal defense law firm, but he came from family law when he was just starting. He's represented a lot of athletes who have gotten themselves into sticky situations, and if he's worried . . . I should be, too.

"Don't show him your cards, Kristin. Don't let him know you have a clue. This is what he wants."

"I'm trying to be fair and get this over with! I want to be divorced already! I want my life back—without his voice in my head."

Danielle squeezes my hand. "It's time to play his game, but smarter."

"How? I don't think like that."

She raises her brows. "It's a good thing you have three best friends who have your back. You will not be alone with him. One of us will be here as a witness for any interaction you have, he doesn't have a case if every aspect can be refuted."

"This is crazy."

She shakes her head. "No, honey, this is war."

CHAPTER THIRTEEN

KRISTIN

ONCE I'VE CALMED MYSELF, I go back to cleaning the house. Danni is sitting at the island, watching me as I scrub the counter with so much effort, I might wear a hole in it.

"Kris?" she calls my name as she laughs. "I'm pretty sure it's clean."

I stop and sigh. There's so much I want to tell her. The fact is, Danielle has always been the one I run to when something happens. I share everything, and I'm dying inside to tell her about last night. It's killing me, but I worry about saying anything.

Not because she might not approve but because if this comes to some battle in court, I don't know if telling her is right.

She moves over beside me, placing her hand on my shoulder. "It's going to be okay."

I look up, opening then closing my mouth.

"You've got that look . . ."

"What look?" I play dumb.

"The I've-got-a-secret-and-it's-killing-me look. Spill it."

I drop the sponge in the sink and face her. "I'm not sure it's a good idea."

"Because?"

"How opposed are you to perjury?" I test her.

Danielle throws her hands in the air before they fall to her legs, making a loud *slap*. "Oh, dear God!"

"I'm asking hypothetically here." I cross my arms over my chest.

"Hypothetically?"

If we speak in the abstract, maybe I can share. "Yes, *hypothetically*, what would happen if someone kissed someone?"

Danielle's eyes widen. "Would that someone be asking because that someone is worried about a possible issue with a divorce?"

I shrug. "Maybe. I mean, this someone could just be asking because she's curious if that's considered cheating in the eyes of the law . . ."

Her smile grows, and she tilts her head to the side. "From what Peter says about the law, it's only intercourse that is considered adultery."

I nod. Well, at least I'm good there. I'm slightly glad that my life-altering kiss can't be used against me, but then again, I'm glad Scott is even stupider than I thought. There's nothing I've done wrong. "Good to know. What if she went out for . . . say . . . a dinner with a client?"

"Dinner is not adultery. Did your friend attend this dinner recently?" Danielle pushes.

"She did."

"Did she happen to see someone she knew?" She grins.

"She might have."

Her jaw drops. "Is your friend trying to kill me? Your *friend* has done nothing wrong by what you've shared so far."

"My friend appreciates the advice."

Danielle laughs. "Your friend is welcome. Your friend should also know that it's only during the marriage and if the friend used joint finances to facilitate her affair. At least that's my understanding."

"Well, my friend is totally in the clear." I bite my lip and wait. "She's not having any intercourse with anyone."

Danielle is ready to burst out of her skin, dying to know more. "Please tell me your friend kissed Noah Frazier, and that's who we're talking about!"

And there she blows.

"She did!"

"Holy shit! How? How does this happen to Heather and then yo—ur friend? Did I miss the hooking up with celebrity course in high school? Does Heather know? Oh, God, was it amazing? It looks like it would be amazing. Those freaking lips, man."

I pull her to the table and fill her in on the whole thing. Clearly, she knows it's me, and I'm almost giddy while I tell her the events leading to the amazing kiss. Her head falls to her fist as I tell her about the dance on the beach. She laughs when I explain the night at Heather's and then my random singing in the car.

My body feels as if I'm floating when I go into details about the kiss itself. Seriously, normal men don't kiss like that, and if they do, I've been missing out.

"You know what I hear through this whole thing?" Danielle asks.

"What?"

"My friend is back."

I run my hands through my hair. "I don't know what you mean..."

Or at least I don't want to admit what I think she's saying.

Danielle leans forward and touches my leg. "You've been a shell of the girl I've known my whole life. I don't think I knew it until now. When was the last time you were silly? When was the last time you sang in the car? Drank and danced? Were allowed to choose something you wanted and actually got it?"

I close my eyes with my head dropping down. "I don't want to think about this."

"I know you don't. I just want you to hear yourself. You may not see it, but I do. In the last ten minutes, you came to life. My best friend was finally here."

Tears begin to pool. "I never left."

"Scott took you away."

"No—" I start to deny.

"Listen to me, you were the happy one out of the four of us. Nicole is crazy. Heather is dependable. I'm the cynic. You were the one who smiled. Captain of the cheerleaders, homecoming committee, and . . . I forget all the other crap you did. It doesn't matter. It was you that kept us grounded, but he put you in a box, Kris. He made you smaller until you fit into what he wanted, and I'm so sorry I let that happen."

I look at Danni, the one who never cries but who currently has tears in her eyes. "Danni," I say softly.

"No." She wipes her face. "I didn't say anything. I thought you were happy. You weren't, though. Nicole would push to say something, and I'd shut her down."

"You couldn't have swayed me." I try to assure her. "I loved him. I wasn't ready to leave."

She nods. I hate that she's trying to take even an ounce of the blame for this. The reality is that until I was ready to be done, I would've stayed. They only would've made me angry by trying to get me to see what was happening, and my first reaction would have been to defend him. I really had believed it was my fault, that I wasn't good enough.

"I could've tried." Danielle looks away with shame.

"I love you for that."

"I love you for it all."

I pull her into my arms and rub her back. "Who knew your black heart could shed tears?" I joke.

This at least gets a laugh out of her. "I'll deny this ever happened."

"There's my girl."

"You're going to be happy again, Kris. I know it. Don't let Scott rob you of anything you want in life. If you like Noah, go for it. If you want to sow your wild oats, do it. No matter what, I've always got your back."

I'm beyond blessed to have the relationships I have. "It's too soon for me to date."

"Says who?" She scoffs.

"I'm not even divorced yet!"

Danielle rolls her eyes. "Who gives a shit? There's no timer on recovery. If you like him, why can't you date him?"

"Do you remember why you showed up here in the first place?" I remind her.

"Did your friend screw anyone while she was still living with her husband?"

We're back to the friend thing again. "No. Never. She was loyal to a fault."

"Then, I'll get complete clarification, but she should be

fine. And the only thing we'll worry about is if she's insane for walking away from a guy that looks like that!" She points to the file folder with Noah's picture on the front.

The doorbell rings, and we both stand. I'm excited to see my kids, but I know who's waiting with them—him.

I look to Danni, who nods. Here we go.

When I open the door, Aubrey's smile causes me to forget all the worries I had. She's the bright light in this dark storm. "Mommy!" Her arms are wide, and I scoop her up.

"I missed you so much!" I bury my nose in her hair and breathe my little girl in. "Oh, did you eat vitamins and grow?"

"No!" She giggles. "I'm the same."

"Finn!" I crouch low, and he puts his arm around my neck. "Hi, buddy."

"Hey," he says with a huff. "Can I go to my room?"

"Sure." I kiss his head, not caring that he's too cool for it anymore.

Aubrey gives me another squeeze as I clutch her tight. I don't think I truly allowed myself to feel how much I missed them. My heart feels so full having my babies with me.

I look over, and Scott's frame fills the door. "Hi," I say as I put Aubrey down.

"Hi. Right." He snorts.

The urge to roll my eyes is strong, but I shove it aside. He thinks he has something, and he has no idea that I know. "Honey." I squat, taking Aubrey's hands in mine. "Why don't you go take your bag to your room and put your things away?"

"Okay, Mommy." She looks back to Scott and rushes toward him. "Bye, Daddy."

"Bye, baby. I'll see you soon, okay?"

Her head drops, and she nods. "I love you."

He kisses her head. "I love you."

At least he can still be a good father. I stand here with my hand over my heart as she rushes to the back, giving us a moment.

"Have a good weekend with them?" I ask. My goal is to lead the conversation.

"I did. I hear you had a great weekend, too."

"Did you?"

I'm not giving him a damn thing. He wanted a divorce, he can deal with the actuality of what that means. My life is no longer his damn concern. "So, I'll see you in two weeks." I place my hand on the edge of the door, but he doesn't take the hint.

"How long have you been seeing another man behind my back?" Scott folds his arms across his chest.

I let out a short laugh. "I don't know what you're talking about, however, two days ago you were saying how we needed to meet at a neutral location to"—I lift my hand and make air quotes—"keep things separate."

He glares at me. "Ha! You admit to fucking another man behind my back? How many times? Is that why you refused me so many times?"

I hear someone clear their throat from behind me. "Oh, hi, Scott," Danielle says with a sweet tone. "How are you doing?"

His eyes meet mine and then go back to her. "Danielle, I didn't know you were here."

I turn my back to him. "Scott is under the impression I was unfaithful."

"Unfaithful?" she says with shock. "That's crazy."

"I know." I look back, meeting his eyes. "Especially since it was him who had a bunch of questionable texts, long weekends, and large gifts on the credit card for his co-worker."

There's no way I could miss the flash of awareness that plays across his face. Yeah, that's right, I suspected.

She *tsks*. "Why would you ever think she was having an affair?"

He cracks his neck and mumbles under his breath. "Tell me, Kris, how was your date with Noah Frazier?"

"You mean my meeting for the article I'm writing?" I hope he feels like the idiot he is. "I'd really love to talk, but I have company and need to get the kids settled. Thanks for dropping them off." I move forward while I push the door. He is either going to move or the door will close on him . . . his choice. "You can pick them up on Wednesday from Danielle's for your weekday dinner. Bye, now."

He moves backward with his mouth open. "Are you—"

"See you soon," I say when there is less than an inch of space.

The satisfaction rocks through me. I'm not the meek little housewife he wanted. I'm on my own, starting over, and I'll be damned if his voice will fill my head anymore.

Danielle stands there with her fingers on her lips. "Wow," she breathes.

"Was that bad?"

"No, that was epic."

I fall into the chair, feeling drained but proud. I stood up to him. I didn't fall apart or try to explain away his accusations. Maybe Danielle is right and I'm getting the old Kristin back. One that has been smothered and refuses to stay down any longer.

Watch out world.

CHAPTER FOURTEEN

KRISTIN

I STAND at Erica's desk while she reads over the article. My nerves are through the roof as I wait for any feedback. It's so different from what I did years ago. I don't just go where the story is and wing it. No, not only do I have to smash everything important into fewer than a thousand words, but I also need to make it catchy enough that people won't click away from it in two seconds. Television storytelling is a whole other world.

"Hmm," she says and puts the paper down.

"Is that a good hmm?"

Erica places both hands in the air, moving them around a bit. "You've had a change. The coloring is different around you. Very pink."

Here we go again. This girl needs meds and to lay off the acid. "I'm wearing blue."

"I know what you're wearing, Kristin, but your aura is adjusting to whatever is going on in your life."

Ah. My aura, again, I should've known. How silly of me.

Erica moves around the desk, standing very much in my space. "I like the article. You were funny and got more than I thought you would. He isn't known for being open in interviews. This is all good, and he must've liked you—"

"Liked me?" I interrupt.

She moves over to where she has rolled yoga mats. "Yes, he called this morning."

My eyes go wide, but I don't say anything. I have no idea what would make him call my boss, but there's no shortage of inappropriate things that could have prompted it. What if he told her I kissed him or got drunk and pulled him into the pool? I should've known this was never going to work, even if he did kind of promise that we were going to start over.

Damn it.

"Relax, Kristin." Erica giggles. "Get a mat and sit with me."

Not wanting to get fired, I begrudgingly grab the other yoga mat and take my place beside her. She's sitting criss-crossed with her hands resting on her knees. "The key is to find your center."

"Right. Center."

I'm centered in hell right now.

"He said he'd like to do another piece with you writing it," she says with her eyes closed. "He'd like to do a much larger exposé and really delve into a more meaningful story."

The words fail me. I had hoped after the article I wrote, he'd go back to New York, and I could pretend this weekend was just a dream. Now he wants me to write some large story about him? This cannot be happening.

My self-control is not that good. We had one working dinner, which ended with us sucking face. An in-depth exposé where I need to be around him for longer periods of time will not bode well.

Although, sleeping with Noah is certainly not the worst thing that could happen.

I mentally slap myself. Yes, having sex with the man I'm supposed to write an article on would be inexcusable and totally unprofessional.

However, it would be a very authentic way to find out what women want.

Okay, I definitely need a shrink or a vibrator.

"I'm sure there's someone more qualified than I am." I try to push it off.

She starts to hum, and I stare at her. After a few more weird sounds, she blows out a long breath and turns to me. "He wants you. This is a good thing." Erica's hand touches my leg, and she continues, "Noah is the pot of gold at the end of the rainbow. You have no idea how many times he's denied interviews."

"Right. So why the hell does he suddenly want to do this and with me?"

"Who cares?"

"It doesn't make sense. Why now? Why me? Why not interview with Barbara Walters if you're going to do something for the first time? It's crazy and I'm sure his publicist will never sign off on this."

Erica shrugs. "I have no idea why, but he likes you and felt like you were the right fit. I'm not going to lie, I'm over the moon. This is the break of a lifetime."

Then it hits me . . . he thinks he's going to get into my pants. If I get this big article that could get me out of blogging for a gossip site, I would be in his debt and fall in his bed.

"I can't do it," I say, unwilling to put myself in a position to fail.

Erica raises her brow. "You don't have a choice."

"Erica, you can't tell me this isn't a little bizarre."

"Hollywood is off its rocker. They're not like you and me. We live very normal lives and are not crazy like they are," she says with a straight face.

She thinks she's normal? I try not to laugh, but I fail. A giggle explodes from my lips, and I cover my mouth quickly. "Sorry, the imagery was funny."

She's the strangest bird I've ever met. People don't meditate in the office just because or believe no shave November applies to women as well, but she does. If she's normal, then the world is screwed.

"Hollywood in a rocker is funny," she laughs.

Lord help the future.

"So, you'll tell him he has to work with Pam or you?" I push hoping she'll relent.

"Not a chance. You are officially on assignment, and the piece is due in a month. I want a really in-depth article. Something that blows people's pants off."

"Socks," I correct.

"What? I don't wear socks. Too constraining on your toes."

I shake my head and close my eyes. There's no hope with her. "I don't feel comfortable with this idea. I don't even know what to write."

She shrugs. "Welcome to celebrity journalism. You take what he gives you and make it sound like more."

I internally groan. Apparently, she isn't going to budge. "Can you give me some idea of what you're looking for?"

Erica stands and then places her hands on the ground with

her ass in the air. "Just follow your gut. I need to finish here and then I'm on a flight to New York."

"New York?"

She lifts her one leg and arm, stretching them toward the ceiling. "Yes, I'm meeting a friend for a protest."

I'm not caught up on current events. My days consist of this, and my nights are homework and whatever awful show Aubrey puts on. In the back of my mind, I know that I'm going to regret asking her for any details, but Erica has piqued my interest.

"What are you protesting?"

She comes back to standing and smiles. "It's a legit important issue for my generation."

The way she says it clearly means I'm too old to understand. "Oh?"

"We're protesting because they're talking about making us pay a monthly fee for a social media app."

I have no words. Literally—none.

"I don't get it." She huffs. "Why do they think it's okay to charge us to use something that costs them nothing? It's crazy. I feel like this is another way that proves we're all just part of some experiment, you know?"

No, no I do not.

What she's talking about is business, but I don't point that out. Clearly, she wouldn't agree.

Erica continues. "If they wanted us to pay for it, then they should charge up-front so we can decide to become addicted to the app. Now, to suddenly decide . . . it's wrong."

I nod and hum because I don't trust myself to speak and not call her a crazy person.

She looks at the clock. "I'll be back in a few days. I'd like to see notes next week. Noah said he'll be waiting for your call."

"Okay," I say with disappointment. I really don't want to be around Noah. I know exactly what he wants. Well, he's in for a rude awakening. I'm a pro at avoiding sex—just ask Scott, it's been cobwebs growing for years.

I PACE around the living room, trying to prepare myself to ask Heather for Noah's number. Of course, he didn't give it to Erica. Instead, I have to call my best friend as if I'm in high school.

Fuck it.

"Hey!" Heather says as she answers.

"Hey."

"What's up?" she asks.

Oh, just calling because your boyfriend's friend is trying to mess with my head—I think.

"Not much. What are you up to?"

"Just waiting for Eli to get back from the store," she tells me as a bunch of pots bang in the background.

"Is Noah with Eli? I need to talk to him, and I was wondering if he was there?" A long pause stretches between us, and I look at the phone to see if the call dropped. "Heather?"

She clears her throat. "I'm here. Sorry, I thought you asked me something about Noah and since he mentioned you today as well . . . I'm just trying to put the pieces together. So, tell me, dear friend, did you do something naughty?"

It is nothing compared to what she did the first night she met Eli. I didn't sleep with him, run off, and then pretend as if it never happened. Nope. I kissed him even though I told myself I wouldn't and now am in denial about whether I feel a damn thing for him.

Totally different.

"Don't start. He called my boss and wants to do some bigger story. Since I did a good job the first go around, she gave the story to me."

Her laughter is so loud I have to pull the phone away. "These guys." She laughs harder. "I swear. They're insane and don't know how to handle the word no. You're so screwed, Kris. I mean, you're like totally fucked if he's set his sights on you."

I don't know that she's right. I wasn't really clear on the whole no-chance-at-a-relationship thing since I did stick my tongue in his mouth, but we'll leave that out for now. Some things don't need to be shared.

"There are no sights set. This is work."

"Oh." She laughs. "That's all? So, you didn't kiss him?"

Shit. She knows.

"I'm sorry." I make a crackling noise in the phone. "Bad connection."

Heather is the last person who will snub her nose at me, but the more people who know, the more excuses I need to make.

"Don't go into acting if this blogging thing doesn't work out, you really suck."

I flop back onto the couch and let out a loud huff. "Would you hate me if I said I didn't want to talk about it?"

She pauses. "Never. I get it."

I start to say something but there's a knock at the door. "Hey, I'll call you right back," I tell her as I get up.

"I'll be here."

We disconnect, and I open the door, thinking it's a package or something. Instead, Noah Frazier in all his ridiculous glory is smiling at me.

CHAPTER FIFTEEN

KRISTIN

"WELL, well, well, if it isn't my new assignment," I manage to say without drool dripping down my chin.

Noah is one of those men who looks hotter each time I see him. He's gorgeous on a bad day. However, the sight of him in a navy T-shirt that is practically painted on, khaki shorts, and two days' worth of stubble on his face makes me want to fall into a pool just so he can strip me again. Only this time, I'll be sober so I can actually enjoy it.

I need to get laid.

His hands brace on both sides of the door, and he leans forward. "Aren't you going to invite me in?"

"I could, but what would be the fun in that?"

"I'm pretty sure we could have fun." He smiles.

Oh, I don't doubt it. "I'm going to pretend you're talking about the article I'm apparently writing about you."

Noah lets out a throaty chuckle. "What else would I be talking about? Is there another kind of fun that involves the two of us that you're thinking of?"

I'm onto his game. "The only fun between us will be posted online."

He rights himself and removes his sunglasses, showing me his bedroom eyes. Damn him and his sexiness. His voice is low and sultry with an edge of humor. "I figured since you didn't give me your number the other night, I should stop by so we can get the next few weeks figured out."

"How sweet of you," I allow the sarcasm to flow. "I get an article I didn't ask for, and you've managed to ensure we'll spend weeks together."

Noah takes a step closer to me, but I hold my ground against the intensity between us. The closer he gets, the more my legs shake. My stomach has millions of butterflies in it and my throat is dry. The musky sandalwood cologne hits me, reminding me again of what it was like to be in his arms.

Pull it together, Kristin. You can't go down this path.

"Do you worry about being around me?" he asks.

"No. Why would I?" I retreat, but Noah follows, denying me the space I was going for.

"Why are you trying to get away now?"

I clench my fists and force myself not to give another inch. "I'm not going anywhere."

He smiles like the cat that ate the canary. "I'm not, either."

That is exactly what I was afraid of. Heather was right—I'm so fucked. I have no idea what Noah's game is, or if it extends past his bid to get into my pants, but I can't deny the attraction between us. His gaze rakes over my face and then down to my chest. My breathing is accelerated, and he'd have to be blind to miss all the signs that I'm both turned on and terrified.

"Well—" My voice cracks, making me have to clear my throat. "I guess we better get to work."

"Yes, I'm ready to get to work."

I shift over to the side and focus on breathing. Having distance is the key to this. When I'm not so close, it isn't so bad. Sure, short of putting a paper bag over his head, there's nothing I can do to make him less hot, but space will keep me from doing something stupid.

Like leaning forward and pressing my lips to his.

I make a mental list of rules to ensure success for the project. Noah is smooth, sexy, and kisses like a God. The way he touches me, tastes, and scatters my thoughts will be what makes this train go off the tracks. I can't think about how his fingers felt digging into my back or the way his lips moved with mine.

And now I'm keyed up.

Way not to think about it, Kris.

The list. Yes. I need a list of rules.

"We need some ground rules," I say, lifting my hand so he'll stop encroaching on my much-needed space.

He laughs.

"I'm serious. If you want me to write this article," *Not that I have a choice,* "then you'll need to agree to my terms."

He struts closer. "I'm listening."

"None of this." I point to him. "No trying to be close to me with your sexy moves and whatnot."

Noah stops and raises his brow. "You think I'm sexy?"

"Yes, I mean, no. You know what I'm saying, damn it! You're all flirty with me. No being flirty!" He knows exactly what I'm saying.

"Okay." He stands straight. "No flirting."

Good. I think.

"Next rule, no dates. You can't take me out and *schmooze* me, thinking it'll lead to sex. We're *not* having any kind of sex." I put my hands on my hips.

Noah's lips form into a panty-melting smile. "What I'm hearing is that you think about sex with me."

"I don't." I lie.

He moves closer. "Then why worry about a date?"

"Because we're not dating. I'm writing about your life."

"And you've already told the world that I have feelings for someone, haven't you?"

I knew this article was going to be a mistake. He gave me that piece of info, knowing I would have to publish it but not be able to say more. My pulse quickens as he takes another step toward me.

"Not the point. And you're being flirty again!"

He grins as he continues to inch closer. Stupid smirky bastard is making my thoughts scatter.

"They'll want to know who it is that I'm suddenly chasing after." His head tilts to the side.

"All the more reason for no public appearances." I shake my head. "Do you agree to the terms?" My feet shift back until I hit the back of the couch. I'm trapped, and he's still pursuing me.

"No." His voice is low.

"No?"

"No, we'll have food because we'll need to eat. We'll be in public because I'm not going to spend the next month hiding, and it's going to be very hard for you to keep your hands off me if we're always alone." His voice is full of mischief.

Bastard might be right. It will be harder to keep my . . . *wait a minute.* "Keep my hands off you?"

He shrugs. "You are the one who tried to kiss me the first night and told me about how amazing you are in bed. By the way, I'm happy to test that theory out if you need confirmation."

My jaw falls open. He tried to kiss me. Heck, he *did* kiss me. It was him who initiated all of this. Plus, that night I was toasted, so nothing I did should be held against me since I only remember fragments. Now, the other night, yeah, I kissed him *back.* Not first.

"Your memory is a bit off, pal."

"Pal?"

"You know, buddy, pal, bro, homey . . ."

Why am I having to explain this?

Then he laughs.

You would think with the way our exchanges go that I'd never dealt with a man before. I'm starting to wonder if I'm just incapable of human interaction at this point.

"You can call me anything you want if you kiss me again," Noah offers.

"Kiss you?" I scoff. "No."

"Then you can only refer to me as 'Man I have feelings for but refuse to admit it.'"

Like that's ever going to happen. "Or I can refer to you as 'Delusional actor who thinks he's hot.'"

"You've already admitted you think I'm hot."

"You're all right." I try for nonchalance.

While he's near me, he's followed the first rule and has stayed back more than I thought. I'm grateful for the distance because the yearning to kiss him strengthens the closer he is.

"Your mouth says one thing, but your body says another." His eyes drift to my breasts.

Sure enough, my nipples are poking out like two mountain peaks. "I'm cold."

"I'll let you have your lies."

"How nice of you." I cross my arms over my chest. Stupid boobs.

Noah takes a few steps back, and I look to the ceiling, praying for divine intervention. I have three weeks of this torture, but then he'll be gone. This isn't his home, New York is, and the last thing I have time for is some guy who will breeze in and out of my life.

I have two kids to think about and a divorce hearing in a week. Noah Frazier is the least of my worries.

"I read the article," he says as he turns to face me.

I'm surprised he read it, but I'm not sure if I want to know what he thought. His face isn't giving me any clues. "And?" I can't help myself.

"I think the title is funny," he smiles.

Mission accomplished. Eli has mentioned that they never read the tabloids, claiming that it's better to pretend you don't know what people are saying about you. I've seen some of the comments about Noah online. It's horrible that anyone thinks they have the right to judge his life. So what if he eats unhealthy once? Why is Noah subjected to being told that his acting isn't up to par with someone? Access to celebrities is a luxury I never had as a kid, but I'd like to believe if everyone treated them the way they would face to face, it would be a better place.

"I didn't know you read articles about yourself," I say as I make my way to the couch.

I'm sure he has thick skin, but he isn't made of Kevlar. Words can hurt, I know this better than most. Scott may have never physically assaulted me, but he planted seeds of doubt that bloomed into roses with thorns. Each prick drew blood, forcing a new rivulet of pain to flow, showing me that there were possible truths to his words. Even once those wounds healed, there was a scar to remind me that it happened. I would do anything in my power to never feel that way again and I completely understand why Noah would protect himself by not looking at articles.

He shrugs. "I don't, but I wasn't concerned with reading a bunch of bullshit. Plus, I needed to know if I had to discredit you with the information I have."

My head hurts from this conversation. Him and his information. No one is going to care about what I do. Plus, he seems to forget I may not be able to say what was off the record, but I sure can use it to make his life hell.

Instead of arguing, I go back to the beginning of this discussion. "About the rules—"

"Yeah about that." He cuts me off. "I think they're dumb, and I'm not interested. We'll just do this my way."

Seriously? He doesn't get to decide that. I'm the one leading this article, so there needs to be some sort of order. Plus, I don't care if he's interested, this isn't up for debate.

"No rules, no article."

"Again, I'm going to call bullshit." He grips his chin with his hand. "When I talked to your boss, she was excited about this. I have a feeling you really don't have a choice, do you?" He grins, and I fight the urge to punch him.

"Why is that, Noah?" I can't wait to hear this one.

"Not a clue. I was simply helping out a friend. You know, job security is a rarity in this industry."

Sure, I believe that one.

Noah walks into the living room like he owns the place.

I watch him, letting the one nagging question come back to my mind. "What made you decide to do this anyway? You've never done any kind of major press, so what could possibly be the reason you suddenly feel like telling your life story?"

"You."

My lips part. "What?"

"Because of you," Noah repeats.

I look for some sign that he's joking, but there isn't any. He's completely serious. For a fleeting moment, I think it actually could be me, and then I realize I am being ridiculous. There is no reason for it to have anything to do with us; we're nothing.

He wouldn't stay in Tampa for weeks just for me, would he?

If he is, what the hell does that mean?

"Why would you say that?" I ask while touching my throat.

He pushes off the table and stands before me. "I'm being honest. I find that there's no reason to beat around the bush. If you ask me a question and we're not on the record, then you'll never have to question my words, Kristin. It's because of you that I'm here."

I stare at him, hating that my life is so fucked up. That I'm so fucked up. If it were another time and place, I'd be all over him. In a few short days, I've felt more for Noah than I have for anyone in years. When he's near me, I forget the rules of what I'm supposed to be . . . I just am.

But giving in to him would be a mistake. One I'm not prepared to make.

I'm damaged inside, and there are far too many bruises and broken bones left to heal before I can put myself out there.

"I know you think that, but you have no idea what I'm really like."

Noah's hand lifts and skims my cheek. "I know that your laugh makes my heart race. The way you smile when you think no one is watching stirs something inside me that makes me desperate for more. The way your entire face lights up when you talk about Finn and Aubrey. I know what it feels like to have you in my arms, touch your lips, and fuck, I'd be lying if I said I'm not wishing for it again. I think about you more than I should. I know that you think you're weak, but I see a strong, beautiful, and smart woman who deserves a man to worship her. More than any of that, Kristin, I should walk out and let both our lives be a hell of a lot less complicated than trying to start something, but here I am. You're worth complicating things."

My breath hitches and I tingle from head to toe. "I do-don't —" I stutter. "I'm . . . you're . . ." The words I want to say won't come out because each thought I have gets cut off by another.

His dark green eyes are open and expressive. His tone is playful, but his gaze isn't. I see the desire, hope, and wonder there, and they stun me.

What were my reasons again? I can't seem to remember them.

Noah inches closer, causing my heart to accelerate so fast I'm worried I might pass out. My thoughts are jumbled, my chest is tight, and I don't know how to respond. I want him, I want him when I know I shouldn't.

My divorce hearing is in a week, my life is a mess, and this is too soon. I shouldn't have feelings for this man. I shouldn't want his hands all over my body.

I should be pushing him back, forcing myself away from him because I don't know if I can endure yet another heart-break. The man I loved failed me, what is to say he won't?

Noah's eyes stay on mine, almost as if he can read the confliction that stirs within me.

His lips turn to a grin and he straightens, breaking the intensity. "I need to head out and meet someone. I'll be back in a few days, and we can begin then." Noah leans in, kisses my cheek, and lifts my chin so my eyes meet his. "Okay?"

"Huh?" I question, not comprehending what he said.

"Three days?" He smiles.

"Sure. Days away. I'll be here." Days away? What the hell is wrong with me?

"Perfect." His lips move toward mine, and I freeze. He's going to kiss me, and I'm just standing like a statue, unsure if I want this or at least trying to pretend I don't want this. Instead of touching, though, he holds still as our breaths linger. His voice is barely a whisper, but I hear the words as if he's yelling. "I'm going to win your heart, Kristin. Be ready."

His touch is gone a second before he turns and walks out the door.

I grip the back of the couch and try to catch my breath because I'm in no way ready.

CHAPTER SIXTEEN

NOAH

"I WANT you to be happy, Noah," Mom reiterates in our weekly video chat. She believes it's her mission in life to keep my feet on the ground.

She forces me to call the same time and day no matter where I am. Right now, I'm sitting in the car outside of a condo I'm looking at leasing in Tampa. The realtor is standing at the front of the car, clearly pissed.

What can I say? I'm a mama's boy, always have been.

"I am happy." I give her my best reassuring smile.

"You're lying." She pulls the phone closer as if she'll be able to see me better. "I know you better than that."

She's the only person in this world who loves me beyond all my faults. She has also spent a great deal of time drilling that into my head, but it's true. When my life fell apart, she forced me to move on. Losing Tanya was a crossroads in my life where if I went the easy path, I'd be God knows where. Mom wouldn't allow it.

I owe her everything. If one call a week is the only thing she asks for, I'll give it without reservation.

"What could I be sad about?"

She looks off to the left and sighs. "That's for you to figure out, but maybe it's time for you to open yourself up a little. It's been a long time, Noah. A lot of things are different, you're different."

I don't want to talk about this. "I'm moving that way," I say, hoping she'll shift the conversation away from Tanya.

"Oh? How so?"

When my mother can see my reactions, it makes it harder to blow her off. I'm pretty sure this is why she insists on video chats instead of phone calls. "A few things, Mom. I got another project on the docket, I auditioned for it a few months back, not thinking much about it."

She smiles. "Tell me about it."

I fill her in on all the details of the movie. I've done a few small roles in film, but nothing spectacular. This would be a lead, and it's working for a director I highly respect. The film isn't a genre I would've typically looked for, but since it was Paul Skaggs as the director, I took a chance. Hopefully, I don't fuck it up and this is the transition into more film than television.

"I feel as though this is a good move for you, Noah," Mom gives me her beaming smile that's filled with pride. "Tell me what else is new. I feel like there's more you're purposely leaving out."

She's like a shark who smells blood in the water. "There's not much to say, it's very new."

"You've met someone?"

It's easy to forget that my family and real friends don't read the shit on the internet. They're not worried about what new drama the media has created to sell magazines. If there's news, they hear it from me.

"You'd like her."

I know I do.

"Tell me." She smiles. "What's her name?"

Trust isn't the issue for why I'm hesitant, there's nothing in the world that would make my mother betray me, but naming Kristin means opening myself up to a million questions.

"Noah Frazier, why are you making that face?" Mom asks after I've been quiet too long for her liking.

I never could lie to her, which is sad since my job is acting. "Her name is Kristin, she's a single mom, has two kids, and lives here in Tampa."

Her lips purse. I knew it. "Single mom?"

"I know what you're thinking, and I would never do anything to hurt her or the kids. I'm aware of what it means."

My father left my mother when I was four. He took every penny she had, the car, and never looked back. She somehow was able to push on with her life. My mother worked two jobs but was at every soccer game I had, and I had no idea we were poor. The older I got, the more she would share about being a single parent and the reasons she wouldn't date.

One being my father hadn't returned and she still felt he was her husband. That was, and still is, the most ridiculous thing ever, but I think there is more to it than I know.

My mother's eyes are full of concern. "That's not my worry, Noah. It's that you live a life that isn't family . . . friendly. Are you ready to even consider something where you are more stable in where you live? If she's from Florida, how are you going to have a relationship?"

I clench my teeth so I don't say something rude. "I'm sure if it gets to anything more than friendship, which is all we are at this point, we'll figure all of that out. It's all just happened, and I'm not sure that she'll even warm up to the idea of dating."

She laughs. "You're crazy if you believe she won't see what a good man you are. I think you need to be careful, though. Not just for yourself, but for her and her children. A mother doesn't take chances when it comes to the hearts of her babies."

Who knows if it'll even come to that. At this point, Kristin doesn't want to chance anything. It's clear that she has feelings for me, but I see the hesitation in her eyes. Proving myself won't be easy, but then again, nothing worth having is.

I smile, remembering her face the other day. Her mouth opening and closing when I let her know what my plans were. Wait until tomorrow when I really turn on the charm.

"Don't worry, Mom. I've waited a long time for a girl like her, I won't be taking any chances."

Her lips turn into a flat line, and she releases a breath through her nose. "Lord help her . . . and you. I hope to meet her soon."

"I hope so, too."

THIS MEETING IS TAKING FUCKING FOREVER. I keep scrolling through my phone for anything interesting as they drone on about the movie and filming schedule. Focusing is damn near impossible when all I seem to think about is Kristin.

"And you understand this means we'll start filming much sooner than we originally planned?"

It's been almost a week since I've seen her. I'm trying to play this cool, not asking for her number, not emailing her, pretending like I'm letting her lead a little, but I'm anxious to see her again.

"Noah?" My agent elbows me.

"Huh?"

"I asked if you were fine with the schedule adjustment."

I glance at the paper, now being that asshole who comes to the meeting and doesn't pay attention, and nod. "Looks good."

My agent clears his throat, and I push Kristin out of my mind. This is my career, and I can't screw this up.

The meeting resumes, and we talk about the locations, and the female lead stares at me from across the table. She's pretty, but definitely not piquing my interest. Her smile is soft, but it looks like she's trying. Her eyes are blue, but not with the shine that Kristin's have.

Fucking hell.

Again.

I'm right back to where I started—thinking of her.

My phone screen lightens, and it's the realtor.

"I have to take this," I explain as I'm already out of my chair.

"Hello?"

"Hi, Mr. Frazier, it's Sommer," she says nervously. "How are you?"

"I'm in a meeting but wanted to take your call."

"Oh," she says quickly. "I won't keep you. I wanted to let you know that if you want the condo, it's yours. The owner is motivated and, well, you were approved."

This is the craziest thing I've ever done to be close to a woman. I'm renting a fucking condo in a town I have no intention of staying in, just to be around her. I kind of had to after I told Eli I would do the first article, but when I decided to be an idiot and allow the second article on me, that was because of her.

Everything I've been doing is because of her.

Yet, I wouldn't change a damn thing.

I'll force her to do another article, rent another condo, or whatever it takes until she gives in. I'll be as patient and persistent as I need to be.

I'm a fucking goner.

Sommer clears her throat. "Sorry. So . . ."

I think about being closer to Kristin and there's really no other answer.

"I'll take it."

CHAPTER SEVENTEEN

KRISTIN

"HOW LONG HAS it been since you've seen or heard from him?" Nicole whispers as we wait for the judge to call me in.

Six days and fifteen hours.

"Why are you asking about this?" My voice is quiet but full of frustration. I'm about to have my divorce finalized, and she's worried about when I last saw Noah.

She shrugs. "I'm curious. What else would you like to talk about?"

I look at her as if she's lost her mind. "I don't know, the fact that my marriage will be officially over in a few minutes."

Nicole leans forward, glances to where Scott and his two lawyers sit, makes a face, and leans back. "Good riddance. Now you can think about the deliciousness that is more than willing to take a bite of your peach. Maybe he'll even lick it a little or drink your nectar." She wiggles her brows.

After over twenty years of friendship, I should know better than to bring her in public. However, it doesn't stop the burst of giggles that escape my mouth.

"Shh." She takes my hand in hers as I try to get myself under control. "You'll get us in trouble."

"You're the one talking about drinking my nectar."

"I'm the one you called because you knew I wouldn't be all sad." She nudges me. "I'm your friend that takes the shit and turns it to diamonds."

She definitely is that person, and it's why I had her come with me. Nicole may be the only one of us who stayed single, but I'm the only person who knows why. I was the one who held her hand on her darkest day, so I wanted her to see me at my low point.

Today, I will endure watching the man I thought I'd grow old beside end that dream. I wanted Nicole to remind me that even when I'm down, I'm not out. She's living proof of it.

"Thank you for being a diamond." I squeeze her hand.

"You're welcome."

———————

"THE JUDGE WOULD LIKE to call Scott McGee and Kristin McGee forward please," the court clerk announces.

"This is the end." I stand and fix my skirt.

"This is the beginning, Kris. The end to misery and the start of something you get to determine. I love you, and I'll be here when you're done."

I nod and hug her.

My lawyer places her hand on my shoulder and nods. We walk in silence, my heart pounding against my chest as we enter the courtroom. I stand on one side and Scott stands on the other. It's sad that this is where we are. After all the years of trying to close the gap between us, it's now an ocean, and I can't see the land.

There's no denying the anguish that flows through me. I look at his profile, remembering how much I loved him. Memories of us when we were young assault me. The smiles, laughter, and silliness that I thought would never end. How his eyes were filled with love as I walked down the aisle of the church in my wedding dress, believing I would love him until the day I died.

Maybe I did die. That naïve girl is long gone. I'm not the same as I was, just as he isn't.

The judge speaks, reviewing all the paperwork, but I can't focus on it. It seems so easy when you hear your marriage broken down into bullet points. We're just two people. Assets, visitation, alimony, and numbers.

We were more than that once.

My lawyer taps my arm, forcing my attention back forward. "Mrs. McGee, are you aware of the change of filing grounds regarding the dissolution of your marriage?"

I glance at my lawyer and she shakes her head. "No," I say with confusion.

Who changed the grounds? My lawyer didn't say a word.

"Mr. McGee submitted the paperwork late last night claiming that you committed adultery during the duration of your marriage, and you're not entitled to any support due to the financial constraints this caused. He claims it should be on the record that you used his finances to fund your affair."

My lungs won't fill with air. I can't believe this. He is out of his goddamn mind. "That's completely untrue," I tell Clarissa. "I've never been unfaithful."

Scott's lawyer pipes up. "Mr. McGee has just learned of this, which is why we haven't submitted proof."

The judge shakes her head. "So, this is an accusation? One you thought you should file just in case?"

Tears fill my vision as I stare at Scott. Is he that unglued? He'd try to hurt me this much? When Danielle said this was possible, a part of me didn't believe it. No way would he want to do that to his children. Seems I was stupid to think he gave a shit about anything but himself and money.

"One that, if we were granted enough time to further investigate, we could prove the validity."

No, he couldn't because it isn't true. I've never done anything questionable. I loved him even when he made me feel small. I didn't seek comfort in another man regardless of how unworthy he told me I was.

She chuckles. "Mr. Sheridan, am I to believe that you submitted a charge against Mrs. McGee without any sort of receipts, text messages, or testimony to back your client's claim? You thought that by stating it to be true, then your client wouldn't have to pay his financial share. Am I right?"

"If we could have an extension, your Honor—"

"No." She cuts him off. "There will be no extension. If you actually had a shred of evidence, you would have presented it."

My attorney, Clarissa, grips my hand and squeezes. I close my eyes and breathe in through my nose. Scott isn't the only one who has the ability to change the claim. Peter called Clarissa and sort of instructed her on what route to take.

We spent the last week gathering information in case he tried to pull some shit.

"Your Honor," my attorney speaks. "If Mr. Sheridan would like, we have sufficient evidence to prove the emotional abuse that Kristin McGee endured throughout the fourteen years of marriage to Scott McGee."

Her eyes meet mine, and I see a flash of empathy. "Really?"

"This is unfounded and ridiculous!" Mr. Sheridan shouts.

The judge looks back to him. "You see, Mr. Sheridan, it isn't unfounded if she is able to provide documentation and such."

My lawyer presents the various letters from friends and family, screenshots of emails, text messages, and the transcripts of a voicemail he left that proves he was screwing Jillian while we were still married.

I didn't want to do this. It was a necessary precaution, but he left me no choice. It's all in black in white, the years of hell I've worked hard to hide and the lies I've told everyone about how great Scott was, are all refuted in her hands.

He wasn't great.

I was just too weak to walk away—until now.

The judge reads through it, removes her glasses, and pauses. "Divorce is always emotional. It's my job to remove the emotion from it and be fair. I've been doing this a long time, and this is my least favorite type of case." Her eyes move between Scott and me. "I can't presume to know what happened to bring you both here today, but I can say that there are two people in your lives who don't yet know the real ramifications of your choices. Your children are going to struggle, but you have the power to decide how much they suffer."

Everything inside me hurts when I think about Finn and Aubrey. While we're adjusting to living without Scott, I see the difference in their eyes. My goal has always been to protect them, which is why I never wanted to present him in a bad light. That doesn't mean I deserve to be raked over the coals because he's a selfish asshole.

She clears her throat. "I don't like games, Mr. McGee. I don't like liars. More than those, I don't like people who think it's okay to put others down in order to build themselves up. If you truly thought your wife was having an affair, why wait to file until the day before? I'll tell you why," she says before he can answer. "You knew it was completely false. So, after reading the evidence and lack of evidence, it's my discretion to decide what it all means in regard to the division of assets and the best interests of the children." Her eyes meet mine. "Mrs. McGee, did you work throughout the marriage?"

"No, your Honor. My husband felt it was best I stay home with the kids since we could afford to lose my income."

"And you and the children vacated the house?" she asks.

"Yes."

"Mr. McGee," she calls his attention. "I do not believe your wife was unfaithful. I do, however, believe that you were emotionally abusive based on the information that was presented. I urge you to seek counseling for the welfare of yourself and your children. With that said, you are to pay durational alimony for the next seven years, child support, as well as provide medical coverage for both Mrs. McGee and the children."

Scott lets out a low noise, and I breathe a sigh of relief. My job is great, but the pay is not the best, and I can't expect Heather to let me live in her home forever. This will allow me a little breathing room.

The judge finishes the paperwork, and we're done.

We're divorced.

Scott walks over to me with anger radiating off of him. "This is your fault. All of it."

My first instinct is to cower, but I stop myself. Noah's words echo in my ears: *"You think you're weak, but I see a strong, beautiful, and smart woman who deserves a man who will worship her. More than any of that, Kristin, I should walk out and let both our lives be a hell of a lot less complicated than trying to start something, but here I am. You're worth complicating things.*

I stand a little taller and look him in the eyes. "I'm sorry you feel that way, but you're not my problem anymore, and in all honesty, I don't give a flying fuck."

My legs feel like jelly as I walk away. Each step I take away from Scott gives me a bit more strength back.

Nicole gets to her feet as soon as I come into view. "Done?"

"It's done. I'm single, and we're done," I say, and my lip trembles.

"Not here." She takes both my hands in hers. "He doesn't get to have any satisfaction. You smile right now, okay?"

I push back the tears and plaster a fake smile on my face. Scott walks past, glaring at me, but I stay strong. He won't see me break ever again. He's seen enough of that.

It's time to rebuild the bricks he tore down.

"WHAT THE HELL?" I laugh as all my friends, who are gathered in my living room, toss confetti in the air.

"Happy divorce day!" Heather yells as she wraps her arms

around me. "You're not going to be alone tonight, and we're going to celebrate."

I don't know whether to laugh or cry. My heart is severed in half, each side is at war with the other, trying to see whether I'm broken or can be healed. There is no guidebook on how to handle a divorce. I hate that there's even a sliver of sadness. Scott doesn't deserve even that much from me, but denying it won't change the fact that I am sad.

"I'm not sure guys," I say, which makes Danielle's lips turn down.

"Do you remember when Heather and Matt's divorce was final?" Nicole asks. "Wasn't it you that organized the intervention to ensure she wasn't sitting at home eating her disgusting cookie concoction?"

I hate when they're right. I hate it even more that I did for Heather what they are doing for me now, and I don't want it. "Still, I'm tired."

Heather shrugs. "Slumber party it is!"

There are no boundaries with this group. We don't care if someone wants to be alone or wallow in self-pity, we'll just join in without an invitation. The kids are with my parents for the weekend, and they aren't leaving, so I might as well make the best of it.

We grab the bottles of wine and park our asses on the couch. For the first hour, we talk about plans for Heather's wedding, which is in a little over two weeks. She got engaged a few days ago, seriously Eli is ridiculous with being so good to her, and I try to focus on how happy I am for her. Each detail she shares about the things he's doing allows little pieces of sorrow to creep in. She's my best friend, whom I love more than I can say and who deserves to be happy, but I wish I weren't so newly single.

"I still can't believe you're getting married in less than a month and then moving to Canada!" Danielle shakes her head.

"I know, it's insane, but Eli got the movie role and I want to be with him."

"I'd want to be with him, too," Nicole adds on.

I bob my head in agreement. "For real. Don't let a man like him out of your sight."

Danielle raises her glass. "It's like when I decided that I should go to college away from Eddie. Big mistake. Beginning of the end."

Here we go again. Danielle, when she drinks, talks about her ex, who she swears was her literal soulmate. The one God hand-picked for her and as a punishment for not being nice to him, sent him away.

"Oh, for the love of God!" Nicole bursts out laughing. "You know he's married with kids and . . . so are you! You were that whacko who would've married him when you were fifteen."

"At least when I was fifteen I could've married someone," Danni counters.

And then the fight between Nicole and Danielle begins while Heather and I shake our heads.

The conversation shifts for the next hour as we laugh about the stupid things we did when we were young. I don't know how these stories never get old, but they don't.

"Do you think Mrs. Yoder still has nightmares about Nicole?" Danni asks. "That poor woman retired from teaching after you."

"She was crazy! She needed someone to show her that she was losing her damn mind."

Heather waves her hand and bounces. "What about when Nicole got caught having sex with Mr. Fink under the stairs!"

I laugh, snorting wine from my nose. "Oh my God! I forgot about that. I really hope you got an A in physics. I mean, you earned that shit."

"Why are all these stories about me? Oh, wait, because I'm the one who actually does shit that's story worthy." Nicole pulls her knee to her chest. "Unlike you boring asses."

She's always been the one doing crazy things, but she makes no apologies for it.

"Calm down, Scary Spice." Heather sighs. "We've all done our fair share of stupid crap."

"Hell yeah, you all have! I've got stories because when you three do something, guess who you call? Me. You call me, so I know *all* your secrets."

The three of us look at each other with wide eyes. What the hell have they done that I don't know about?

Nicole bursts out laughing as we study each other. "I love you guys so much. Let's find out what we really want to know." She grabs my hand. "How bad did Scott have to pay?"

They let me go this long without questions, I guess it's time to fill them in on the drama that today was. I recount the divorce hearing for them, loving the faces they make. It's still a little surreal to think he tried to accuse me of cheating on him. There isn't a chance that he believes that shit.

"I'm so glad we're never going to have to be around Asshole anymore," Nicole says as she props her feet on the coffee table. "I really would like to chop his nuts off."

"Seriously, maybe he and Matt will become best friends." Heather giggles.

I drain another glass of wine before refilling it again. "Well, I still have to deal with him every other weekend. I'm sure he'll parade Jillian around now that we're divorced and he can throw it in my face."

The more I drink, the more I realize how much I hate him. He is a prick for trying to screw me out of money like that. I left the damn house. I never said a word about his slutty secretary he was banging. I didn't ask for jack shit, and he feels like I'm entitled to nothing after fourteen years of marriage? Fuck that.

"Don't worry about her, honey, you've got Noah Frazier sticking his tongue in your holes!" Nicole laughs and slaps my leg.

"What?" Heather gets to her feet.

"Nicole!" I screech. "Do you seriously not know how to keep your mouth shut? So much for all our *secrets*."

She shrugs. "I'm pretty sure that your mouth was what was open."

I roll my eyes and throw a pillow at her as she wiggles her tongue.

"Hello! You kissed Noah?" Heather demands my attention. "When? Where? Why didn't you tell me?"

I really thought she knew. "It was no big deal."

Danielle coughs with a laugh. "Until he told you he's going to win your heart."

"Jesus Christ! You guys suck!" My hands fly in the air.

Heather stares at me with her hands on her hips. Thanks to big mouth one and two, I might as well tell her.

"Fine. Yes, I kissed Noah when we went to our dinner

thing. Then he came over here the other day, telling me how he felt and that he had feelings for me. *However*, I haven't seen him since then."

A slow smile spreads across her face. "Then tonight is your lucky night. Eli and Noah are on their way here to pick me up."

Of course they are.

CHAPTER EIGHTEEN

KRISTIN

I'M IN THE KITCHEN, hiding like the chickenshit I am.

I haven't seen Noah in what feels like forever. I don't have his stupid phone number so I couldn't call him to coordinate our next meeting, and I wasn't asking Heather or Eli. Now, I'm half drunk, which around him is never a good thing, and emotionally unstable.

Again, a bad idea.

I heard a car door shut and suddenly needed to search for food.

"Kristin!" Danielle calls.

"What?"

"Stop hiding, he's not here!"

They all start to laugh, and I stick my tongue out at the wall. "I'm hungry not hiding!"

I really need to go food shopping, there's nothing here. I'm on my hands and knees, digging in the bottom cabinets, scouring for some chips. A bag of Cool Ranch Doritos is what I need.

"Looking for something?" Noah's deep voice scares the fuck out of me.

I jump, slamming my head on the wood. "Ouch," I say as I rub the spot I hit. Seriously, one damn time I'd like to be totally normal around him. I'm not asking for much.

"You okay?" He chuckles.

"I'm great, it's just another moment to beat myself up over later."

I carefully extricate myself without further injury and sit back on my heels.

"Hi." I give a sad smile. His hair is cut a little shorter, but his facial hair is grown out.

I like it. I like it a lot.

Noah returns my smile as he squats so we're eye level. "Hi."

I look around the kitchen, waiting for one of us to say something more.

Silence continues, stretching into the realm of uncomfortable.

"So, how are things?" I ask.

"Shouldn't I be asking you that? I know today was . . . *the* day and all."

Is that why he didn't try to get my number to call me? I didn't even think about that. He knew my divorce was this week, and maybe he was giving me time to process it without him . . .

"Yeah, I'm single." I shrug. "Officially *on* the market."

Noah fights a grin, but I see the mischief in his eyes. "It's a good day for all men."

"All men, huh?"

He cocks his head to the side. "Well, at least I know one who's happy about it."

I pull my hair to the side and play with the ends. "He is?"

Noah's finger elevates my chin. "He is, and he missed you."

That's sweet.

He's sweet.

The things he said to me last week got me through today. I should tell him that. Seeing him right now brings everything I tried to bury back to the surface. The pieces of my heart that were trying to draw their battle lines are starting to pick sides.

I need to show him in some way that I may not act on it today, this week, or even this year, but he isn't the only one feeling this. The mistakes of my past shouldn't distort my possible future.

"She missed you, too. Maybe. A little." I smile.

His hand drops, and I miss his touch. When I'm around Noah, it's as if the issues in my life don't exist. I don't understand it, but my worries are easier to carry because he's here.

Which is the most ridiculous thing, considering I barely know him. Yet, everything inside me tells me to trust my gut.

Something comes over me, and I have to kiss him. I push up quickly, fusing my lips to his. The force of my attack causes Noah to fly onto his back, and I land on top, kissing him. He holds me against him, and I allow myself to feel everything.

The way his tongue slides against mine makes my heart race.

He rolls us so we're on our sides and takes over the kiss. I can't move, and I don't mind, either. My leg wraps around his hip as both of us lose control.

I've never had sex on the kitchen floor, but I'm game right now.

"Oh!" Nicole practically screams. "Well, okay then."

I quickly sit up, pulling my clothes back to where they should be as she grins at me. "I was just looking for a snack."

My hand slaps against my forehead. *Really, Kristin?*

"It looks like you found one." She laughs. Nicole glances at Noah and then back to me. "We're heading out, wanted to say goodbye."

"Of course, we were coming."

Nicole bursts out laughing. "You're making this too easy."

Noah gets to his feet and then helps me up. "You're dead to me," I whisper to Nicole as I pass her.

Once we're all in the living room, Danielle hugs me and heads home. Nicole follows right after with her parting words of sexual appreciation. Heather, Eli, Noah, and I stand in the living room.

"So?" I shift my weight.

"We should get going," Eli says, nodding at Heather.

"Yeah," she agrees. "Noah?"

I look to him, not wanting him to leave. We need to talk about what just happened. I freaking attacked him on the floor. Normal people don't do that on the day they get divorced. What is wrong with me?

"Do you think—" I say, but he speaks at the same time.

"I was going—"

Heather snorts. "Why don't we leave you guys to talk? I know you're behind on the article, right?"

I love her. She's now my favorite.

"Yes. That's what I was going to say." I look to him. "We should probably talk a little and make plans for how we're going to handle things."

"Of course," he agrees.

Eli lets out a mix of a laugh and a cough. "Good thing you brought your own car, Noah."

I was so stupid to think I was going to be able to stay away from him or that he was going to make this easy and walk away. It's been clear from the beginning there is something between us.

I don't know what it means.

I don't know if this is the right thing.

But he makes me feel as if I'm strong enough to find out.

"I'll call you tomorrow." Heather pulls me into her arms.

"Okay."

Her eyes are filled with a warning, but then her lips lift to a smirk. You'd think I was fifteen and about to have sex for the first time. Hell, we aren't going to have sex now. We're going to sit like adults, with a wooden table between us, and talk.

That is what must happen.

No sex.

They leave, and my nerves grow with each second we're alone. My chest is tight as Noah and I look at each other. So many things to say, but I can't speak.

I want to ask him what this is and why are we unable to stop it. I want to know if this is normal. If I would still be this attracted to him if I weren't divorced.

"Can we talk?" I finally speak.

"We probably should."

"At the table," I clarify.

He takes a seat, and I walk around to the other side. There's no way I'm sitting close to him. I'll probably attack him again and break my furniture in the process.

"Okay, I don't know what came over me in the kitchen, but clearly, I don't know how to use my brain around you. I know

I'm sending all kinds of mixed signals, and I'm sorry for that, but you make it hard to think," I blurt out. "I'm a thinker, Noah. I think a lot, and this is weird and unlike me."

He runs his hands through his hair. "You don't exactly have me doing what I want to do, either. It's been a long time since I've been this crazy about a girl."

"You're crazy about me?"

He leans forward with a sexy grin. "I thought you'd have realized that by now. I rented a fucking condo here this week."

I'm not sure what that means because he's supposed to be staying here for a few weeks anyway, so it makes sense he'd rent a place. "Okay . . ."

Noah rubs his forehead while shaking his head. "I had no plans to stay here. I was visiting Eli for a few days and then going back to New York. Now, I'm signing leases, doing press shit, and thinking of excuses to see you."

"Which is nuts! This is too fast, and I can't get hurt again."

"I don't want to hurt you."

No one ever means to hurt someone, but it's reality. I can only carry so much pain before I'm going to break. "I don't think you'd do it intentionally," I say, twisting the ring on my thumb. "You're the first man in a long time to make me feel pretty."

Noah's eyes flash with anger. "Kristin," he starts, and I hold my hand up.

"Let me finish, please." I wait to see him relax so I can get all this out. "My ex-husband was abusive in ways I never saw. He put me down all the time, made me believe I was worthless to the point that I was . . . sad and lonely. He broke me so that the small scraps of love he gave felt like meals. I could live off one compliment for months because they came so rarely. I don't ever want to be that woman again," I say as I fight back tears. "I shouldn't want you. I shouldn't even be thinking about another man because I'm scared."

He leans forward with his palms up. I want to place my hands in his, but instead, I just touch the tips of his fingers. "You aren't the only one scared here. Trust me, I'm not sure what to think half the time. But I can promise you this"—he pushes forward so our hands are now joined—"I will never make you feel small. You won't ever be lonely, Kristin. I promise you that, if you give this a chance, I will treat you like you should've been treated all along."

"And when you leave to go on with your life?"

Noah shrugs. "We'll cross that bridge then. Look, you might go on another date with me and realize it's you who doesn't like me."

"Not likely."

"It could happen. All I'm asking for is for us to spend the next few weeks figuring it out. If you fall in love with me, that's on you. The possibility is real." He grins. "My money says you'll want to keep me."

That's the issue. My wanting to keep him, and him not wanting to cherish me.

I look at our hands and then back to him. "It's not that simple."

"Nothing is, but I'm not walking away from someone who has lit a fire inside me that I thought died out. I just need you to give it a chance."

Why does he have to be so great? He's the polar opposite of Scott. Everything he says is filled with so much meaning. It's terrifying because what if I do give him that chance and he leaves me? How could I ever recover?

I'm only crawling today because I couldn't get any lower than my ex-husband shoved me.

This isn't fair to Noah, though. He deserves to be happy with someone who can give him more.

"Noah." I sigh, pulling my hands back. My heart is already broken, might as well pulverize it and push him away. "I'm the last thing you need."

He gets to his feet without saying a word. I watch him move around the table, making his way to me. My heart beats so loudly I worry it's going to explode.

My mind is reeling, and with as much as I want him to tell me I'm right and walk away, I don't. I want someone to fight for me—just once.

When he reaches me, my breath stops. I want to scream that I didn't mean what I said, but he cups my face, moving his thumb on my cheek. "Maybe you're right. Maybe neither of us needs any more complications, but you're the only thing I want."

I'm pretty sure I just died.

Has anyone said anything as perfect as that? If they have, I don't care because my entire world has shifted.

"I want you, too." For the first time, I'm completely honest with him.

I want him.

I want him to want me, and God help me, I want it all.

Fear ruled me for too long, and I won't allow it to do so for one more second. Noah and I might not last. We could be a flash in the pan that fizzles out before it gets going, but if I don't try, I'll never know.

"Yeah?" he asks with surprise in his voice.

"I'm scared, but yes, I would like to see whatever this is between us."

"I'm glad you said that." He grins as he leans closer. "I was getting ready to really put the moves on you."

If this was him not trying, I can't even fathom what the hell I'll be in for.

The truth is, I don't care.

"Shut up and kiss me," I demand.

Noah brings his mouth to mine, and I slip my hands behind his neck, holding him to me.

CHAPTER NINETEEN

NOAH

I KEEP WAITING to wake up.

It has to be a fucking dream that Kristin is in my arms. Her fingers press against my neck, pulling me closer while I kiss her lips.

"Noah," she says my name as her mouth moves to my neck.

This wasn't my intention when I came here. I wasn't even sure if I should come with Eli, but I needed to see if she was okay. Kristin stirs every protective urge I have. If that prick had hurt her, I was going to bury him.

I'd made a deal with myself that if she had been upset, I would give her time without me pressuring her. The last thing she needs is another person fucking with her head. We'd be friends, I'd do the article I was an idiot to suggest, and then we'd part ways.

When I saw her on the floor, smiling and happy to see me, there was no way I could walk away.

"I've thought about you all day," I tell her as I kiss my way down her neck. "When my plane landed, all I could do was find a way to see you."

She moans and drops her head back. "You have no idea . . ."

"About what?"

Kristin's blue eyes meet mine, and I watch the confliction swirl in her gaze. "How much I think about you."

"You're not the only one, sweetheart."

"Good." She smiles as I drop my mouth back to hers, loving when she opens her lips and I can dive back in. I taste the sweetness of the wine against her tongue. Her fingers slide down my back, but they can only go so far since she's still sitting.

My hands cup the back of her thighs, and I lift her. She yelps when I sit her on the table, giving me the angle to kiss her better. Instead of giving in to my urge, I take a second to look at her, amazed at all she is. How the fuck did I get this lucky?

How could one drunken reporter find her way into my heart with just a smile?

She runs the pads of her fingers against my cheeks. "I like this," she muses as she scratches my semi-beard.

I like her touching me. I like everything about her.

"Yeah?" I ask.

She nods with her bottom lip in between her teeth, not meeting my eyes.

"What else do you like?" I ask as she moves her thumb across my lip.

"The way you kiss me."

Well, I can gladly give her that again, but I know Kristin's biggest issue is she was silenced. I won't allow that. I want her to be confident and never worry that she has to hide anything.

"Like this?" I brush my lips against hers, pulling back when she moves in and tries to take over. She lets out a small whimper, and I wait for her to answer. "Is that what you want, sweetheart?"

She shakes her head, but that isn't going to fly tonight. Nothing will happen unless I hear the words. I'm fighting every impulse to lay her on the table and make her lose her mind. I want to make her feel good, worshipped. My muscles are aching from restraining myself from doing just that, but Kristin has to lead how far this goes.

"I can't hear you," I urge.

"No," she finally says.

"What do you want?"

There's no mistaking her hesitancy. She wants to say it but doesn't know how. I have to push her without breaking her. I'm not sure what the right move is to do that, so I move my mouth back to hers.

Her legs wrap around me, pulling me flush against her. My cock strains against my pants as she digs her heels into my ass. She breaks the kiss and runs her tongue against my ear. "That's more like it," she rasps.

"Fuck," I groan as she repeats the motion against my other ear.

I'm teetering on losing my restraint and taking over. Instead of fucking this whole thing up with her, I have to stop this now.

I start to pull back, but she clutches me tighter.

"Kristin," I say as I pull her wrists down. I take a few steps back, giving us a little space to breathe. Fuck. Fuck. Fuck.

What am I thinking? She got divorced today, and I'm here dry humping her on her goddamn table. "I need . . ."

"What did I do wrong?" she asks with pain in her voice.

"What?" I ask, moving back toward her.

"You . . . you stopped. I-I'm . . . I don't know what I did. I'm sorry."

Jesus Christ. She thinks I stopped because she did something wrong? "You didn't do *anything* wrong, Kristin. I was wrong to do this to you today." I move my fingers against her slightly swollen lips.

She takes my hand in hers, dropping it to her legs. "Do this to me?"

"You got divorced today, and I'm an asshole for touching you."

Kristin lets out a mix between a snort and a giggle. I don't know what the fuck it is, but it's cute as hell. "You think you're an asshole? First of all, I attacked you in my kitchen. Even if we take that out of the equation, you are the absolute last person I would call an asshole today. You want to know something?"

I want to know all her somethings. "What?"

"You helped me today without even being there. Scott, my ex," she clarifies without needing to, "he tried to make me feel . . . well, like he'd normally make me feel, but you stopped it. What you said to me the other day, it meant more than you'll ever know."

Kristin's eyes fill with tears, and my chest starts to ache. "Don't cry," I beg. A crying woman is my freaking kryptonite. Do you hug them? Tell them it's okay? I've made that mistake before, told my girlfriend it would be all right before an explosion of how not all right it is happened.

She wipes her cheeks and sniffles. "I'm telling you that you're not an asshole, Noah."

"You don't really know me yet." I try to lighten the mood with a joke.

"Idiot." She laughs.

"I am that." I smile and remove the tear that's about to fall.

It's in my DNA to fix things. I'm a man; it's what I do. If there's a problem, then the solution is somewhere, and I'll find it. Kristin crying because I stopped kissing her isn't one I've encountered before.

I also don't think kissing her to make it stop is the right choice.

Do I stand here?

"I . . . I liked kissing you."

Maybe she does want me to kiss her. "Kris, I'm more than happy to kiss you," I say pushing her brown hair back. "I'll kiss you all night if it means you won't cry."

Her eyes lift to the ceiling and she grumbles. "Great. Now I'm guilting you into making out with me."

I take her face in my hands, bring her head down, and wait for her to look at me. She looks lost. The free, sexy, confident woman who took what she wanted is gone. I want her back and will do whatever I have to in order to accomplish that.

"I want nothing more than to bring your lips to mine. I want to kiss every inch of you, make you forget everything except me, and then make love to you until we collapse. You don't have to guilt me, you just have to say the word, and I'm right here."

CHAPTER TWENTY

KRISTIN

IT'S BEEN TOO long since I've felt so desired. A part of me doesn't believe it's possible, but there's no mistaking the look in his eyes.

Noah wants to do everything he said.

He doesn't move a muscle as he waits for me to say something.

Instead of speaking, thinking, or talking myself out of this, I feel.

My hands move from my lap to his stomach. Our eyes stay locked as my fingers make their way under his shirt. I take my time exploring his chest, feeling his muscles beneath me as we both breathe each other in.

I slide my hand higher, pulling the hem with me as I go. He doesn't say a word as he removes his hands from my face and raises his arms, allowing me to inch the shirt higher and then over his head before throwing it to the floor.

"You ready to make good on your promise?" I ask with more bravado than I actually have.

I'm ready to live.

I'm ready to feel.

I'm ready to give myself permission to take chances.

Noah gives me his cocky smirk, which sends a current through my veins. His hands grab my ass, and he pulls me against his very noticeable erection. "What do you think?"

I think I'm about to pass out, that's what I think.

"I don't know how to do this," I admit.

For years, it's been a chore. One that, according to Asshole, I wasn't good at. I've learned to sort of sit back and take what I can get. Noah clearly doesn't want that, but I'm terrified I'll disappoint him. I'm not sure I could survive being mediocre to him.

"You're in control," he tells me as his lips ghost over mine. "Take what you want, sweetheart. I'll give you as much or as little as you say."

"What if it's not what you want?" I whisper, hoping he maybe doesn't hear.

Noah shifts back enough to look me in the eyes. "I want *you*, Kristin."

My pulse races, but there isn't a chance in hell I'm going to walk away now. He emboldens me to take what he's offering. I've never felt as safe as I do right now. He does want me, and I want him. I'm going to do what he said and take charge.

I push Noah back a little and get to my feet. Our chests touch and my hand slides to the back of his neck again, bringing his lips to mine. I lose all sense of time as both of us fight for control. He gives it to me and then takes it back as if he can't stop himself.

Just knowing he's relenting a little makes my heart race.

Noah brings his lips to my neck, his tongue traces my collarbone and tastes the skin across my shoulder.

I take his hands in mine and start to walk backward. He follows me as we make our way to my bedroom.

Nerves plow through me like a freight train as we reach the door.

"Are you sure?" he asks.

How do I answer that? Do I want him? Yes. I don't even think it's a choice anymore, it's a need.

"Yes, I'm sure," I reassure him.

"We don't have to do this." Noah gives me another out, to which I smile, running my fingers over his short beard.

It's my turn to be vulnerable with him. He's given me words of encouragement that have carried me through. The fact that he's still cautious with me is answer enough. Noah cares about me. Not about getting laid, but my heart and soul. He's the thread that won't patch my heart, he wants to heal it, eradicating the scars.

"No, we don't have to, but you're what I want. The smile you say you love is there because of you. The laugh you hear, only started when you came around. I was drifting for so long, afraid to grab on to something because nothing was sturdy enough. I don't know if you'll be what tethers me, but right now, I know that I want to find out."

He crashes his mouth to mine, kissing me hard, slamming my back into the door. I fumble for the knob, and I fly backward into the bedroom.

Noah doesn't stop, and neither do I, we keep our lips fused as we blindly make our way to the bed. My legs hit the mattress, and he lifts me into his arms and places me in the center.

"I'm going to make you feel so good," Noah promises as he stands in front of me.

I have zero doubts about that.

"He might have been right, Noah. I could be really bad at this," I warn him.

"I very much doubt that." He grins. "Take your shirt off."

Seems I'm no longer in charge. However, the raw sexuality he's exuding makes me totally okay with that. I do as he asks, taking my time, loving how his jaw ticks as he waits impatiently. "You know, you could always help." I gaze at him through my lashes.

He moves toward the bed slowly, settling on the bed so his knees are straddling me. My hands move on their own accord, touching his bare chest. His muscles tense beneath my fingers as I make my way higher.

Noah grips my wrists, hoisting them over my head. "Keep them there," he demands.

My chest rises and falls as he grips the bottom of my shirt, raising it slowly. He runs the back of his fingers against my sides, just barely touching me.

"I've thought about what you looked like in that bathing suit every single day. I've imagined touching your breasts, taking them in my mouth," he rasps.

I make a soft moan, feeling his words everywhere in my body. "You don't have to imagine anymore." I'm all for the touching.

The fabric goes over my head. He reaches behind my back with his lips against my ear. "That's not the only thing I've thought about." He unhooks my bra but doesn't move to pull it off. "Bring your arms down, and show me how fucking perfect you are."

My arms fall, and I grip each strap, letting them fall, but holding the cups to keep me covered. I watch his eyes turn hard as I let it drop. Noah's breathing accelerates, and once again our mouths find each other. He shifts forward, covering my body with his, bare chests rubbing against one another.

It's as if he reminds me with each kiss how intimate this is. The talking, promises, and glances are hot as hell, but each time he kisses me, there's more hidden. It grounds me to him, and even if it isn't conscious, it keeps me here.

"Touch me, Noah," I plead.

It's all he needs, and the next second has his hands cupping me, his thumbs rubbing against my nipples. I've always had sensitive boobs, but this is off the charts for me. I could orgasm from this alone.

His head lowers, and his tongue rims my nipple. "Oh, shit," I pant.

Noah repeats the motion and then does it to the other side. My eyes close as he blows across the wet skin. If I knew it would feel this good, I would've jumped his bones earlier.

I squirm beneath him as his hands roam my body and his mouth works its magic on my breasts.

His fingers inch down to my shorts and run along the band.

"How much more do you want me to touch you?" he asks before flicking my nipple with his tongue.

"Don't stop," I beg.

"I didn't ask that." He breathes the words against my skin.

What did he ask? I can't concentrate on anything other than how fucking good this feels. "I can't remember . . ."

He lifts his head, and my eyes fly open to see why the hell

he stopped. "I want to know where you want me to touch you, sweetheart."

Even in the heat of the moment, Noah cares about what I want.

Others may not understand why this matters to me, but it's everything. He isn't trying to get his and move on. The power in this moment breaks any walls I had built.

My fingers glide through his hair, and I hope he sees in my eyes the gratitude I'm feeling in my heart. "Everywhere. I want it all, Noah."

The fingers that were resting on my stomach find their way under my shorts. "Here?" he asks.

"Yes."

Lower he goes with our eyes still locked. "Do you want me to stop?"

I shake my head. "No," I say, remembering he wants to hear the words.

He slides his finger against my center, finding my clit, and I no longer can keep my eyes open. My head falls back as he drives me higher than I've been able to do on my own. When he inserts a finger, I can't stop the sound from escaping my throat.

"Do you like that, sweetheart?"

Do I sound like I don't? I'm a mix between a cat meowing and a sheep baa-ing. However, I couldn't give a shit less because it feels too good.

"Don't stop," I command.

Noah does exactly that. His hand goes still, and I want to cry.

"I said don't. Don't stop, *please* don't stop." I push up on my elbows to find him grinning.

"Oh, I'm not stopping. I'm just getting started." Noah hooks his thumbs into my shorts and starts to pull them off. "I want you naked. I want to see every part of you, touch every inch, and I'm going to taste you."

My anxiety spikes, knowing I'm about to be completely naked. Obviously, this was going to happen considering what we're doing, but he's . . . gorgeous and I'm . . . not.

He seems to sense my shift and looks up. "You're the most beautiful thing. It's like you were made for me."

"Noah," I say hesitantly as he spreads my legs, moving his head closer.

"Feel free to scream my name while I fuck you with my tongue."

I gasp at his words, and then the sensation of his mouth overtakes everything. He isn't tentative as he eats me out—he's ravenous. Noah sucks, flicks, licks, and slides his tongue against my clit.

He moves back and forth, and the edge I've been trying not to fall off comes even closer. I grip the comforter, hoping to hold myself back for just a little longer, but then he slides a finger inside me, and it's too much.

"Oh, fuck. Shit. God. Noah!" I scream as my back arches off the bed.

I'm done.

Who knew that lack of sex would result in the most intense orgasm of my life?

Dear God.

I will never recover from Noah. If he leaves and we never do this again, I'm going to have to do something to erase my memory. Nothing will come close to the things he says, the way he touches me, or makes me feel.

I'm not even sure if I have bones anymore. Maybe they've disintegrated. He climbs back up my body, kissing my skin as he goes.

My fingers tangle in his hair and then slide down his back as he gets higher. "You're killing me, Kristin." He pants the words against my ear. "You're perfect, and I want all of you."

He's not the only one that wants it all. I move my hand to his ass, pulling him against me. "I don't plan to stop."

He rolls me on top of him and holds my face in his hands. "I don't want today to be about anything else."

I look in his eyes, trying to figure out what he means. "Today is about what we want it to be. It's about us."

Confliction plays across his face, and then he speaks. "Today you lost something."

I wonder if he's bringing up the divorce to see my reaction or for some other reason, but I haven't thought of that once. All of my mind is on Noah and what he gives me. I don't want what happens here tonight to be something he ever doubts.

"No." I shake my head. "I gained something. You're the only thing I'm thinking of. You're the only thing I care about today. I want you. I want this."

His head lifts, and he kisses me. With each touch of our tongues, my fear ebbs, leaving me with desire.

We break apart, and I lean back. "Now, I think you should lose your pants."

"By all means." He lets me go and puts his hands under his head. "If you want them off, you're going to have to do it."

All right then.

I slide off the bed, enjoying the view of Noah lying there. He took his time, and I plan to do the same. It's my turn to make sure he remembers tonight. I pop the button of his jeans open and smile as the sound of the zipper fills the space.

He lifts his hips as I pull the clothes off and toss them to the floor. Noah is even better than I pictured. I remember thinking he was packing the good stuff when I was in the pool with him, but I didn't do him justice.

"Talk about perfect." I grin.

"I'm all yours." He stays still, letting me look.

For as long as you want me.

My hands slither up his legs, and I grip his cock.

Now, it's his turn to make noises.

"Fuck, Kristin." His fingers grip my hair as I bring him into my mouth.

Noah grunts, groans, and curses as I bob up and down. His hands vary from being in my hair to slamming on the bed as I work to give the best blow job of my life. I take him as deep as I can, and his fingers tangle in my hair. He's losing it and I'm loving every second.

"You . . . stop . . . Kristin . . . fuck." It's about time I'm not the only one who can't speak.

I lift my head, and his emerald eyes meet mine. "Want me to—"

Noah sits up quickly, cutting off my ability to finish and tosses me to the other side of the bed. I squeak as I hit the pillow, and then we're nose to nose. His breathing is labored and our mouths collide.

My fingers dig into his shoulders, and his cock moves against my pussy. I need him inside me—now.

"Noah, now. Please," I beg.

"Please what?" he rasps.

"Take me. All of me. Take me."

He grabs the condom from his pants, rolls it on, and we gaze into each other's eyes. Noah watches my face as he slowly enters me. The look of ecstasy on his face is something I will never forget.

We make love, moving through different positions, exploring and learning each other's sounds. It's like nothing I've ever experienced before. Having someone so committed to making me feel so special. Between the immense amount of pleasure and emotions, I'm spent.

If wine and chocolate had a baby, it would be called Noah, both are satisfying and do my body good.

Noah's arms are wrapped around me as he sleeps. I inhale, loving the mix of musk and sweaty sex that clings to his skin. He cocoons me in his warmth, and I could stay like this forever. I turn my head, listen to his heartbeat, and drift to sleep with a smile on my face.

CHAPTER TWENTY-ONE

KRISTIN

"YOU NEED TO LEAVE." I giggle against Noah's lips. It's almost three, and I need to grab the kids from my parents by five.

"When can I see you again?" he asks and then kisses me.

We need to stop before I say screw it and have sex—again. It really is like riding a bike, you get back on and go again. I woke to find him in the kitchen, cooking breakfast, where I thanked him on the floor since that was where we sort of started last night.

Then, when he found out I'd never seen *A Thin Blue Line*, he forced me to watch two episodes as he said his lines in my ear. That led to an incredibly long shower with lots of . . . soap, but now I have to get my kids.

I push against his chest, and he chuckles.

My hand goes to his mouth before he can try again. "Tomorrow?"

A sly smile paints his face, and he takes my hand in his. "I was thinking tonight?"

"Noah!" I shake my head. "I have kids. It's way too soon for them to see me with another man."

He squeezes my hand. "I could sneak in."

"They could wake up," I counter.

"Then you'll have to be very quiet." His voice is low and drips with sex.

As much as I want to chastise him, now that he's said it, I kind of want to take him up on the offer. Damn him and his sexiness.

I take a deep breath, step back a little, and focus on something other than what I could do to keep my mouth too full to speak. "The article is due in three weeks so we'll need to actually work tomorrow. I need material and then a week to assemble it."

Noah releases a heavy sigh and nods. "I can *try* to keep my hands off you."

"You won't be the only one trying," I say under my breath.

He laughs. "Well, if you weren't the best sex I'd ever had, it wouldn't be so hard."

"Shut up!" I smack his arm.

"What?" He raises his hands. "I'm serious."

"Whatever."

I get drunk one time in front of him and give him enough material for any situation.

Noah walks over, wraps his arms around me, and kisses my forehead. "I'm not kidding, sweetheart. Last night was hands down the best I've had."

I search for the hint of a lie, but he's dead serious.

His hands move to my butt, and he pulls me against him. "That's what you do by just making me think about how good you feel."

My smile grows when I feel how hard he is. "You should know that you hold the top spot for me," I say, looking in his eyes. I love how tall he is. There's something positively sexy about how he looms over me, casting a shadow with his body.

I raise up on my toes to touch my lips to his.

Noah groans as he breaks away. "We need to stop before I toss you over my shoulder and take you to the bedroom."

Would that be so bad?

I open my mouth to object, but he says the only thing that could stop me. "Finn and Aubrey probably need you."

He's right. They know that their dad and I needed to do something yesterday, but they, well, Aubrey doesn't know what it means. Finn is all too aware, and I think there's a little relief that he can finally say we're divorced instead of not living together. It's the period at the end of the sentence so we can all move forward.

"We could do Monday," I suggest.

"That's two days away."

"Tomorrow?" I circle back to my original suggestion.

"Tomorrow." Noah nods, gives me a quick kiss, and makes his way out the door.

I stand here, hand on the wood, head resting on it with no idea how this is real. Noah Frazier is walking away after the most unbelievable night and still wanting to see me again.

He opens his car door and smiles when he sees me watching him. "I'll see you tomorrow, sweetheart."

"For the article . . ."

"And maybe a little fooling around." He smirks and gets into the car.

I am in a world of trouble.

"KRISTIN!" Aunt Nina calls as I walk in.

I scream and run toward her and throw my arms tightly around her. "I didn't know you were visiting!"

"I told your mother." She rocks me back and forth, squeezing me tight.

My aunt is the coolest person in the world. She was the person I could talk to about everything my mother wouldn't be able to handle. The first time I had sex, she was who I called to talk about it. When I turned eighteen, she took me for my tattoo. There's nothing that my Aunt Nina doesn't know about me. It's crazy that she's my mother's sister.

"She didn't tell me. When did you get here?"

"Just today. Jackson, Catherine, and the girls are out back, too."

"Really?" I smile. "I can't believe I didn't know! Are Uncle Brendan and Reagan here?"

My cousins and I are around the same age. They moved a lot, but when I was twelve they were stationed at MacDill Air Force Base and we all grew extremely close. Then they left, and it sucked only seeing them for the occasional holiday.

It's been too long since I've seen them.

"I am, I am!" Reagan comes out of the kitchen with Aubrey in her arms. "Look what I found!"

Aubrey squirms, reaching for me. "Mommy!"

"Hi, baby!"

I squeeze my peanut and then hug Reagan.

"Grandma made me wait to go in the pool until you got here." She huffs. "Can I please go in the pool *now*?"

There goes any chance of the talk I planned, but then

again, I'm happy to put that off. "Sure, go get changed, and I'll be right out."

Aubrey runs off screaming to my mother, and Reagan takes my hand in hers.

"You look amazing," she says. "Seriously, Kris."

"Look at you!" I touch her hair that she cut to right above her shoulders. "You lost like ten inches."

"It was time." She shrugs.

"This haircut looks good on you," I note.

"I think you mean divorce," Reagan smirks.

"Well, it's apparently a look we both wear well."

Yeah, there's that. We're both newly divorced from asshole men.

"You can't even say hello?" Jackson's deep voice booms.

"Jackson!" I yell and launch myself at him.

He lifts me and spins around. "It's been too long."

"No one told you to move to California and never come back."

They all moved out to California a few years ago. Jackson owns a security company that does God knows what, and he opened an office there.

"I would've wound up there if I were still active duty, anyway."

We all try to forget his time as a Navy SEAL. I'm pretty sure this is what caused me to have the insane fear when it comes to Heather and her job. Why does everyone think getting shot at is a good career choice?

"Where's Cat?"

"She's got the kids in the pool."

I give him a look, wondering if he's lost his damn mind. "And you're in here?"

He lets out a laugh and then pulls me against his side. "You'll protect me."

Yeah right, he's on his own.

We get outside and Finn has their oldest daughter, Erin, in his arms as he moves around the pool. "Hey, buddy!" I smile and wave.

"Mom, look! Erin likes me." His face illuminates.

"She does."

It's been a long time since I've seen that smile. Erin and Aubrey are a year apart, but God forbid, he plays with his sister that way.

He'd probably drown her.

"Hi, Mom." I give her a kiss on the cheek. "Did the kids have fun?"

"They always do. You know your father spoils them rotten." She pats my father's arm.

"Hi, Daddy."

"Hi, Krissykins." He pulls me into his arms. "How's my favorite daughter?"

I love that no matter how old I am, he still looks at me as if I'm his whole world. My father would slay dragons for my mother and me. He loves with his whole heart.

Sometimes, I wonder what's wrong with me to have ever thought the way Scott treated me was right. I have the perfect embodiment of love in front of me. Yet, I was willing to take not even an eighth of what my father and mother have.

My father's eyes narrow as he studies me. "You look awfully happy."

"I do?"

"You have fun last night?"

Lying is not something I'm comfortable with. It makes me

feel gross inside, but lying to my father is abhorrent. I was the world's best teenager because I couldn't lie. Sneaking out would never happen because I would go right back in or tell them I had just done it. Nicole hated me in high school for that part. I was always ratting us out.

However, sex is even more uncomfortable to tell your father about.

"I did," I say simply, hoping he'll drop it.

"Good. The girls came over?"

Short answers. I have to give him short and pointed answers. "Yup."

I'm biting my tongue to avoid offering more information than needed.

"Glad you weren't alone." He pats my leg before turning and yelling, "Brendan!"

I release a huge sigh, which doesn't go unnoticed by Reagan.

Shit.

Thankfully, Reagan doesn't say anything for the rest of the night, and we all enjoy each other's company. Mom and Aunt Nina laugh about old times, Catherine and Jackson are getting the girls ready for bed, and Reagan and I enjoy a glass of wine by the fire pit.

She tells me about her job, and I tell her about mine.

"Wait, so you're getting paid to stalk hot guys?" She laughs.

"In theory."

"Here I am, a divorced lawyer with no chance of making partner, and you're writing about celebrities and getting to hang out with Four Blocks Down. Man, I got fucked."

"You're nuts."

"This is true." Reagan grins. "So, don't think I didn't see

you blush when Uncle Dan asked you what you were doing last night. Spill it."

"Not on your life."

She taps her fingernails on the glass. "You had sex, didn't you?" she whispers—loudly.

"Oh my God," I groan.

"You did! With who?"

Like I'm ever going to tell her that. Hell no. I don't even fully believe it happened myself. But the soreness in my legs—and other places—tells me it did. It's the most liberating thing I've ever done. But I'm not telling anyone about it, not yet.

"There's nothing to tell you."

"You know it's my job to read people," she reminds me.

"Read people doing what?" Jackson returns, taking a seat next to us.

My family is so invasive sometimes. "Nothing. We're not talking about anything."

Reagan smiles before drinking her wine.

"What are we not talking about?" Catherine sits on his knee.

Great. A former Navy SEAL, a lawyer, and a publicist all ready to ask me questions. I feel like this is the beginning of a bad joke. One where I'm the punch line.

CHAPTER TWENTY-TWO

NOAH

I'M DRIVING BACK to my condo after watching basketball with Eli, and I make a right when I should've gone straight.

Then another right.

Before long, I'm a few blocks from Kristin's house.

It's half past midnight, and this is the last place I should be, but it's the only place I *want* to be.

How pathetic am I? I'm like some lovesick puppy.

I park out front and lean my head back. What the hell is wrong with me? It's only been a few hours since I've seen her. However, the only thing I've been able to think about is what happened between us.

Last night was . . . unexpected.

When I went there, my intentions were honest. I didn't think we'd have a sexfest for almost twenty-four hours. Beyond that, I didn't think I'd be this consumed by her. Instead of scratching an itch, it made it worse.

I have no idea how she feels now that she's had time to think. I pray to God I didn't fuck up to the point that she hates me. Then I remember we still haven't exchanged phone numbers.

Grabbing a piece of paper, I write my number down and then head to the porch. I figure I'll stick it in the mailbox and hope she'll see it.

When I lift the lid, a light in the living room flicks on and the curtain moves across the window.

Now I'm a fucking stalker that's going to be arrested. My publicist will love that.

The door opens, and Kristin comes into view, holding an umbrella cocked as if it were a baseball bat. "Noah? What are you doing here?"

Reclaiming my balls. "I forgot to give you something, so I was dropping it off."

"It's almost one in the morning," she says, stepping out onto the porch.

It's dark out, but I can still see how beautiful she is. Her dark brown hair is pulled up, she isn't wearing any makeup, and there is the cutest pair of glasses perched on her nose, making her sexier than ever.

"I wanted to see you."

Kristin looks away, but I catch her smile. "I couldn't sleep," she explains. "I wanted to talk, but it was late . . ."

"And you don't have my number," I tack on.

"That, too."

I step toward her, not able to keep my distance. My hand touches her cheek. "I'm here now. What's on your mind?"

Her tiny hand wraps around mine, and she moves to the steps. We both sit at the edge, and she rests her head on my shoulder. I try to wrap my mind around what's happening between us.

"You. Us."

"We're both thinking the same things," I reassure her.

"Yeah?"

I laugh. "Yeah, sweetheart. This wasn't exactly my plan when I came to Tampa. I thought I'd hang out with my friend, and then I met you."

Kristin squeezes my hand a little. "I feel as though it's all a dream. That I'm going to go to sleep, and none of this will have been real."

"Look at me." My voice is low and firm. "It is all real."

"You're the first thing in a long time that feels right."

She humbles me. She brings me to my fucking knees with that statement. I don't deserve Kristin. I don't deserve a second chance, but I damn sure want this one.

"Then we figure it out together."

Kristin lays her head back down and sighs. "What does all of this mean?"

"What do you want it to mean?"

I need her to tell me first because I'm afraid I'll scare her off. There's no way to describe how intensely I feel about her, and even if there were, I don't think she's ready to hear it.

I'm an overthinker by nature. I like plans and for those plans to stay on track. It's how I've done well in my life. A task is presented and I tackle it head-on.

Kristin is the anti-plan. She's the walk-off home run that no one expects. She's the winning lottery ticket. She's the girl I swore that, if I ever found her, I'd do anything to keep.

"What I want and what reality is are two different things. You're a celebrity, and I'm a . . . well, I'm a sort of journalist. It's my job to write things about you, and then we had a lot of sex.

Like, stripped my sheets because they smelled like a whore house."

I chuckle and nudge her leg. "Been to a lot of whore houses lately?"

"Shut up." She laughs. "I'm awkward, and you're perfect. I'm divorced with two kids, and you're a bachelor. You're rich, and I'm far from it. I live here, and you don't. It's incredibly stupid of me to think this is more than just some pretty mind-blowing sex."

That's where she's wrong. If I wanted mind-blowing sex, I could get it anywhere. I'm not dumb enough to tell her that, but it's true. There are perks to being rich and famous, women want to fuck celebrities. I didn't fuck Kristin.

"It was more than that for me, sweetheart." I move so that she can see the truth in my eyes. "You're not some easy lay for me. I don't need easy. I don't care that you're divorced from some asshole who treated you like shit. You've got a past, and so do I. If I thought for one minute you cared about money, we never would've made it past the first night. As for you being awkward, that's what makes you perfect."

"And then you say that." She slaps her hand over her eyes. "Could you not be so damn perfect? Just . . . a little flaw. Something to stop me from falling for you. Anything really. I had hoped you had a small dick, but that didn't work out."

"Sorry to disappoint you," I say and then burst out laughing.

"I didn't mean . . . I give up. I'll blame it on the lack of sleep. You have a *very* nice penis."

I pull her closer and kiss the top of her head. "I'm glad you approve."

Kristin nestles herself a little closer. "I haven't found anything about you that I don't approve of—yet."

"I'm sure you'll find something soon enough."

Which is what I'm worried about.

She sighs. "Tell me about your family."

"My dad left when I was a kid. I'm not ashamed to admit that I'm a mama's boy, and that's about it. What about you?"

Kristin shifts out of my hold, pulls her knees to her chest, and then wraps her arms around her legs. "My parents are amazing, they live in Tampa. They both grew up here, so they stayed, kind of like me. My dad was a salesman, Mom stayed home and was . . . seriously the perfect wife and mother ever. We have a small family, but by the noise we produce, you'd never know."

I always wanted more family around. My father moved my mother to Illinois when they got married. Her entire family was in Kentucky. I asked her once why we didn't go there, and she said she needed to stay put just in case.

That's the one thing I wish I could give her—the years of wasted time, waiting for someone who was never coming back.

Kristin giggles a little. "It's funny, I never saw the parallels until now. I think I envied my mother for so long that I tried to be her. Married the first boy I fell in love with, had kids, quit my job, tried to be Supermom, but I failed."

"You're not failing," I tell her. "What did you fail at?"

She blows out a deep breath. "I don't know, giving them stability?"

"You'd have stayed with him for them? You think that would've been a better situation than you being single?"

Asking this is a loaded question. I don't really want to know the answer, but then again, I do.

Kristin's eyes meet mine, and she shakes her head. "No, I was done. I wish they didn't have to leave their home and start a new school. No matter what anyone says . . . one day, they'll blame me. I'm the one who left."

Relief floods me because the last thing I want to be is the guy she wishes were her ex.

"You're also the one who told me that when Aubrey was sad you had a dance party. What about when Finn was struggling in math and you watched four hours' worth of YouTube videos so you could explain it? Those are just the things you told me about last night. Leaving him is the best thing you could've done. They'll see him for what he's worth one day. Trust me."

I did with my father. It didn't take long for me to open my eyes to the reality. He left us. He walked away for whatever bullshit reason he concocted in order to justify it. I didn't need my mother to say a word, which she never did, to see him for what he was.

"Maybe, God only knows what their father will convince them of in the meantime."

She told me a little about her marriage last night between rounds, and I want to beat the ever-loving hell out of him. Who the fuck treats a woman like that? Telling her she's fat, can't cook, is a shitty mother, and has let herself go. I'll fucking show him what he let go.

A man doesn't do that.

A man fights for his family.

A man treats a woman with respect.

Cowards tear people down to build themselves up. I'm not a fucking coward.

I turn to her, wanting her to hear my words very clearly. "You're nothing that he says you are. You are the woman who tucks those kids in at night, encourages them, and has a mock concert in the living room to cheer them up." I brush my thumb against her palm. "You're so much more than he ever saw, sweetheart."

Her lips part and Kristin rests her forehead against mine. "You're more than just one night for me, Noah. You're the whole damn thing, and that scares me. I don't want to be scared anymore."

She can be nervous because I'm not, for fifteen years I've searched for her. Now that I've found her, there's nothing I won't do. "I have enough courage for the both of us."

She lifts her head, and her eyes are filled with unshed tears. "Jesus. I never had a chance against you, did I?"

I run my hands up her back, pulling her closer to me, brushing my lips against hers.

"Told you I was going to win your heart."

CHAPTER TWENTY-THREE

KRISTIN

"NOAH, STOP," I complain with a laugh as he tries to sneak his hand up my shirt.

"I like touching you," he explains.

And I really like touching him, but I need to get work done before the kids come home.

"We have three hours."

He stands and lifts his shirt. "Let's get to work."

"Sit down." I giggle. "I mean three hours of *work* before you need to be gone."

"Plenty of time for sex and talking, sweetheart."

I'm not arguing that, but I'm chasing a deadline. So far, we've only scratched the surface of his acting history. Nothing personal, nothing that I can write some fabulous article about. If Noah and I fall apart, I still need a job. Therefore, I need a fantastic feature that will blow people's socks off.

"Not today. Today, I need to learn more about you."

Noah plops back into the seat like a dejected child and I can't help but laugh. "This sucks."

"This was your idea!"

He glides his hand over my shoulder, causing me to shiver. "This was my plan to get close to you." Noah's lips graze my ear. "It worked."

I'm never going to get work done this way. When we're touching, it's too much. "Okay, new rules."

He laughs. "The rules again?"

"Yup. New rule, no touching during interview time. If I miss my deadline, I'll get fired."

Not that I love my job all that much, but I need money.

"If you want me to stop touching you, then we need to leave the house."

What the hell does the house have to do with him restraining himself? "We agreed . . ."

"No, you requested and I refused," Noah says as he gets to his feet. "Come on, we're going out."

Out? No. We can't go anywhere in public. Not happening. People will photograph us, and I've seen firsthand how people behave around celebrities. It's as if all self-control doesn't exist. People scream, cry, jump around . . . it's insane.

Noah already has his keys in his hand and I'm still sitting at the table. "Kris?"

"I'm not sure us going out is such a great idea," I say as I clasp my hands in front of me.

"Because?"

"Because you're Noah Frazier," I say with my brows raised.

"And you're Kristin McGee."

Oh, how funny this man thinks he is. "You know what I mean."

Noah puts the keys in his pocket and comes closer. "Right now, we're the only ones who know anything. Your friends, your family, my family are all in the dark. What people do know, is that you're a reporter and I'm an actor. I told you that we need to eat because people do that. If it raises suspicion, I'll get it squashed. My people are very good. If you want to stay here, know that you'll be naked beneath me . . ."

I roll my eyes. "You're ridiculous."

"You're gorgeous."

"Again, ridiculous."

His fingers brush across my neck and down my throat. "You choose, sweetheart. I'm happy to stay here, strip you, kiss every glorious inch of your body, or we can go out and deal with people."

My body tingles at his promises because Lord knows I'm a cat in heat around this man. "People it is."

He smirks. "You can't resist me."

That is a fact. "You're no better. Let's go lover boy."

Noah lets out a low chuckle. "I'll make good on that later."

We head out the door without losing any clothing but gaining a lot of nerves. I'm not sure what we are, but he knows I'm in no way ready to make this a label. Right now, we're having mind-blowing sex, enjoying being together, and for the first time in over fourteen years, I feel like I have choices.

I may be alone, have a job that is ridiculous, and be a single mom, but losing the two hundred pounds of asshole husband was the best decision I ever made. Leaving may have been hard, but staying would've destroyed me.

Plus, I wouldn't be having the best time of my life with Noah.

"You okay?" Noah asks as he turns into the parking lot of the restaurant we went to for our first meeting.

I shift my body and decide I need to speak what's in my

heart. "I like you, Noah. I like you and I like what we have going here." My voice is full of worry.

"I like you, too," he smiles.

"I worry that I'm going to like you too much and then I'll wish I had stayed away."

Noah shrugs and releases a breath out of his nose. "I can't promise anything just like you can't, but you're not the only one who worries about this. I can tell you that being around is what I want. We have no guarantees, but at the same time, I would rather risk it all than look back with regrets."

"You think you'd regret walking away from me?" I ask with a racing heart.

Each time I'm around him, I realize how wonderful he is. He doesn't have a problem being vulnerable with me. It's a rarity that I treasure more than he'll ever know.

"I want to kiss your lips right now, show rather than say the words, but I know without a doubt that I couldn't have walked away. I'm telling you that you're the first girl in over twenty years that I've talked to my mother about. I know you're scared, sweetheart, but a life without risk isn't one worth living. One day, I want to see the mistrust disappear from your eyes, and I'll only be able to do that with time."

My throat goes dry and tears well up on my lashes. "I want to trust you. I do trust you more than you might think."

Noah's lips move into a small grin. "Then trust that I won't put you in a position I can't get you out of. If I thought this place was swimming with reporters, we would have stayed home. But, look." He ducks his head to look out the windshield, and I follow his movements. "It's empty, it's a small step, will you walk it with me?"

I realize right then he's asking for more than just one

thing. If I say no, he'll turn around and we'll leave, but if I go with him, it's saying more.

Do I want more with Noah? Yes, but I am scared.

If fear is the only voice I listen to, I'll never have the life I want. The only four-letter word I want yelling in my head is hope. Hope that I can have more. Hope that love will be something I share again. Hope that Noah will be careful with my heart.

So, I let that voice speak from my lips. "Yes."

The look of appreciation in his eyes causes my stomach to clench. I hope one day making him happy doesn't make me so happy or this could be really bad.

We enter the restaurant, and it's pretty empty. Tampa's in the off-season, and it's past the lunch hour rush. They seat us at a table with a view of the ocean and my nerves start to quell. Noah knew, and I took a step with him toward something more.

~ Two weeks later ~

NOAH

You look beautiful.

My heart races as I look around the boat for him. Our eyes meet and my chest constricts. He doesn't look good, he looks other-worldly. His tuxedo looks tailored and fits him perfectly, it probably was. His gaze moves back to Eli and he laughs but then finds me again.

> You're not so bad yourself. I wish I could be close to you right now.

I send a reply back as I walk around the other side of the room. Both of us have kept our distance and it's been torture. Today is about Heather and Eli, not my new relationship with Noah. When they got engaged, we decided to spend that time being sure whatever was growing between us could survive.

Now, I'm not sure that I can endure another minute apart from him.

NOAH

> I have every intention of being very close to you tonight.

I grin and put my phone back in my bag. I can't text him and keep myself on the other side of the room. It's too much of an effort as it is now.

My three best friends are all acting like idiots on the dance floor, singing and dancing in a circle. It was a million years ago when that was me in the white dress, happy, thinking life was going to be perfect from that moment on.

The music shifts into a slow song, and I seek Noah out. I watch as Eli heads toward Heather, who stands there with her arms open for him. I lean against the wall, smiling as my best friend steps into her husband's strong hold. The music talks about a life of devotion, love, and promises.

My eyes meet Noah's, and the intensity burning between us sucks the air from the room. Every part of my body is pulled to him, and when our eyes lock, it's as if everyone else in the room drops away, leaving just the two of us.

I take a step toward him, unable to stay where I am, and

Federico, one of the cops Heather works with, steps in front of me. The air expels from my mouth as though I've been punched in the gut, and I attempt to smile.

"Hey, Kristin, I was hoping I'd find you. Would you like to dance?" he asks.

Noah shifts out of the corner of my eye, and I try to move around Federico to get to where I was going. "I would love to, b—"

"Great." He smiles and takes my hand. "I'm glad your dance card was open."

Shit. Now I feel like a bitch if I finish my sentence. I give Noah an apologetic look and head to the dance floor with Federico—reluctantly.

"You look great, Kris," he says as he wraps his arm around my back.

"Thanks."

Federico is nice, but I have absolutely no interest in him. There's only one man I want to be dancing with right now, and I can feel his gaze on me.

"Sorry to hear about you and your husband."

"It's for the best."

Federico's hand moves up my back slightly and guilt floods me. I find Noah, who is watching me as he slowly takes a swig of his beer. I see the anger in his stance while he moves his weight from one leg to another.

In my eyes, I hope he sees what I'm feeling and knows it's him I want.

"So what do you think?" Federico's voice breaks my stare.

"Huh?"

"I figured since we're both divorced, maybe you'd like to have dinner . . ."

"Oh," I say taken aback. "I appreciate the offer, but I'm kind of seeing someone."

The truth is, I'm kind of falling in love with someone. Everything today has shown me that my heart wants Noah. My head wants to never again feel the pain of losing a man I trusted to love me. I'm battling both parts of myself even though Noah is nothing like Scott. It's more because there's still so much we don't know.

The longest song ever ends, and Federico's hands fall. "I hope he treats you right," he says, and I nod while biting my lip.

He does treat me right.

He treats me better than anyone has before.

How can I feel this strongly when the relationship is this new?

It doesn't matter how much I tell myself this is a bad idea, I crave him. Not just the sex, which is freaking unreal, I crave *him*. His smile, his words, his touch, and the way he makes my whole shitty situation not feel so . . . shitty.

I look for Noah, but he's not where he was. Butterflies fill my belly, and I keep looking around.

"Don't dance with anyone else," his deep voice whispers from behind me. "I can't watch another man hold you, touch you, feel you in his arms."

I nod. "Same goes for you."

The heat from his body is against my back, warming every part of me. And then a split second later, it's gone.

I turn quickly, but all I see is him walking away.

Thankfully, the reception is almost over, and less than an hour later, we're on the dock, bidding farewell to our best friend.

"Thank you, guys," Heather says as the four of us stand in a circle.

"You did it for all of us," Danielle says. "Well, almost all."

Nicole sticks her tongue out, causing us to laugh.

"You're off to Vancouver next week?" I ask, trying to hide the sadness.

Heather's bottom lip curls. "I am, but I'm not staying the *whole* time he's filming. I'll be back in two months. I'll miss you guys."

We all group hug, like we've done since we were little girls. They're the closest thing I've had to sisters, and the last two years, we've grown even closer.

"If Eli were my husband, I wouldn't ever come back. He could just do me all day," Nicole says unapologetically.

Danielle slaps her arm. "You're so crass."

"You wouldn't have me any other way." Nicole puts her head on her shoulder and kisses her cheek.

Heather and I give each other a look and smile.

"Ready, baby?" Eli comes up behind her and slides his arm around her middle.

She nods. "Okay, loves. I'll see you in a few weeks!"

We all take turns hugging and kissing them both. She grabs my wrist before I can walk away. "Hey," she says quietly.

"What's wrong?"

"Nothing, I hope. Are you and Noah okay?"

Her question stuns me a little. "Okay? Sure, we're working on the feature."

She tilts her head and grins. "Are you going to lie to me? Me? Of all people?"

I should've known she'd see through my very bad acting. Tonight was absolute hell trying to stay away from him.

"We're not saying anything right now. It's new, and I didn't want your wedding to be where you found out."

"Found out?" She laughs. "I've known since it started. Hell, I saw the writing on the wall the minute you two saw each other. It's hard to hide that kind of chemistry."

I can almost feel Noah's presence. Sure enough, I look over to see him talking to Eli but looking at me.

"I could love him, Heather. If I let myself, it would be so easy."

She takes my hand in hers. "I'm pretty sure he's already in love with you."

"It's too soon."

"It's never too soon when it's right. I know how hard it is to take chances after you've been hurt, but take them. If I didn't have Nicole pushing me toward Eli, I would've missed out. Don't miss out because of fear. If Eli and I had fallen apart, I wouldn't have regretted one minute I spent with him. And the only thing you'll regret is not following your heart."

Heather was strong enough to trust Eli, and that worked out for her. Who knows, maybe Noah is my second chance at happiness.

I pull Heather into a huge hug and pull back without letting go of her shoulders. "I love you so much. You give me hope, and as much as I'd like to tell you all the excuses I could come up with, I'm not sure they matter. I think we both know I'm falling in love with him."

She touches my cheek and offers a knowing smile. "Yeah, I knew you were screwed."

I'm counting on that tonight. "He's really good at doing that, too."

"Kristin!" She bursts out laughing.

"What?"

Heather's shock is slightly amusing. I was raised to never talk about what goes on in the bedroom. When all my friends were sharing their extremely intimate details, I would stay silent. One time, I got hammered and they somehow got me to spill all kinds of things, but other than that, I'm tight-lipped. I also never had anything worth sharing when it came to Scott. Our sex was lackluster at best.

Then it became nonexistent.

"I love this new you."

Truth be told, I do, too.

"You girls done yapping? I'd like to have sex with my wife," Eli says while tapping his watch.

"Go screw your husband," I tell her.

We say goodbye again, and I stand, watching as Noah walks toward me with purpose. The closer he gets, the faster my heart races. It's been hours of being near him, but not close enough. Now, there's nothing keeping us apart.

When I can't take it another second, my feet start to move. Knowing how I'm feeling, I don't want to be away from him.

Each step breaks another link in the invisible chain that was holding me back.

I'm not tethered to my past.

My head and my heart start to yell the same thing.

When we're just a few feet apart, I move faster, and we collide. He catches me as I leap into his arms. Noah holds me as I clutch his face in my hands, bringing our lips together. In the middle of the parking lot, Noah solidifies himself in to my heart. I kiss him in short bursts as he keeps my feet off the ground.

"I hated this," I tell him before bringing my lips back to his. "I hated not being near you when you were close."

He leans down so I can reach him easily, his hands travel up my spine and tangle in my hair. "All I wanted to do was take you in my arms. Kiss you. Rip you out of that man's hands and claim you as mine in front of everyone," he says, and then our lips are too busy to talk.

Noah fills my senses. The scruff on his cheek scratches my hands. The salt air mixed with his cologne makes my head dizzy. Each swipe of his tongue fills my mouth with the taste of the beer he was drinking.

Our lips break apart, and Noah's breathing is somewhat labored. "Your house or mine?"

I rest my hand on his chest, sliding my fingers against the placket of his suit shirt. "Well, we can be at mine in five or yours in twenty. Which do you prefer?"

Noah's hands move to my ass and he pulls me against his erection. "What do you think?"

"My place it is."

CHAPTER TWENTY-FOUR

KRISTIN

"STOP!" I try to swat him off as his fingers keep finding their way down my pants. I'm trying to make breakfast, but it's a little hard when he's made it a new game to see how many times I'll blush in one morning. "Behave."

"You didn't say that last night," he says gruffly against my ear.

Last night was not about behaving. Hell, we didn't even make it to the bedroom. We were both out of control with need. We made it to the couch where we passed out with me on top of him for the night.

Which was fine by me.

Now we need sustenance, but it's hard to think about food with his finger rolling my nipple. My head falls back to his shoulder, and I moan. "If you don't stop, we'll never eat," I warn him, not caring at the moment.

"I'll eat."

"Noah!" I move, pushing his hand away. "Now, go sit over there, while I—"

The doorbell rings, followed by a few loud knocks.

"Expecting someone?" he asks.

"No, it's probably the damn neighbor kids. They don't understand the whole don't ring the doorbell before ten thing." I turn the burner off and head to the living room.

"Kristin!" Scott's voice echoes as he pounds loudly again.

My heart sputters, and fear almost chokes me. What the hell is he doing here? I look at the clock, and sure enough, it's way too early. Noah is here. Noah is here, and my ex-husband is banging on the door.

"I need to drop the kids off, Kristin!"

Fuck. My mouth hangs open as I turn to see Noah coming out of the kitchen in nothing but his boxers as he eats a piece of toast.

The bell rings again. "You going to get that?"

I shake my head. "My kids. They're—" I look at my tank top and boy shorts and want to hide. They can't see me like this. Finn may be ten, but he isn't stupid. He knows his parents are divorced, and now to see me with another man . . . damn it. "Shit."

"Your kids?" Noah asks.

"Yes," I whisper and push him to the bedroom. "You have to hide in the closet or . . . I don't know, go out the window. Damn him for just showing up."

Once we get to the bedroom, I toss on a pair of pants, put a bra on, and try not to look like a hot mess, which I fail miserably at.

Noah stands there, looking at me.

"Umm." I point to his lack of pants. "Clothes and then hide."

"I'm not hiding." He smiles.

"I don't have time to argue, Noah. My kids aren't ready to see me with another man, and . . ."

He walks toward me and then places his hands on my shoulders. "They're your kids, Kristin. They're who you are, and we don't have to tell them anything, but I'd like to meet them."

I'm so not ready for this. "Noah—"

"No, sweetheart. They're your life, and I'm really hoping you're a part of mine. Is it ideal? No, but I'm not hiding in a closet, and I'm not climbing out the window. It'll be fine. We're friends, and I'll be here a lot the next few weeks for the feature, it isn't a stretch."

I huff as my phone starts to vibrate against the floor where it must've fallen. I can stand here and argue or stop delaying the inevitable. "Fine. Put pants on and stay in here until Scott leaves."

Noah kisses my forehead and releases me.

Time to go face the firing squad.

I get to the front door, draw a deep breath, and give my best smile.

"Nice of you to open the door," Scott grumbles as he thrusts Aubrey's backpack at me.

How I ever loved this man is beyond me.

"Nice of you to drop them off on . . . oh, wait, you're only eight hours early."

Scott grabs the other bag sitting on the porch and tosses it in the entry. "They demanded to come home, and I have stuff to do, so I said fine."

Why? I know they don't have the most fun there, but they love their dad. For them to want to come home this early makes no sense. "You should've called. You're supposed to have them until a certain time, and I'm not going to have you violate the custody agreement because you have stuff to do."

Before he can respond, the kids are climbing the steps.

"Mommy!" Aubrey smiles and rushes toward me. "Did you have fun at Aunt Heather's wedding?"

I scoop her up into my arms, loving how excited she is to see me. "I did!" I kiss her cheeks. "Did you miss me?"

"Yup." She giggles, trying to push me away so she can talk. "I always miss you, Mommy."

"I missed you, too."

Finn walks in with a strange look on his face. I can't tell if he's angry or crying. "Finn?" I call out to him.

He doesn't say a word, just walks to the couch without even a backward glance. I put Aubrey down, and she rushes back toward her room, probably to make sure I didn't throw out her stuffed animals I hate so much.

I look back to Scott, who appears irritated as he stares at his son. "What happened?"

Scott glares at me. "You made us wait out here for fifteen fucking minutes, that's what's wrong."

I start to laugh incredulously. "Yes, well, I doubt that's his issue, but I'm glad you're being so helpful in finding out what's wrong with our son."

The one thing I've learned is that he doesn't actually like confrontation. When I kept quiet, he felt empowered. Now, I'm not afraid of him. There's nothing he can do to hurt me. My kids are legally in my custody, I have a roof over my head, and he has to pay me or I can put him in jail.

"I don't have time to stand here and argue." He looks back to the car where I see Jillian in the front seat.

That took a lot less time than I thought it would. "Wouldn't want you to keep Jillian waiting . . ."

Finn snorts. "Yeah, we wouldn't want her to be upset."

Okay, something happened, and I don't care if he has plans, the kids come first. They have to be our priority. "Why are you angry, buddy? Did something happen that has you acting like this?"

"Ask him." He points to Scott.

"Enough, Finn," Scott snaps. "You've had an attitude for two days, and I'm tired of it."

"Like you care," he mumbles.

I look between them with a sinking feeling. Finn might be struggling, but this is a whole new level. "Finn?" I push.

"He doesn't want to talk about it." Scott crosses his arms over his chest.

"Scott!" Jillian yells through the rolled down window.

"One minute," he tosses back to her. "I've got to get going."

"Too bad. You can wait." He's a damn parent . . . time to act like it.

Every time Finn comes back from Scott's, this is what I get. It takes me hours to get him to finally lower his walls enough to actually give me more than one-word answers.

"Look," Scott's voice rises, "I'm not going to stand here and let you tell me what to do. I've dealt with your shit—"

"Mom? Is that?" Finn calls, stopping Scott's yelling. I don't need to turn around to know what he sees that has his voice filled with bewilderment. I see Scott's reaction as he spots what I'm hoping is Noah with clothes on.

"Noah Frazier," he says walking toward Finn with his hand extended. My eyes are wide, and I'm screaming at him in my head to get the hell in the closet, not go sit on the couch. He

looks at me and smirks, basically answering my silent screaming. "You must be Finn."

Finn stares at him with wide eyes and his jaw open. "You're
. . . Noah Frazier. From *A Thin Blue Line!*"

"I am. Your mom and I were working on our article, and I
was hoping we'd get to meet."

The two of them talk a little, and Scott watches with anger
rolling off him. I don't know what he's pissed about, but that's
his issue. None of this would've happened if he hadn't just
shown up here.

This is going to be so bad.

Scott's voice drops low enough so only I can hear him.
"Isn't this an interesting turn of events."

"What? That I'm working on a Sunday?"

"I bet you're working hard for that money."

Oh, so now I'm a prostitute? Good to see he thinks so
highly of me after all the years we spent together. Instead of
going back at him, I take the high road. "I can't change your
opinion of me."

"You get a check from me each month and find yourself a
new wealthy boyfriend."

"It's always about the money."

Jillian exits the car, and it's clear she isn't happy that
she's been kept waiting. "Jesus Christ, Scott. We have
to go."

"Hi, Jillian. Nice to see you again." I smile.

Her eyes move to the couch where Noah is getting to his
feet. "Oh." Her hand flies to her throat. Noah moves toward
the door, and Finn goes silent, glaring at Jillian. "Isn't this a
pleasant surprise seeing you again so soon."

"The restaurant, right?" Noah asks with mock perplexity.

He may be a good actor, but I know what he's like when he isn't pretending.

"Yes." She smiles.

"I'm Noah." He extends his hand to Scott and then drops it when he refuses to shake. "Anyway . . ." He laughs. "It's great to meet you."

"It'll be nice seeing each other more regularly, it seems." She places her hand on Scott's arm, ensuring I can't miss the huge diamond sitting on her hand.

I don't want to be upset, but I'd be lying if I said it doesn't hurt just a little. Not because I want him, but because it's her. They really do deserve each other.

"I see that congratulations are in order." I point to the engagement ring.

Scott shifts a little.

"I'm assuming that could be what has him upset?" I throw that out there.

Jillian huffs. "We don't have time for this crap. If he's upset, that's his issue."

I might just punch a bitch. My hand clenches into a fist, and I start to count, hoping to calm myself so I don't end up in cuffs today.

Finn stands and throws his bag to the floor, making a loud *thump* and breaking me from my anger. "I hate her! Everything is changing, and you don't even care!" he yells at Scott.

"Buddy." Scott steps forward, but Finn kicks the bag, shocking us all.

I've never seen him act like this. He's the silent one who lets his feelings fester.

"No! You don't. You're marrying her and having a new

baby! What about Aubrey and me? You don't love us because you love *her*!"

"Finn!" Scott calls, but my son is already running to his room.

A lot of information was said, and I want to process it all, but my heart is in my throat.

"Pregnant?" I look at them both.

"She's four months."

It doesn't take me long to do the math. There's no denying anything about their relationship anymore.

"Four months ago, we were still married. He's not stupid, and he is in no way ready to have you remarried and have a new sibling. No wonder he's pissed."

Scott looks at Noah and back to me. "Yeah, it's all my fault. Could have nothing to do with finding his mother with a new guy."

I want to beat him with his own arms. As far as Finn knows, Noah is a friend. This is ridiculous, and he knows it. I can't believe he'd do this to our kids.

"That must be it. It couldn't be that he found out that you're having a baby, getting married, and clearly something was said to him about it."

"We handled things in our home the way we chose." Jillian rolls her eyes. "It's obvious where he gets his dramatics from."

I move forward, but Noah grabs my arm before I can do anything stupid. My breathing is labored, and the sound of my heart is deafening. I can't believe he'd do this to the kids. For everything that's awful about him, he's loved them. I might have been expendable, but I never thought our kids would be.

Everything I hoped for to keep things civil is gone.

"This is a *family* matter. It's not about you or your time, it's about our *son*," I say through gritted teeth. "Nothing else matters but him, and you're unbelievable to be so selfish not to see this would hurt a ten-year-old boy."

"I'm selfish?"

Scott turns to her. "Go to the car, Jill."

"Excuse me?" Her jaw drops.

"Go wait in the car," he demands. "Kristin's right."

My eyebrows shoot up. There is no way I heard him right.

"You're taking her side? Are you kidding?"

He pinches the bridge of his nose. I know that look all too well—she's about to see Scott in all his glory. That was my cue to stop whatever it was I was doing or saying or I'd have to listen to an hour-long speech of all the things I do wrong. "Shut up." He pulls his arm out of her grasp. "This isn't about you or her, it's about my *son*. Now, go to the car."

She shoves his arm and stomps away like a toddler who didn't get their way. Scott runs his hands down his face.

"I'll give you guys space," Noah offers.

I want to cry. How can this man still be here. He has to see the insanity of my life. There's no denying that this divorce is a fucking mess. Our marriage may be over, but our lives are intertwined. I wouldn't blame him if he ran far and fast.

Hell, I'd like to run right now.

There's so much I want to say, but when I open my mouth, Noah touches my arm. He tilts his head to where Finn ran off to. "Go. He's what's important. I'll wait."

He's right. Finn is all that matters. He's hurting, and I can't waste my energy on Asshole and his slutty fiancée.

"Thank you." He's so good to me. Noah is ten times the man Scott will ever be. Instead of worrying about himself, he cares about Finn, which is more than I can say about the woman who will become a part of my two children's lives.

Noah smiles and heads through the door.

I look back to the man I don't even know anymore. "Let's go try to fix this mess," I say as Scott and I head back to Finn's room.

CHAPTER TWENTY-FIVE

NOAH

KRISTIN'S EX is something else, but that Jillian chick is a whole other level of fucked up.

She's been back there with Finn for about ten minutes and I'm not sure what the hell to do but wait. I can hear the three of them going back and forth—Scott's voice is loud but not loud enough to make out what they're saying.

After a few minutes, the door swings open, and a little girl with big blue eyes that match her mother's is looking right at me.

"Who are you?" the little girl, who I assume is Aubrey, asks.

"I'm Noah." I smile and put my hand out. "I'm friends with your mom."

Her tiny fingers wrap around mine, and she smiles. "I'm Aubrey Nicole McGee. I'm six, and I'll be seven next because seven comes after, and then I'll be eight. I can count to one hundred without stopping. I'm small, but Mommy says good things come in little packages. Do you know that I have a zoo?"

She's also the cutest thing I've ever seen. She's Kristin's clone. "You do?"

"Yup. I have lions, elephants, giraffes, and lots of other animals in my room. Mommy said I can't have a whole zoo, but I do. And then, I'll get more and have two zoos."

"Very cool." I smile at her. Her voice is sugary sweet, and Aubrey has a faint lisp, which just makes her even more adorable. "I like the zoo."

"Me, too." She puts her hands behind her back and twists. "I wanted to get a snack, but Mommy and Daddy are talking to Finn. Do you think *you* could get me something?"

Umm. I'm not sure, but do I tell her she can't eat? I can't imagine that would go over well.

"Are you allowed to have a snack?" I try to get a little more information from her.

Aubrey shrugs. "If I promise to eat my dinner, I can."

Sounds reasonable, and since it's breakfast time, I don't see a problem. "Do you promise?"

Her blue eyes grow bigger, and she nods quickly. "I promise. I would like some cookies."

Is that normal? What are the rules with kids and cookies? She did promise to eat her dinner, so I doubt it matters, maybe. I look at her as she gives me the puppy-dog eyes.

Shit.

I decide to go with it and hope this is one of those get-out-of-jail-free moments if this is against the rules. "Are you allowed to have cookies this early?"

"Yes." She smiles.

I would bet my ass I'm going to be in trouble, but she's tilting her head and batting her eyelashes. There's no way I can say no. I don't think six-year-olds lie anyway. That comes later . . . I think. "Okay then."

The way her entire face brightens makes me want to let her eat cookies all day. I find the package, get a cup of milk, and head to the table. I take the first cookie and dunk it, and she mimics me.

I try not to laugh when she double dips and sticks her entire hand into the milk. When Aubrey's hand comes out, milk drips all over the table.

Yeah, I'm in trouble. This was definitely a bad idea.

"More?"

Might as well go big since I'm toast with Kristin.

"Yes, please."

She continues to dip her hand into milk and eat cookies— a lot of cookies.

I look at the door, hoping Kristin is doing okay with Finn and they are working through it. The way her eyes filled with pain was impossible to ignore. She looked as if someone punched her in the gut. I've seen that look of sheer disappointment on my mother's face many times.

Each birthday when she hoped he'd call. On Christmas when we spent another year without a word. Or their anniversary that went without notice. Years that he hurt her and never gave a shit.

Then there is Finn. You can't fake that kind of hurt, and it brought it all back for me. I was a little younger than he is now the first time I lost it. I would scream at my mother, asking what was wrong with me.

No matter how powerful love is, anger is louder and can drown out all reason. It took my mother's constant reassurance to finally believe that it was not my issues, but his.

Aubrey tugs on my sleeve and studies me. "Are you going to marry my mommy?"

If I was eating or drinking, I would've choked. "Why would you think that?"

She grabs another cookie. "Daddy is marrying Jillian."

This is the absolute worst conversation I could be having. I'm definitely not the right person to talk to her. Hell, I'm feeding her cookies just to keep her happy and get her to like me.

I try to think of a safer topic. "You know that I'm friends with Eli?"

"You are?"

"He and I are good friends."

"Do you know Aunt Heather?"

I nod.

"She's the best." Aubrey smiles. "Uncle Eli is on TV," she tells me.

I smile. "I know. I was on the show with him."

Her eyes go wide and her mouth falls open. "You were?"

"Yup."

"Do you know Charlie?" she asks.

"Umm . . ." I know a lot of people named Charlie but no six-year-old would know those. "Charlie?"

She takes another cookie and nods. "From *Good Luck Charlie*. I love that show. Mommy says I can watch it if I behave. She's the best person on TV! Do you know her?"

I have no freaking clue what show that is. I rack my brain but come up short. However, I really want her to like me. Where's Kristin? She'd know what I should say.

"I'm sure I know someone who does," I tell her.

She claps her hands together.

Aubrey opens her mouth to ask something else, but Kristin and Scott's voices stop her. They're hushed, but I hear the crack in her voice. The front door closes, and Aubrey hops down, wipes her hands on her shirt, and swipes her arm across her mouth.

There's no hiding the cookies, she's literally wearing them now.

A few seconds later, the door swings open.

Kristin's eyes land on me, then the table, and then her chocolate-covered daughter.

Busted.

"Aubrey!" She puts her hands on her hips.

"Noah gave me cookies!"

"Hey!" I poke her in the side, and she giggles. "You promised."

I was played. She realized I was a sucker and totally took me for a ride. She's good, and I'm going to be in trouble with her mother. Kristin puts her hand to her head and mumbles under her breath about the death of her.

She tries to look angry but fails, clearly fighting a smile. "You know better than that."

Aubrey's eyes are soft, and that bottom lip pushes out. Man, she's a damn pro. I'd give her anything she wanted with that pout. "Sorry, Mommy."

Kristin doesn't seem fazed at all. "No more snacks until after lunch, and the zoo needs to be cleaned."

"Noah is on TV!" Aubrey tells her mother with a hint of satisfaction.

"I know. Remember that big article I told you about?" she asks as she wipes the cookie crumbs off her daughter's arm and shirt. "He's who I'm writing about," Kristin whispers and points at me.

Aubrey walks over and throws her arms around my neck. "Thank you for the cookies. I like you." She kisses my cheek, and I'm toast.

This little girl just stole my heart. Seems that this girl is more like her mother than I first thought.

Yup. I'd buy her anything she wants. A pony . . . done. I'll get her an entire barn full. If she wants to meet this Charlie person, I'll track them down and it'll happen. And the zoo is happening, whatever her mother says, I'll find a way around it.

She lets go and heads out.

"Is Finn okay?" I ask as Kristin leans against the counter.

"Not really. It was bad enough that his parents got divorced, but . . . this is too much. Marrying her? Pregnant. He just kept saying he hates us both."

"He doesn't hate you. He's mad, and boys say stupid shit when they're upset."

If she knew the shit I said to my mother, she'd understand this is normal. I was a little bastard for a period of time. There wasn't a rule I felt applied to me, but I learned.

"I don't know. I can't believe this. I mean . . ." Kristin's head drops into her hands.

I step forward, pulling her against my chest. "It'll be okay."

She lifts her head and reveals the tears pooling on her lashes. "How? How is this okay? We haven't been divorced more than a few weeks, and now he's marrying his pregnant girlfriend? Then there's the fact that he got her pregnant when I was still living in that fucking house with him."

I'm doing my best to let her work through this in her head.

Finding out something like this has to be difficult, and I'd be an asshole to push my own doubts on her. Knowing all that doesn't stop my unease. She has a right to be pissed, but I'm still a guy.

"The situation isn't okay, but your kids have you. My mom is the only reason I survived the shit with my dad. Trust me."

She drops her head back onto my chest. I hold her because that's all I can do. There's nothing to make this better except be here.

"How are you not running for the hills?" she mumbles into my shirt. "I told you I'm a mess, and now you get to see it all."

Kristin is the woman I want, and I'll take everything that comes with her. "I told you before that I'm not going anywhere."

A tear falls down her face. "You did." She plays with the button on my shirt. "I just didn't believe you because it was easier not to."

"And now?"

"Mommy!" Aubrey yells, and we break apart, moving to opposite sides of the kitchen.

"What, honey?"

The door flies open, and Aubrey runs in, carrying her animals. "The zookeeper didn't feed them!" Her lips are pursed, and she huffs.

Kristin bursts out laughing.

"It's not funny," Aubrey scolds.

"No, not funny. I'm sorry. We should get a new zookeeper."

Aubrey looks at me and a smile forms. "You could do it, Noah. You could give them cookies and make sure they get two kisses each before bed."

Oh, Lord. I look to Kristin, but she stands there, covering her mouth with her hand.

I squat so Aubrey and I are eye to eye. "I have to ask my agent if I can take the job, but if he says yes, I'm in."

"Yay!" she yells and runs out.

I walk back to Kristin, who lets her laughter fly. "I needed that."

"Hey, I'm her new favorite person," I inform her.

"Yeah, you fed her cookies!"

But look what it got me . . . a new best friend who thinks I'm awesome. Sure, she knows she can totally bend me to her will, but that's pretty much any woman.

"Whatever works. Now I'm the zookeeper since you were fired."

Kristin shakes her head. "I'm sorry our day is ruined."

"It's not ruined. Why don't we do something? Get the kids out of the house?" I suggest.

Kristin raises a brow. "You want to spend the day with me and the kids?"

"What did you think I was going to do?"

This is just one more reason I hate her ex. One minute, she's brave, ready to take on the world, and then the next, she doubts everything.

"Honestly? I don't know."

"Do I lie to you?" I step closer.

"No."

"Do I ever make you question what I want?"

She shakes her head slowly. "No."

I take her hand in mine, remembering that some piece of shit spent years trying to break her. "Okay then, let's take them somewhere. Do something they enjoy, any suggestions?"

Her smile grows slowly and now I'm scared. "I know the perfect place."

CHAPTER TWENTY-SIX

KRISTIN

"CAN YOU GIVE ME A FEW MINUTES?" I ask Noah, jutting my chin in the direction of Finn. He's standing against the wall with a sour face. I'm going to put an end to this.

"Of course."

"Aubrey, do you think you could show Noah where the map is? He's never been here before."

Her eyes brighten, and she takes Noah's hand and tugs. "Come on! I can show you."

Noah doesn't seem to mind, and after a few steps, he lifts Aubrey into his arms as she points toward the information area. Another brick around my heart pulverizes. Seeing him with my children means more to me than anything. They are my heart and soul and him trying matters.

I look back over to Finn and sigh. I don't want to push him, but I raised him better than this. Noah tried to engage him in a conversation several times, and he was rude. I don't tolerate my kids being disrespectful.

I nudge Finn's arm, and he turns to the side a little. "Hey, you ready to go inside?"

"I don't want to be here."

My knee-jerk reaction is to tell him too freaking bad, but I would like him to be less of a turd. I hear my mother's voice in my head, telling me to pick my battles.

"I know you're angry, and you're allowed to be, but you're *not* going to be rude to my friends, do you understand?" I ask him.

His eyes narrow, and I see the defiance swirling. "Fine."

"I mean it, Finn. Noah and I are friends, and he wants to hang out with you and your sister."

We're friends who are trying to figure out where we go from here, or I am, at least.

"I said fine." Finn continues to pout.

There are times when he's so grown up, and then there are times like this, which remind me how young he really is. He's in so much pain, but he doesn't know how to process it. Instead of talking, Finn shuts down. It's heartbreaking to watch my sweet little boy struggle with things beyond his control.

"Okay then. I hoped you would be a little happy since you love this place."

Finn crosses his arms against his chest. "Dad took us here."

And there it is. "Don't you think your dad would be happy you're here?"

He looks at me with his lip trembling. "I don't want a new Dad. I don't want a new Mom."

Asshole is the most selfish person I know. The only reason the kids found out he was going to marry Jillian is that Finn heard her screaming at him about the wedding.

Scott tried to explain that nothing will change for them, but Finn isn't stupid.

"Noah just wants to be your friend." I look at Aubrey, who is now leading him to another one of her favorite spots, the gift shop. "He was hoping to talk to you more about the show . . . what is it called again?"

He fiddles with the cord of his headphones. "You don't have to pretend."

This kid is too smart for his own good. "Okay, I'm just saying you love Noah's character, and here's your chance to hang out with him."

Finn smiles but then seems to remember he's supposed to be pissed off at the world. "Why? Why does he want to know me?"

I shrug. "Maybe because I told him how cool you were."

Finn may have done his best to ignore Noah, but I caught him looking at him with wide eyes a few times. Heather and Finn watched *A Thin Blue Line* marathon, and he was hooked.

"Can you smile and try?" I ask.

"I'm so excited." At least I know the kid can nail sarcasm.

I didn't want to have to do it, but he's left me no choice. I need to pull out the big guns.

I blow a raspberry against his cheek, and he makes a noise. "Mom!"

"Don't be a grump, and I won't kiss you in public." I grin.

"You're so weird."

"You say weird, I say coolest mom ever."

Finn rolls his eyes. I take pride in his reaction to my goofiness. I've always been this way with him, and it's kind of our thing. I'm over the top, and he lets me know how uncool I am. "No way."

"I'm cool. I'm friends with Noah Frazier, and you're not." I stick my tongue out. "That makes me cool."

"You're crazy."

"Don't make me hug you and yell your name."

He puts his hands up in surrender. "Fine. Let's go have fun."

Mom wins again.

We start to walk toward where Aubrey has Noah holding about twenty different stuffed sea animals in his arms. The look of sheer panic in his eyes at my tiny maniac daughter is hilarious. She continues around the bins, stacking the animals higher as Noah follows her.

"Mom? Is Noah your boyfriend?"

I don't want to lie to him, but I don't even know what we are. "No, right now we're friends who are getting to know each other. But I like him and want you guys to get to know him." I tell him the kid's version of the truth.

"So, you're not getting a new family, too?" Finn asks with fear in his voice.

You would think I just got hit by a car with how much that hurt me. He must be suffering so much with the anxiety he's feeling.

"Never. Even if Noah and I decide to become more than friends, you and Aubrey are my family. *Always*."

Finn nods. "Okay."

"Okay, let's go save Noah before Aubrey convinces him to buy the aquarium." I smile.

We walk over and Aubrey looks like she won the lottery. You can barely see Noah's face over the pile she's accumulated.

"What mess did you get in?" I ask while biting my lips to keep from laughing.

"Mommy, look at all the toys Noah said I can get!" She twirls.

I turn and look at him, wondering what exactly he told her.

"If I say no, she makes this face," he tells me.

"Yeah, that's called being six and a girl." I start pulling the stuffed animals out of his arms and tossing them back into their bins. "She already knows how to use her cuteness as a weapon."

I turn to my daughter, prepared to be the bad guy. "No toys, we're here to see the fish, not create an aquarium at the house."

"Okay," she says with a dejected tone.

She's a mess. Aubrey has this down to a science and is very good at getting what she wants. I couldn't believe when she was able to do it to my father. He had to stop taking her to stores because she'd come back with a bag full of whatever she asked for. If I hadn't known better, I would have thought he'd never dealt with a little girl before, but according to him, Aubrey is different. My parents were strict with me, but my kids rule the world.

Noah looks over at Finn. "Have you seen the Harry Potter movies?"

I hold my breath, hoping Finn gives him a chance. His room is filled with all kinds of things from the books and movies. We've gone to the theme park countless times. Finn has read the series, seen every movie, and can probably recite most of the lines.

"Have you?"

"Heck yeah!" Noah smiles. "Who is your favorite character?"

"Who is yours?" he counters.

Noah grins at him. "Sirius. Hands down."

Finn looks to me and then back to Noah. "Me, too! Did you cry when he died?"

The two of them start talking about the plot and what they would've done if they were each character. Noah and Finn take turns laughing at the ideas they come up with and the reasons why.

Aubrey and I follow behind them, and for the first time in a long time, I feel whole.

Even with all the crap that happened today, it's as if my life just clicked into place. My son is smiling, even though a few hours ago he was in tears. My daughter is happy and smitten with Noah. And I know how lucky I am to have found this man.

As we walk, people stare, whisper, and a few take photos, but he doesn't acknowledge anyone. He only gives the three of us his time.

"You having fun?" Noah asks as the kids run off to see the sharks.

I wish I could kiss him right now, but this isn't the right time. We're in public, and the kids are in no way ready to see anything close to a relationship. "I am. I miss our bubble, though."

He leans against the railing beside me. Our arms brush against each other, which is the most touching we've done. "I do, too. I liked our privacy."

"Hi, Mr. Frazier, I was wondering if I could take a picture with you?" A girl in her early twenties asks, giving him the face Aubrey uses.

"I'm sorry, I'm here with some friends, and we're trying to

stay low-key." He politely declines her question, but she still pouts a bit as she nods.

"Oh, sure. Thanks anyway."

When we went to dinner weeks ago, he said he doesn't like to turn fans away. I'm confused about why he would do it now. "You could've taken a photo."

He leans in, and I feel his breath on my face. "Not when we're together, sweetheart. When I'm with you or your kids, I'm just Noah. There's no photos or any of that, it's us."

My eyes meet his and even in the dark, I see the meaning behind his words. Noah is choosing us over anything else. He's giving us his time, his heart, his attention. Things that matter. If I could bottle this feeling, I would.

"You have no idea how much I want to kiss you right now."

Noah smiles. "I'm pretty sure I can guess."

"You'll just have to make up the lost time."

"Yeah?"

I move my finger so it just touches his hand. "I'm thinking tonight."

"Noah!" Aubrey yells with her hands on the glass. "Come see! The shark is going to eat Finn!"

He hooks his pinky with mine. "You're on."

I lean my head back and wonder what the hell I did in this life to deserve him. Here's a man who could get any woman he wants, and yet, he's with me. I'm sure Noah's life is filled with invites, parties, and probably no shortage of indulgences, but he's at an aquarium with two kids and a divorcee. Life is good, and I'm a lucky bitch.

CHAPTER TWENTY-SEVEN

KRISTIN

"FUCK, YOUR MOUTH IS HEAVEN," Noah says as I bob. "That's it, sweetheart. Take me deeper."

I do. I take his cock back as far as I can, and he groans. I love the way his face scrunches when he's trying to keep himself in check. There's something gratifying about a simple girl like me being the reason the vein in his neck is swelling.

His eyes find mine, and I take him deep to the back of my throat. "I'm going to make you come so hard," he promises. "I'm going to see how many times your body releases for me. I want to taste you, fill you, love you until you can't take it. Do you want that?"

I moan, knowing the vibrations will cause him to lose it.

Noah's head falls back, and I run my tongue along his shaft as I move up and down. My hands pump him, and he grunts. Then I cup his balls, and he almost loses it. "You. Shit. I can't. Holy hell." He can't get any words out, and I take great pleasure in seeing him out of control.

I lift, sliding my tongue around the head. "You like that?" I ask as I do it again.

"I want to come inside you," he tells me. "Don't make me come yet."

"So, you don't want me to do this?" I ask as I take him back into my mouth, going as deep as I can before releasing him. "What about when I do this?" I lick the underside of his cock and then his balls.

"Kristin." He groans and then pulls me off.

I look at him with a satisfied grin.

He struggles for breath and then crushes his lips to mine. Our tongues duel, knowing that he enjoys me pushing him just as much as he likes to be in charge. Each time we're together, it's different. Noah allows me to be myself without any apologies. If I want something in bed, I have to ask, and he is damn sure to let me know how he feels.

I don't have to wonder if he likes something, and he doesn't hold back. Noah constantly lets me know how I make him feel both physically and emotionally.

Right now, his mouth is telling me everything I need to know. He's feeling feisty and domineering.

Our lips break apart, and I'm ready for him. I need him inside me. I move down so I can ride him for once.

"Don't move." He grips my hips, stopping himself from entering where I need him most.

Oh, this is going to be good. I like bossy-in-the-bedroom Noah. He gives me control sometimes, but I'm more than happy to hand it over to him.

My pulse is racing as he moves his hands from the backs of my thighs to the front. Slowly, his finger feathers against my pussy, but he doesn't touch enough to give me any release.

"Noah," I beg. "Touch me."

"I am touching you." I hear the smile in his voice. "You played your game; now I'm going to drive you fucking crazy."

I moan as his other hand moves to my back, pushing me onto my knees. He's going the wrong way. I want him to fuck me, not move me farther from his dick. Right when my lips part to tell him, he starts to rub circles against my clit.

Damn it. I can't think of anything but the immense pleasure that's coursing through my limbs.

"So good," I pant.

"You're going to have to keep it down," Noah warns as he pushes my knees farther apart and starts to slide toward the bottom of the bed. "When you come this time, no screaming."

I've never had a problem keeping quiet before, but with him, I can't control myself. It's like a switch inside me has been flipped, and the more we make love, the more vocal I become. Noah makes it his mission to ensure this continues as well.

I'm. A. Lucky. Bitch.

My fingers slip in his hair, and I hold on. "I'll be quiet, don't you worry."

Noah's eyes spark with a challenge. "We'll see about that. Get up here and let's find out if you can handle it."

I'm not sure what he means. Up where? I start to slither to where he is, but he stops me.

"No, sweetheart. I want you to sit on my face."

I was about two seconds away from an orgasm before, but now I'm going to lose it. How in the hell is this my life? The sexiest man I've ever seen is in my bed, telling me to sit on his face . . . someone needs to slap me awake.

He grips my hips and positions me exactly where he wants me.

The first time his tongue brushes my clit, I fall forward, holding the headboard for support. Then he repeats it again and again until I'm biting my tongue so hard I'm seeing stars. Or maybe that's the fact that each time I get close to release, he stops. He's playing cat and mouse with my orgasm.

"Noah," I moan. "Don't stop. Fuck. Don't stop."

My nails dig into the wood as he continues to drive me crazy. His hand slides up my stomach, and he rolls my nipple. My muscles tighten before I shatter to pieces. Somehow, I'm able to keep myself from screaming, but there are some nice nail marks in the wooden headboard now.

Noah flips me onto my back, pushes my knees wider, and enters me. My eyes close as I'm filled to the brink.

"Look at me."

My God, his voice is so damn seductive that I have no choice but to do what he asks. I look at the lust swirling in his green eyes, and my pulse pounds in my ears. Noah starts to move slowly as neither of us disconnects our gazes. His hands glide up my legs, and then we're nose to nose.

Something shifts between us. It's no longer just sex. I don't know if it ever was, but there's no denying it right now. His fingers cup my cheek, and I hold the back of his neck. Noah's lips touch my nose, my forehead, my cheeks, my eyelids, and then finally my lips.

"You're so beautiful," he tells me as he moves slowly. "You make it impossible to think of anything but being with you."

"I want you so much," I tell him.

"You have me, sweetheart. You have me." He continues to make love to me, whispering about how good it feels and how much he cares about me.

I'm overwhelmed.

Every part of me is becoming his. There's no denying how I feel anymore. Whether I wanted to or not, I've fallen in love with him. He's everything I could've ever wanted to find. In his eyes, I see all the answers to the fears I have about how he feels. Neither of us needs to say the words to speak them.

"I can't hold back much longer," he tells me.

I lift his head, waiting for him to look at me. When he does, I let all the remaining walls between us crumble. "Love me, Noah. Love me and don't hold back."

Our foreheads touch and Noah falls over the edge.

I lie here, totally spent loving his weight on top of me. My fingers make patterns on his back and he kisses my neck. "We were pretty loud," he says with an impish grin.

"If we woke the kids . . ."

Both our heads move to the door, hoping no little feet are visible. "I think we're clear," Noah laughs quietly.

I hope so, that will be a conversation I'd love to avoid until the kids are . . . forty.

We clean up, and I go double-check to make sure the kids are asleep. Relief consumes me when I find them both passed out exactly like I left them an hour ago. I tiptoe back to my room, feeling like a teenager who is going to be caught by her parents.

He's still in my bed with his arm behind his head and a smile on his lips.

"And?" he asks as I climb in next to him.

Noah's arm wraps around me as I lie against his chest. "Both are sound asleep."

"Good."

My legs tangle with his, loving the way he lets me wrap myself around him like a vine. The closer we get, the more secure I feel. I have so many questions about what we're doing, but I never know when to bring it up.

There are truths that aren't going to go anywhere, no matter how hard we wish things were different. I live here, my kids live here, my life is in Tampa, but Noah's isn't. I've told myself this whole time it didn't matter because I wasn't going to fall for him.

That clearly didn't work out.

It's time we talk.

"Noah?" I run my finger across his chest. "When the feature is done next week, then what?"

He goes still, and I wish I could take the words back. Knowledge isn't always power, sometimes, it hurts and is dangerous to your heart.

"Then we have to make a plan."

Okay, plans aren't bad. Unless it's a plan to figure out a way to end this, then I would like a new architect working on this.

I lift my head. "Does that plan involve us being something other than the great friends we are now?"

He pushes the hair out of my eyes and smiles. "I think we're more than friends, Kris."

"Depends on what you think a friend is," I counter.

"Do you let other friends touch you like this?"

I roll my eyes since he knows the answer to that. "I'm serious."

"I am, too. My feelings for you are much stronger than just a friend. I think you know that."

I hoped. I really hoped, but I didn't know for sure. "Even after today?"

There's no way to explain my embarrassment over the shit-show that unfolded this morning. I still can't believe Noah witnessed all of that.

"Why do you think today changed anything?"

"Because you're a famous actor who could get any girl you want with zero baggage. Instead, you pick me." I shrug. "The drunk girl who falls in pools and has a crazy ex who is clearly an asshole. One of my kids spent an hour being a total shit, and the other one is obsessed with you. Let me know when I land on the part that screams to stick around."

Noah shifts, rolling us so that we're facing each other on our sides. "Do you think I don't have a past? Do you think you're the only one with things that make them less perfect?"

"I think I'm chock full of it."

He huffs. "You're not the only one who worries about the things in your life, Kristin. I worry you're going to run."

My throat goes dry at that statement. What is in his past that he thinks I'd run from? Whatever it is, if he thinks it's worse than my baggage I'm not sure I would agree with him. "I don't know what makes you think that."

"My past isn't perfect. My life hasn't always been Noah Frazier the actor. I've worked very hard to keep my shit hidden."

"Keep what hidden?"

Noah's eyes fill with dread, and my stomach drops.

"I want to—" He stops speaking, sits up, and releases a heavy sigh.

"You can talk to me." I place my hand on his arm.

His hand opens and closes as he battles whatever is raging inside him. "I want to," Noah says. "I'm going to talk. There are things that we need to talk about."

He's scaring me a little, but at the same time, I want to be his safe place. Plus, my feelings for him have grown to the point that I couldn't go back if I tried. Relationships aren't easy, I know that, but he's worth whatever effort I need to put in.

"Okay." I sit up, pulling the sheet with me. "Whatever you have to tell me..."

His eyes meet mine, and his back straightens. "You're what I want. You are everything that I want."

"I want you, too." I smile tentatively. I'm happy I'm what he wants, but I know that's a prelude to what he has to say.

"I hope you still do after I tell you this." Noah exhales and then begins. "I was born Joseph Noah Bowman. Most don't know that because I legally changed my name to Noah Frazier, which is my mother's maiden name. Growing up, everyone called me Noah because Joseph was my father's name. I think it broke my mother's heart to call me that name."

My heart aches for him as he tells me that. I know a lot about his childhood, and I can't imagine what it was like for him. It is a little strange that I'm in love with a man and I don't know his actual name, but it makes sense why he changed it.

"So, you've sort of always been Noah anyway?" I ask.

"Yes, but I didn't ..." He stops and grips the back of his neck. "It wasn't until after..."

I touch his cheek, hoping to give him a little encouragement. I've never seen him like this. Noah has been the driving force throughout the time I've known him. He's pushed his way into my life and never backed down. He's always been so self-assured and confident, and to see him shaken and unsure of himself has me scrambling for a way to reassure him.

"You don't have to be afraid. I'm not going anywhere." I tell him the words he's said to me.

"My feelings for you are unlike anything I've felt before.

I've never told anyone this, at least not anyone in a very, very long time." He looks away. "I don't talk about it because I'm not proud of it. I've gone to extensive lengths to keep it out of the media."

I don't want him to tell me anything he's not comfortable with, and right now we're not Kristin the reporter and Noah the actor. He's the man who shares my bed.

"Noah, I would never . . ."

"I know you wouldn't. I've put my past in the past because I can't change it. I just want you to understand that this is something I've tried to forget. Shit like this ruins people in my line of work."

"Hey." I pull him back to me. "I will never betray you."

"And I will never lie to you or hurt you. I have waited a long time to find someone worth sharing my life with. I need you to listen to everything before you judge me. Can you do that?"

I nod, praying I can actually do what he asks.

"A long time ago, I lost someone who I loved more than anything. It was our high school graduation night, and I was going to propose to her—" Noah's voice cracks, and he clears his throat before continuing. "Tanya was going to college in Oklahoma, and I was staying in Illinois because I couldn't afford college out of state. We had these big dreams about how we'd grow old together. I promised her I'd find a way because she was my entire world. But Tanya was . . . I don't know."

"A teenager?" I offer.

He tilts his head with a sad smile. "Yeah, she was eighteen, wanted to experience college, and in the back of my mind, I knew she would breakup with me after she left. I knew it, and

I couldn't let her go. I figured if we were engaged, it would change things."

This is the part of the story where you know the floor is going to drop out. Noah's anxiety is palpable. I move my hand to cover his and squeeze.

"I told her two best friends I was going to pop the question, and they never indicated it was a mistake. Hell, one even helped me shop for the ring. She agreed to meet me out at the ridge by the river on her grandparents' property. We met there almost every night. It was secluded and gave us some"—he clears his throat—"privacy. We had sex, and I thought everything was perfect. God, I was so damn nervous."

I don't say anything. I'm not even sure I'm breathing. My heart is pounding against my chest as he's lost in his memory.

He shakes his head a little and then continues. "I popped the question as we were lying in each other's arms, not even considering the answer would be no. Tanya got to her feet and started flipping out. She was shaking her head, saying all kinds of shit about how she wanted space and I was trying to trap her. I stood there, listening to her tell me we were done." He wipes his hand across his face. "You have to understand, I was young, but we had been together since eighth grade. I didn't know what the hell to think. I accused her of cheating on me, lying, using me for whatever the fuck teenagers use each other for. She slapped me across the face, telling me I could go to hell. It was the worst fight we'd ever had. Then she started to walk away, and I panicked."

The pain in his eyes causes tears to form in mine. He looks tortured, and I want to take it all from him. His thumb slides under my eye, catching the drop before it falls.

"Don't cry, sweetheart."

"You sound so heartbroken," I explain.

He rubs my arm and begins again. "I grabbed her arm and pulled her to me. I held her, begging her to just fucking stop what she was doing. Honestly, I don't even remember what I said because I was . . . wrecked? Devastated? I don't know the right word, but I both loved and hated her in that instant. Tanya was crying at the shit I was saying about her, and she shoved against my chest at the exact moment I let go of her arms. We were close to the edge, I don't know how we got over there."

"Oh, God." My hand flies to my lips.

"She lost her footing and fell, and I tried to catch her. I tried so hard." Noah finally breaks, and the sound that escapes is the most broken noise I've ever heard. "I had her hand, but she slipped. I practically fell as I climbed down the ridge to get her." Tears run down his cheeks as well as mine.

I never knew this girl, but the agony in his voice shakes me to my core. There's no denying how much this has hurt him or the amount of guilt he's still carrying. I move closer to him, resting my hand on his chest. "I'm so sorry."

He shakes his head, wipes his tears, and forges on. "When I got to her, I refused to believe she was gone. I swear she was alive, and I begged her, I begged her to hang on while I got help." He sighs. "I loved her so much, and I wanted to spend my life with Tanya. I carried her in my arms for a fucking mile. I didn't stop no matter how tired I was. She needed me, and God knows I needed her."

Noah's eyes meet mine, and he comes back to the present. "I would've died if it meant I could have saved her, but I couldn't."

"It was an accident. A horrible accident."

"If I would've let her go, none of that would've happened."

"You can't blame yourself. You didn't mean to hurt her, did you?"

"Never. I would never hurt a woman. I would never hurt anyone."

And I know that's true. I spent the better part of my life loving a man who used his words as weapons, cutting me open at every turn he could. Noah isn't anything like that.

"I know that. If you didn't feel any remorse, then it would mean something else," I tell him as I wrap my hand around his neck. "You carried that girl in your arms to get her to safety. At eighteen, I can't imagine that you'd have done that if you had pushed her on purpose." Our heads touch, and we stay this way for a few minutes, just being together.

The entire situation is horrible, leaving nothing but destruction in its wake. I try to imagine what Noah must've gone through. The people all whispering, accusing him of killing her, and then actually having to endure losing the person he loved.

He lifts his head, holds my face between his palms, and gently presses his lips to mine. When our eyes meet, I see his anguish. I wish I could take it from him, give him some kind of peace. Noah's finger slides across my cheek, wiping away my tear.

"I went through hours upon hours of interviews with detectives and the police chief. I was left in a cold room where it was the same questions repeatedly by different people. They had one detective who would be nice, then the next would flip and be a dick. I was distraught, tired, broken, and all I could do was tell the truth."

I take his hands in mine and try to imagine Noah, being

eighteen and stuck in a room being grilled for an accident. "I can't even think what that must've been like for you . . ."

"I took a lie detector test, and since I was telling the truth, they said I was free to go, but that I had to stay in town in case they had more questions. They interviewed family and friends, but people knew I was madly in love with her. I was never charged with anything especially once the coroner's report stated there was no foul play and police officially ruled it as an accident. But my life was . . . awful after her death. Tanya's family blamed me at first, refusing to let me anywhere near the funeral. If I closed my eyes, I saw her falling, our fingers touching, and then her slipping away."

"Why did they blame you?" I ask.

"She was their only child, and whether it was my fault or not, I was there when it happened. I felt like I lost a family when I lost her. Her father was the closest thing I had to one, and he cut me out."

My lip trembles. "I'm so sorry."

As a mother, I can't imagine the grief they felt, still feel. Aubrey and Finn are my world, and if I lost them like that . . . I'd never get over it. There's no moving on because you no longer have a heart. A parent should never have to bury their child, it isn't meant to happen that way.

I close my eyes and see a young Noah begging for their forgiveness, but the maternal part of me knows she'll never fully be able to.

"I wanted my friends to believe me, which many did, but some accused me of actually shoving her off the ledge, instead of her falling. I wanted to die alongside her."

When he says that last part, my chest tightens. If our roles were reversed, I'd feel the same. People make their decisions on what the truth is without knowing the facts. I see it all the time, and it's sad. We hear one version, taking it as gospel, and never actually listen to anything else. Noah had to walk around with people thinking he was a killer because they only had half the facts. I can't imagine the agony he was in.

"I'm glad you didn't, Noah. I don't want to think of a world without you in it."

Noah's lips turn up just a little. "I don't want any secrets between us. I wanted to tell you before, but it's not something I've ever shared because there was no one worth sharing it with."

I hold his wrists, needing to keep myself connected to him. "Thank you for trusting me."

He stares at me with so much intensity that my stomach clenches. "You don't think differently of me? You don't see me as some bad guy now?"

Why would he ever think that? He's the complete opposite of a bad guy. He's a guy who went through a bad situation.

"God, no." I shake my head. "You've been honest with me. You were a kid, and if you'd done something wrong, then you'd be in jail, Noah. It was a horrible accident, and I'm just so sorry you had to go through all of that."

He's still as he looks for something in my eyes. "I love you, Kristin. I love you, and I know it's too soon, but it's how I feel. I don't need you to say—"

"I love you, too." The words come out without a thought. I opened my mouth to say something else, and I couldn't stop myself. I love him.

CHAPTER TWENTY-EIGHT

NOAH

KRISTIN NUZZLES herself closer to me. My fingers continue to rub up and down against her spine as I lie here, trying to figure out what I'm going to do about our situation.

I'm in love with her.

She's in love with me.

And we have every obstacle in our way between her dick of an ex, my job, her life here, and whatever the media could spin about our relationship.

The only thing I know is my life will include her. There's not any other option.

"Hey." Her voice is low and sleepy.

"Go back to sleep, sweetheart."

She fell asleep about an hour ago, but I've been staring at the ceiling. My mind has been going in circles, working out how I feel. Talking about Tanya isn't something I do, but I knew it was time to tell Kristin about it.

"I need you to stay a little longer," she tells me through a yawn.

I need a lot of things, but we both know I can't be here in the morning. "Just close your eyes," I encourage her.

She listens as if she really didn't have a choice. We're both spent. Between the day she had and then my unloading all my fucked-up baggage, I don't know how I'm awake. After twenty years of trying to forget the way her eyes looked, how she screamed my name as she fell, and the way it was to hold her as I searched for help, I'm not sure sleep is ever coming again.

I talked to my mother two days ago about whether I should tell Kristin. She was the one to tell me I had to and I needed to do it before either of us fell any deeper.

"Noah." Kristin sighs, and her hand moves to my chest.

I smile at the fact that she dreams of me. I adjust her a little when my arm starts to go numb, and she hooks her leg under my calf. She's a clinger when she sleeps. Her entire body is touching me in some way.

Her dark brown hair covers her face, so I push it back to see the curves of her cheek and jaw. She's beautiful, and I don't know how the hell I got so lucky. Finding Kristin was . . . unexpected.

As my fingers touch the soft skin, I tell her more that I didn't say before. "I'm not sure how I'm going to leave in a few days. It's been months since the show ended, and I need to get back to work, but I keep postponing. You've done something to me. You've given me back this . . . part of my heart I threw away. You have no idea how much it's going to kill me to go." I damn near break.

The thought of getting on that plane sends a stabbing pain in my stomach. She worries that I won't want her when I'm right here, telling her daily, and I worry she'll find an excuse to end it.

I close my eyes and let out a deep breath through my nose.

There's no way I'm going to lose her, I just need to figure out a plan.

I tell myself to get out of bed and leave, but I want to hold her for a few more minutes. I would hold her forever if she'd let me.

"Mommy!" A bang causes me to pry my eyes open. "Mommy! Why is the door not opening?" Aubrey's voice sounds muffled.

Fuck. I passed out and spent the night.

"Kris." I shake Kristin a little, and she bolts upright.

"Huh? What?"

"Aubrey," I whisper and point to the door.

"Mommy! I'm hungry, and Finn won't get the milk. Are you in there?" Her little fingers poke through the gap on the floor.

Kristin's eyes are wide as she scans the room with panic. "Shit." She hisses as she covers her face. "Shit, shit, shit."

I look over at the clock and curse myself. It's almost seven in the morning. I knew better than to fall asleep.

She puts her hand over my mouth, even though I wasn't going to say anything, and clears her throat. "I'll be right out, baby. I'm getting dressed."

"Are you sleeping?" she asks.

"I'm awake now," Kristin replies. "Go in the kitchen, and I'll be right there."

Kris jumps out of bed, and I admire the view. Her see-through lace bra lets me see every inch of her perfect breasts, and the thong she's wearing is sexy as fuck. I sit up a bit more, propping myself in the right position.

"Noah, what are you doing?" she whispers loudly as she covers her gorgeous ass with a pair of pants.

"What?" I smirk.

"Get up," she instructs. "You can't be here right now. How am I ever going to explain this?"

I love when she gets flustered. It's when her guard is down and she isn't worried about what flies out of her mouth.

"Relax, sweetheart."

She stands straight, glares at me, and then goes back to digging through her clothes. "Relax? Right. Oh, I know," she rambles on, "Mommy had a naughty sleepover, kids, ignore the big man sneaking out." I chuckle, which earns me another look of death. "You weren't supposed to stay the night."

I know this much, but I am here, and I can't exactly do anything now. "I swear, you were just so comfortable, and I needed to be with you. I didn't mean to stay."

That seems to stun her a little. "Don't be all sweet when I'm supposed to be mad at you. You need to get up."

"And go where?"

She throws a sweatshirt on and shakes her hands. "I don't know. Why do you have to be so freaking hot that I forget that I'm an adult? Couldn't you be . . . anything bad?" Kristin chucks my shirt at me, hitting me in the face. "I'm a responsible mother one day, and then you come along, and I'm dropping my panties like a stripper."

"A very hot stripper with gorgeous tits and—"

Kristin glares at me, pointing her finger. "You are in big trouble." Her voice drops low in an attempt to sound like me. "Sweetheart, I'll just hold you until you fall asleep." She shakes her head.

I smile unapologetically as I get to my feet. "I like holding you," I admit as I move toward her. "I like that you drop your panties." My arms wrap around her middle. "And I like that you love me."

She starts to melt a little, moving her hand across my chest until another knock sounds. "Mommy. I want cereal, *please!*" Aubrey whines.

"Coming, baby! Why don't you get a zoo animal to sit with you," Kristin suggests and then turns back to me. "Clothes, and then you have to go."

"Kris, there's nowhere to go, we'll handle it like adults."

Her eyes narrow, and I realize that wasn't the best thing to say. I clearly am in the wrong for not leaving last night, and she's going to beat me with my own arms. "Remember the window? You're going to use that."

I'm not a small guy by any means. Sneaking out of windows was never really an option. "I'm not . . ." When I get a glimpse of her face, I stop.

Looks like I'll be finding a way to make it happen.

"Go." She pushes my chest. "And then you can ring the doorbell or something, but they can't know you slept here." I'm not even sure what's happening, but Kristin is shoving me in the direction of the window.

"You want me to climb out the window, go around the house, and then ring the doorbell?" I ask for clarification.

"Yes."

"Instead of just explaining to the kids?"

She huffs. "Explain that their mother had mind-blowing sex with the guy they met yesterday?"

"I wasn't suggesting any details, but I'm glad it was mind-blowing."

Kristin runs her hands down her face. "Less talking and more climbing."

The things men do for women are ridiculous.

I lift the window open and look back to be sure she's serious. She moves her hands and shoos, so I guess this is actually happening.

"You're going to owe me." I try to joke.

"You're damn right *you* will." She huffs. "Now, go before my six-year-old finds a way to pick the lock, and if you think I'm kidding, I'm not."

Aubrey might not be able to, but I don't doubt that Finn can. Instead of prolonging the inevitable, I do as she asks . . . demands. Yesterday was a crazy day for the kids, and she's right to keep this a secret. Plus, I'd like to keep my current status with them both for a while.

"I'm going, sweetheart." I kiss her softly.

Here I am, thirty-eight years old and sneaking out of my girlfriend's room so I don't get caught spending the night. I guess you're never too old for this shit.

I sit on my ass, legs hanging a little, but because of my size, there's no way that I won't tear my back up. I flip around to my stomach, thinking if I can touch the ground first, it might not be as bad, it's only a ten-foot drop. I look up, trying to get my toes to find the grass, and see Kristin standing there trying not to laugh.

"You're lucky I love you," I grunt as I feel around.

She heads to the window, takes my face in her hands, and kisses me hard. "Yeah, I totally am."

The bang on the door causes us both to jump a little. "Go," I tell her.

"Mom-*my!*" Aubrey's voice is loud, and she keeps hitting her hands on the wood. "You're taking forever!"

I drop out the window while her back is turned and lean against the siding.

"Sorry, sorry!" Kristin's voice carries to me. "I'm here now."

"What took you so long?" she asks her mother.

"I couldn't get rid of a shirt I really love." I can hear the smile in Kristin's voice.

"Huh?" Aubrey sounds confused. "What shirt?"

"Nothing, honey. Let's get you breakfast."

"You made me throw away my favorite dress," Aubrey continues. "Can I keep it, too?"

Kristin's laughter starts to float away as I try to contain my own.

My phone rings, causing me to jump. I quickly silence it and pray no one heard it as I rush around the side of the house and make it to my car without incident.

"What's up, Sebastian?" I answer when my agent calls for the second time in a row.

"I need you to get on a plane today."

"Today?" I ask, looking at Kristin's front door.

He sighs. "They need you to do a read through for the movie. I know they said a few weeks, but they changed the timeline."

My hand grips the steering wheel, and I twist against the leather. "I can't."

"No, you have no choice."

"It's too short of notice," I tell him. "I've got things here that I'm working on. There's no way I'm leaving now."

Kristin and I have a lot of things we need to talk about. I'm not getting on a plane today when last night I told her everything. I'm not a fool; it'll look like I'm running away. Plus, I haven't told her about this fucking movie. Six months of filming in France isn't going to go over well, not when we're this new.

Something makes a loud noise in the background, and I wouldn't doubt he threw something. I frustrate the fuck out of him. "I hope it's more than eight million reasons as to why you can't get there."

It's his job to be the bad guy and to fight for me.

"This is the third project I've done with Paul, he knows I don't dick around."

Sebastian forgets that I've been a walk in the park until now. I've always done what was asked, and I've never fought back, but this is different.

"If you think you're the only actor that can play this part, you're out of your damn mind. Get on the plane, Noah. Don't fuck this up."

"I'll call you back," I say and disconnect the call.

Staring at Kristin's house, I debate what to do. I think about everything that happened last night, and how the timing couldn't be worse, but I know I should listen to my agent. I got a big contract, and that comes with a level of expectation.

> Sweetheart, I need to head to L.A. for a few days. My agent just called. I wish I could spend the day with you, but I don't have a choice. Not sure when I'll be back, but I'll keep you posted.

A minute later she responds.

KRISTIN

I understand.

I'll call you when I land.

I see the curtain move to the side, and she smiles at me through the window.

KRISTIN

Okay . . . I'll miss you.

I love you.

KRISTIN

I love you.

She lifts her hand, presses it to her lips, and blows me a kiss.

I groan, wishing I could go to her, take her into my arms, and actually touch her lips. Instead, I put the car in drive and fight the desire to quit this fucking movie.

I have to find a way to convince her to come with me or I might be willing to give up the career I've built.

CHAPTER TWENTY-NINE

KRISTIN

"YOU CAN'T BE this stressed out over this feature," Nicole says as she sits at my table.

She has no idea. I've been working on my rough draft while Noah's in California, and I'm on version number six. All of them suck.

"You try writing a huge article about a guy you're dating and not talk about the size of his dick."

It's pretty much impossible. Draft number two wasn't half bad until I started talking about the number of orgasms Noah is able to deliver when he concentrates. As much as I'd love to brag, I'm not sure I need to give women any more reasons to fall for him.

"Feel free to tell me about it." She smirks over the rim of her mug.

"You're the last person I'm telling."

She nods sagely. "That's probably a good decision."

Nicole stopped by, saying she had big news and couldn't wait to tell me. Little did I know it would be about her sleeping with a guy I dated in high school—and his twin brother. With most situations regarding Nicole, I'm never quite sure of the appropriate reaction.

One part of me thinks it's kind of cool that she's so adventurous. The other part says she needs to be careful because she's going to get hurt. These guys aren't worried about her well-being as much as they're concerned with getting off.

"Can I read the latest version?" she asks.

I don't remember being weird about my articles before, but I'm super protective about this one. I haven't shown anyone this. It's Noah. It's the man I'm in love with and am about to share with the world. Well, all ten thousand followers of the blog.

"Not until I'm done."

"Kris." She gives me a look. "How much do you have written?"

"Some." I glance at the paper that is sitting between us. The one with all of two sentences written.

She sees my eyes go to it, and we both lunge. Nicole is faster and grabs it. "Kristin!" Nicole shrieks. "You wrote your names! That's it! You need to write . . . words and all."

"I know." I tear the paper from her hands. "I'm working on it, but my crazy ass friend showed up and started talking about anal. Things deteriorated from there. Can't really write when you're talking about getting it in the ass with my ex-boyfriend and his brother."

Nicole sits back down with a sheepish grin. "Please tell me you've let Noah stick it in your butt."

"If I didn't let my husband of fourteen years do it, what the hell makes you think I let him?"

She shrugs. "Because Scott probably liked it in the ass. I mean he always acted like something was shoved up there."

"I wish you hadn't put that image in my mind twenty minutes before he's supposed to drop the kids off." I laugh.

Scott has the kids for their Wednesday night dinner. I thought I'd get some work done since my deadline is coming and Noah had to go to L.A. for a callback. I haven't seen him in three days, and I miss him terribly.

"Speaking of Asshole, did he say anything about Jillian when he picked them up?"

Danielle let Heather and Nicole know about the incident last week. None of us were overly surprised, but they were all still as disappointed as I had been. I always hoped I was wrong regarding their relationship. It was easier to delude myself than seek the truth. Then I'd have no excuses left, and I would've needed to decide.

"He just said she wasn't going to dinner with them. Finn was relieved, and Aubrey couldn't care less."

Nicole laughs. "I swear, she shits sunshine and farts glitter. That girl is the happiest person I've ever met. I'm going to beat whoever it is that makes her the slightest bit sad."

Aubrey is really her own source of anti-depressants. There's very little that makes her sad, she finds the good in everything. "It'll be a boy," I tell her.

"And I'll kill him."

"I don't doubt that."

Nicole points back to the paper. "You better get to work."

I groan and drop my head on my arm. "I hate this. Nothing seems interesting because he's so much more than I can put into words. He's sweet, loving, has this big heart, and I love him."

"Doesn't hurt that he's well equipped in the peen department."

That would be what she goes back to. However, she isn't wrong. "Truth."

My phone dings, and I'm sure it's Scott telling me he's on his way.

NOAH

My hotel overlooks the aquarium, and all I can think about is Aubrey needing an animal for her collection.

I smile at the fact that he's thinking of us.

She does NOT need more, but I need you to come back sooner rather than later.

NOAH

My master plan is succeeding.

Oh, yeah? What exactly is your plan?

NOAH

I'll never tell.

I start to type back a response but can feel Nicole's eyes watching me. "What?" I ask her.

"Nothing. It's cute watching you get all starry-eyed when he texts you. Do you guys sext? Can I see?"

"No, we don't sext!" I shake my head with a laugh.

"Why the hell not?"

She's insane. "Because I'm not seventeen."

"Your loss. Just ask him for a dick pic then."

Sometimes it's best to ignore her.

I look back to the screen, wanting to ask him a million

questions. Since our night together, we've barely had two minutes to catch up. He's been in back-to-back meetings, and the three-hour time difference has done nothing to help with the lack of communication. Really, there's only one thing I want to know. The rest we can figure out when he gets here.

> When are you coming back to Tampa?

NOAH

> Soon, sweetheart. I know the timing sucks, but I need to be here right now. Trust me, I'd much rather be there with you.

Soon sucks. I want him here now. However, I'm not going to make him feel bad when he clearly has to work.

> Fine, I guess I'll forgive you this once.

NOAH

> This one time, huh?

> Well, you're not just some average Joe.

I giggle at the fact that his name really is Joseph.

NOAH

> Are you sure about that? I did tell you my real name was Joseph.

> This is true, Mr. Bowman, and I appreciate you telling me everything about your past. I know we haven't talked about the accident since that night, but I'm glad I found out from you.

NOAH

You will always hear the truth from me first. It wasn't easy telling you, but I wanted you to know about Tanya. I need to run. I love you, Kristin.

I love you, too.

I put the phone down with a huge grin. I never in a million years thought I'd be in love like this. I didn't know it even existed. Now, I don't ever want to be without it.

"You're as bad as Heather now."

"You'll find a man who makes you feel like this, and then you'll understand."

He's out there. She just has to find him.

She flips me off in typical Nicole fashion. "So I can be like you two? No thanks. Heather took a leave of absence to follow him around. You're over here practically glowing from a text message, and I'm getting double time with twins . . . who is living the life?"

As much as she likes to play the single and loving life card, I remember not all that long ago when she was broken. I take her hand in mine. "I love you, Nic. I think you're the bravest woman I know. Not many could go through the hell you have and still be standing, but love isn't a weapon. Real, true, honest love is precious and can heal the damage others have done. Don't give up on it."

The iron curtains she works so hard to hide behind shift, and I catch the pain in her eyes. As quickly as it appears, it's gone. She pulls her hand back and looks away. "I'm better like this."

Nicole wants to be loved. No matter what she says, that

need is engrained in us. It sucks that the one time she took a chance on it, it broke her.

"You're perfect no matter what," I reassure her.

She nods. "Damn right. Now, let's get your article written before you miss your deadline."

I CHEW on my lip as I read through the final draft one more time. It's due to Erica in the next thirty minutes, and I want it perfect. After I realize I can't nuke it any more than I already have, I send the file and pray it doesn't suck.

"What is that, Mommy?" Aubrey asks as I press send on the email, handing the article off to my editor.

"It's my article about Noah."

"I like Noah," she tells me.

I pull her on my lap and kiss her cheek. "Me, too."

"He hasn't fed my animals, though."

"Because he's not here," Finn answers her as he walks in the living room. "Too bad Jillian doesn't disappear like him."

He really hates her, and I know I can't encourage his attitude, but I don't blame him. Not because she deserves anything, but because her presence is making their visits awful. The more Finn pushes her hand, the worse it'll get.

"I know you don't like her, but your dad is going to marry her."

Finn huffs. "I hate her."

"Why do you hate her, Finn?"

He looks at his feet. "Because I don't know her! And Dad is just going to marry her? He's supposed to love you!"

Oh, my sweet boy. I can't imagine that there isn't some

small part of him that hopes for this grand reconciliation, but it's never going to happen. "Hating Jillian isn't going to make your father and I get back together, buddy. You will always have your dad, but he loves her, and she isn't going anywhere." Even if we'd all like to see her take a dip in a vat of battery acid. Nothing says asshole like enjoying being a homewrecker.

Although, I'm sure it was all my fault.

I couldn't keep him happy. I couldn't keep the house the way he wanted. I was shitty in bed and all the other crap he probably said. Lucky for Scott, he had his assistant ready to service him and his tiny pecker.

Of course, I don't get to say any of that.

"Why does Daddy love her?" Aubrey asks, turning her head so she can see me.

Because he's an idiot who thinks with the wrong head.

"He just does. Sometimes we love people for no reason."

Lord knows I can't seem to find a redeeming quality in her.

Aubrey twirls my hair. "She said you're not Daddy's wife anymore."

This shit is going to stop. I'm tired of the kids coming home and telling me the things she tells them. It's clear she doesn't like my children, so she should stop talking to them and me. Scott is going to get an earful. I won't hesitate in taking him back to court and getting full custody. I bet he'll love having to pay more money for child support.

My kids are not going to be poisoned or made to feel uncomfortable because he's moving on. I'm doing the same thing with Noah, only I'm not shoving him down their damn throats.

I touch the side of Aubrey's face. "I'm not. But I'm still your mommy and he's still your daddy."

"That's good." She smiles. "You're a good mommy."

"I'm glad you think so." I tickle her side.

"Is Noah coming back still?" Finn asks.

"I think he'll be back tomorrow, why?"

I tread carefully because Finn is one of those kids that can take words and twist them. He's going through a lot, and I don't need to walk into a trap.

"There's a Harry Potter marathon on." He scratches his head and looks away.

My chest lightens, and I suppress the smile trying to work its way onto my lips. My son is thinking of Noah. Last night I was on FaceTime with him, and Finn talked to him for a few minutes. It was so cute how the two of them chatted about Hollywood. Finn is fascinated by everything related to film. Noah is more than happy to tell him about it.

I sat there and watched my son's face light up when Noah told him he had dinner with his favorite actor.

I laughed when Noah seemed miffed that he wasn't his favorite.

"I'm sure if Noah's back he'll watch. If that's okay that he comes over . . ."

"Why wouldn't it be?" Finn looks confused.

"I don't know, you don't seem to like Jillian around, I wasn't sure how you felt about Noah."

Aubrey hops off my lap and spins in the middle of the room. "Noah has to come over." She giggles. "He's my zookeeper."

Yes, that is the most important thing to my daughter—her fake zoo and the stuffed animals that reside there.

"Noah isn't like *Jillian*." He sneers her name, and I don't disagree one bit.

"He's nice," Aubrey says and starts spinning again.

They have no idea how good that makes me feel. Noah is important to me, but we're taking things slow with the kids. We both want them to be comfortable with him before we throw things in their face. That's the one thing about Scott I don't understand. Why rush? Why does he have to marry her? If they love each other so much, why not wait even if there is a baby involved? It's not the fifties where you need to get married if you're pregnant.

I love Noah. I love him for more than just today. I'll love him tomorrow and the next day. That's why neither of us feels the need to push things quicker than they're going.

"Besides, I heard them yelling because Dad said he wants to wait," Finn snickers.

I'm not above a little gossip. "Wait?"

"Yup," Finn responds while watching his phone. "He doesn't want to marry her. I heard them fighting. Something about me and being okay with it."

That's interesting. Scott has been trying with Finn since their fight. They've been talking more often, which makes me happy. That's his son, and I want them to all get along. I don't have to love him, but I want my kids to think he's the best man there is. Every child needs the love of their parents.

"Are you happy about that?" I ask.

Finn shrugs, giving me his typical ten-year-old response. Heaven forbid I interrupt his video of a grown man yelling at his computer.

The doorbell rings, stopping our conversation, which was apparently over anyway. Aubrey runs to the door, and I'm right behind her.

"Noah!" she screams and throws her arms around him.

"Hey, cutie!"

Noah hoists Aubrey into his arms, and my heart races at the sight. It's been seven days since I've breathed the same air as him. Seven days of longing to touch him, and he's standing in my doorway. However, we have an audience, so as much as I'd like to kiss him breathless and possibly naked, I can't.

"Hi." I smile and lean my head on the edge of the door.

"Noah! Guess what?" Finn comes barreling toward him. "Harry Potter is on all day!"

"No way!" Noah grins. "Can I watch it with you?"

"Duh! That's why I'm telling you," Finn says as if Noah's missing the point.

I guess my boyfriend got taken away from me—by my kids. Aubrey takes Noah's cheeks and forces him to look at her.

Her eyes go big, and she squishes his face. "You have work to do, Mister."

I giggle, and Noah tries to talk with her still pushing his cheeks. "I do?"

"Yup! The animals are hungry."

"Aubrey, they're stuffed animals! They're not real!" Finn grumbles.

"Okay, guys." I put a stop to the fight that is about to begin. "Let's let Noah in the front door."

He puts Aubrey down, and she props her hands on her hips, staring up at him. "I'll go get them ready for their feeding."

Noah squats, taps her nose, and smiles. "Sounds like a plan. I wouldn't want them to be hungry."

I roll my eyes as she sways her hips. Such a flirt even at six. After she runs off, he moves closer to me, looking even better than I remember. His hair is shorter, but his beard is much thicker, and I like it. Noah shifts his weight at the same time I do. My pulse is racing, making it so I have to grip the door in order to stop myself from attacking him. "Hi." I breathe the word.

"You said that already, Mom," Finn says from behind me.

Damn it. I forgot he was here.

The corners of Noah's mouth lift. "She did," he agrees. "Maybe her memory is slipping in her old age, huh, Finn?"

"Probably!" Finn laughs. "The other day, she couldn't find her keys for an hour. They were in the fridge."

"Traitor."

Noah laughs and brushes his fingers against mine. "We'll say hi again later."

Oh, he's damn right we will.

He's the gift you've prayed would be sitting under the tree on Christmas morning. He's what I want to unwrap and play with, but I have to wait.

CHAPTER THIRTY

NOAH

"WHAT THE HELL could you possibly want?" I say as I answer the phone at five in the morning.

"We have problems." My publicist clears his throat.

Tristan is about to have problems for calling me this early. I get that he's nocturnal, but I happen to like my sleep.

Kristin shifts, pulling the covers over her head as I climb out of bed. The last week I've either snuck over to her place or met her when Scott had the kids for dinner. Since it's his weekend, she finally slept at my place, and we christened the fuck out of my condo. I don't think there's a surface in here I didn't lay her on. It was a damn good night.

One that I need way more than a few hours of sleep to recover from.

"What could be the problem?" I rub my eyes as I stumble toward the kitchen.

Coffee is required. I press the button on my Keurig and watch the much-needed caffeine percolate.

"You know that feature I told you not to do?" he asks smugly.

"The one my girlfriend wrote?" I clarify. Not that I've done any other features.

He lets out a half laugh. "Noah, you need to read it. I'm already fielding tons of inquiries, and I'm doing my best, but we need to put out a statement."

Sometimes Tristan is ridiculous. I get that it's his job to protect my image, but not everything is cynical.

"I'm sure it's not bad."

"I'm sending you the link," he says.

So dramatic he is. Once the cup is done, I grab my coffee and laptop before making my way to the counter. I try not to think about the fact that Kristin's bare ass was right here while I had her legs over my shoulders, but the mental image is too good to suppress.

"Noah?"

"Yeah, yeah, yeah," I groan.

The link loads and the headline causes my head to spin. Across the top of Celebaholic is the headline: Noah Frazier: Hollywood Heartthrob or Teenage Killer?

My head jerks back, and I blink, waiting for this to be an optical illusion.

There has to be some mistake.

This can't be what she wrote about.

Not after everything. She wouldn't do this to me. There's no way.

I scroll the page, reading Kristin's name as the author, followed by the story I've spent twenty years burying. It's like a slap in the face.

There in black and white are photos of Tanya and me at

prom, and then all the gory details regarding her death. Then the information about how I moved shortly after, changed my name and started a new life.

Everything I told her.

My chest aches with each word I read. This is a dream, a nightmare that I'll wake up from, it has to be because the woman I love wouldn't sell me out for a fucking headline.

"Noah?"

"Shut up," I bark back and read more. When I see the line about being an average Joe, I know it's her. There's no other explanation. "I-I—" I stutter, unable to get my words to come out. "She . . . Kristin is here . . . I can't believe this."

"I'll call Catherine and get her there." Tristan's voice is full of pity.

"No." I stop him. "Kristin wouldn't do this. This is a joke or something."

He sighs. "I don't know what to say, but this is a PR nightmare, and I need to get out in front of it. I've already called Celebaholic, and I'll do what I can, but it's out there, Noah."

This is what I pay him for, but I can't believe this is happening. Not after everything she and I have shared. I would know if she was playing some game. It would mean all of this was for nothing.

I think about that night I told her, how she cried for me. There has to be some sort of explanation.

"I need to talk to her first," I tell him.

"Regardless, I'm on your side, and it's my job to put this fire out."

"Do what you have to do, but I'm . . . I don't fucking know."

I'm not sure how to deal with the intensity of the betrayal rolling through me. How the hell could she think this would be okay? How could she take something I told her in complete confidence, with complete trust, and post it?

My hand grips the mug, and I start to shake. Nervous energy fills me, and I need to make sense of this. Tanya's parents received a large sum of money when I got my first big payout as a donation to the scholarship in her name. My lawyers handled it all very quietly with a lot of ironclad rules regarding what they could say about my involvement.

They forgave me many years ago and wouldn't betray me, would they? I can't see why, they knew how much I loved her. Her mother was relieved when I told her about Kristin and me. She said it was time I moved on and stopped living in the past.

I start to go down a list of people who never believed it, but why now? Why after all this time? And how the hell would any of them know about Kristin?

At the end of the day, it doesn't fucking matter, it's Kristin's article. It's her name on that post. I trusted her, loved her, gave her my heart, only to have her destroy me. And for what? Why keep going once she got the information? Why is she in my bed?

I need to talk to her before I lose my goddamn mind.

Each step I take has my heart beating louder. My emotions are all over the place, and it's impossible to get my thoughts in order.

Placing the laptop on the floor, I sit on the side of the bed, staring at her face, and do my best to ignore the stabbing pain in my chest. My throat constricts as I reach to touch her. Once this happens, there's no going back, and if I could rewind right now, I would. I'd stay in yesterday and pray that today never happens.

"Kristin?" I gently squeeze her shoulder. "Kristin, wake up."

She rolls onto her back and smiles when her eyes meet mine. "Hi."

The way she looks at me breaks me. This isn't the look of a girl who just fucked my entire career. She's looking at me like I'm her savior. I need her to give me a reason so I can find a way to fix it.

"Kristin, the article published," I say.

"Oh? I thought it was posting tomorrow. Did you read it?" She sits up, pulling the sheets over her naked body.

"Did you?"

"Well, yeah, I wrote it." She shrugs.

"*You* wrote it?" I ask. "No one else helped you?"

She tilts her head and laughs. "Of course I wrote it, silly. I emailed it to my editor a week ago, and we went over the edits a few days ago. You didn't like it? I thought . . . I wasn't sure if you would, but I hoped . . ."

I close my eyes and take a deep breath through my nose. "You thought I'd be okay with this?"

"Noah?" She touches my arm, and I pull back. "Why aren't you? I don't . . . you're angry?"

"You're damn right I'm angry, Kris. I can't believe you actually wrote that! How the fuck could you?"

Kristin shifts back and hurt flashes in her eyes. "What the hell was so bad? It's the truth!"

I get to my feet and grip my head. She can't be this stupid. I know she isn't. She knows how much it tore me apart. We sat in her bed as I fucking broke down and cried to her. There was nothing in that night where I said she should write about it.

Unable to hold it in, I turn to her and throw my hands in

the air. "I didn't know I should've specified I needed to be off the record when I told you about Tanya!"

"Tanya?" She jerks her head back. "What are you talking about?"

"Don't play dumb, Kris. You admitted not two seconds ago to writing the fucking article."

She gets to her feet, wrapping the sheet around her. "I don't know what you're talking about. I didn't write anything about Tanya."

I'm not sure if it's worse that she admitted to it or that she's suddenly playing stupid. If she were going to sell me out, she could at least stand by it. However, I'm too pissed to say a word to her.

I take the laptop off the floor, open it, and place it on the bed. "Let's not pretend. Don't insult me more than you already have."

Kristin moves to the laptop, and she shakes her head. When her eyes meet mine, they're filled with fear. "I didn't write that."

"No, you already said you did."

Her lip starts to tremble. "I swear. That's not what I sent!"

"Is it not what you sent or did you think you had more time before I read it? I can't fucking believe this. I can't believe you!"

"Noah—" She steps toward me, but I move back. "Noah, please. I didn't write that. It's not my article! I swear! I wrote about your job, the new role you took playing a man who fights for the woman he loves, I talked about how kind you are, and the charities you're involved in, nothing about Tanya! I would never!"

I grip the side of my head as I feel as if it'll explode. My

God, I'm being ripped apart. I want to believe her, but it's all there. "How the hell did everything I told you get in there? It has your name on it, Kristin! I haven't told a soul in twenty years about what happened, and then it's suddenly on the goddamn internet two weeks later? Tell me," I step to her. "Tell me how then."

I'm a rational guy, she says she didn't do it, then I need to see what she did submit. Because right now, there's nothing showing me otherwise.

"I'll show you my email! You can see that I didn't send it." Kristin grabs the laptop, but I pull it away.

Right now, I don't trust anything. I don't even trust myself. All I want is for what she says to be true. But I can't let my guard down, I'm weak to her. I have no idea if she'll delete it or try to cover her tracks. I need to be one hundred percent sure.

"Tell me your password. I'll look."

Her breath catches, and she sits beside me. "You seriously think I would do this?"

"I don't know what to think," I admit.

She drops her head and sniffs. "I thought we were better than this."

"Just show me how the article on your blog, with your name and the details from Tanya's death I told you about, wasn't you, and I'll believe you. The last thing I wanted is this, Kristin. All I fucking want is you, and I'm trying to come up with something that makes sense."

Kristin's blue eyes meet mine, and I hate seeing the anguish swirling around, but she has to give me something, no matter how small, to hold on to. "Fine, open the email and you'll see. I didn't do this to you. I would never do this to you. I love you, Noah." Her voice breaks at the end, which equally breaks me. "Erica is the editor-in-chief, she could override anything. So, I don't know, maybe someone told her, and she edited my article."

I want to be wrong. If this email isn't there, I'll grovel at her feet and then destroy the person who did this. She tells me the password, and I load her email. I go to the sent folder, praying to God the email isn't there.

I scan down and see two emails to Erica. The subject of the most recent one reads: URGENT-Use this for the article.

The email opens, and there's no hope left.

I look to Kristin, who is standing against the wall. "I guess my story was worth more than what we had. Don't worry, Kristin, I won't push you off the ledge like you just did to me. Guess it was my turn to fall."

CHAPTER THIRTY-ONE

KRISTIN

"JUST LISTEN TO ME!" I clutch his wrist as he walks out of the room. "I didn't do this!"

Noah rips his arm away and pins me with a stare filled with disgust. "Stop fucking lying! I can't look at you right now. Just let go!"

Pain slices through my heart as he rejects me. He hates me. I see it in his eyes, and my lips tremble. I need him.

"I'm not leaving!" I stand my ground as I rack my brain for anything to explain this. I didn't send that email. I would never tell anyone about his past. "We have to talk. You can't push me away because I love you!"

He gets nose to nose with me, closes his eyes for a moment before opening them again, and breathes heavily. "We're done. There's nothing more to say. I want you out of my place now."

"You have to believe me, Noah. Please, you *know* me. You love me, and we have to figure this out. I don't know how this happened, but I swear to God I didn't do this! Why would I want to hurt you? Don't you see . . . this doesn't make sense?"

"So out of nowhere, everything I told you is suddenly exposed? All the details of my life are there for the world to see, under your name and sent from your email. Yet, you didn't do it? Do you think I'm that stupid? Did you think I wouldn't find out? Or did you think you already got what you needed and didn't care?"

His words wound me deeper than anything I've ever heard before. He doesn't believe me, and I don't know how to prove it. All I know is I didn't send that email. I didn't write those words, and I didn't tell anyone what he said to me.

"What about the people who knew from your past? I'm not the only person that knows!" I grasp at straws, but that's all that I can reach for.

"You think I didn't consider that? Why would they risk losing everything now? My team handled all of that when I entered this business. And how would they suddenly know your name, Kristin? How would they have your email and send it to your boss? Explain any of that!"

"I know what it looks like, but please," I plead. "Please, give me a few days to figure out what is going on."

"Save your energy. I'll be gone by tonight."

My muscles go still, and I feel faint. He can't leave like this. There's an answer somewhere, and I need time to find it. I reach for him, but he pulls back, and my heart drops. A man, who last night couldn't keep his hands off me, will no longer let me near him.

"I'm begging you. Please, give me a minute to figure out what is going on."

Noah's bright green eyes go hard as he stares me down. "I was leaving anyway."

The smugness in his voice shakes me. He never said anything about leaving.

"Leaving?"

"I'm going to France. I got a role, and I was due there in a few days. Looks like you just made it a lot easier. Thanks for that."

So, he's been lying to me? Making me fall in love and planning to walk away?

"You promised you weren't going anywhere!" I cry out.

He lets out a sarcastic laugh. "And you promised me I was the whole damn thing. Looks like we both lied."

"Noah, don't do this . . ."

Piece by piece, our relationship crumbles around me.

"Don't." He turns with his jaw clenched. "Don't make me the bad guy here. Because right now, I'm doing everything I can not to hurt you. I'm holding back everything I'm feeling because watching you cry is killing me. That's what love is, Kris. I'm willing to have my heart ripped from my fucking chest"—Noah pounds his fist over his heart—"because hurting you makes me sick. I love you. I love *you* despite the fact that *you* did this to us. I'm not the one who is doing a goddamn thing, sweetheart. This is all on you." He shakes his head and storms from the bedroom.

I stand with nothing but a sheet wrapped around me and fall to my knees. My heart pounds against my chest as the tears fall relentlessly. "I swear, I love you," I whisper to no one.

How can this be happening?

How was it not even five hours ago we were making love, and now we're through?

I hear the front door slam, and I flinch. He can't leave me. I won't let him. I get to my feet and rush to the living room, but he's not here. "Noah!" I call out for him, but he's gone.

My already crippled heart has taken its final blow and will never recover.

Each breath is a struggle, but I make it to the bedroom, gasping for air. Losing him is too much. If he'd just come back, we could figure this out. There's an explanation somewhere, but he's given up on me. My teeth chatter, echoing through the empty room as I get myself dressed.

I grab the framed picture of us at the aquarium from his side of the bed and lose it.

Noah has his sunglasses on, I'm behind him with my head over his shoulder, Aubrey is in his arms, and Finn is jumping in front with his mouth open. How can he think this is even possible? How I feel is clear as day in the image. I love him. I let him meet my children. Why would I ever do this?

Maybe he needs time. He'll see this isn't real. He has to.

I wipe my tears and try to stop them from falling. It hurts so much.

Gathering my belongings, I do everything I can to force myself to get it together. I go over every detail of the last few days, and I can't think of anything that was out of place. I sent the email from my home, verified that Erica got it, and then I've been with Noah.

I dropped the kids off at Scott's while Noah waited at my house. Then, we came to his place, had the most intense sex of my life, ate, had more sex, and then everything imploded.

The condo feels cold, all the warmth and love we shared hours ago has evaporated. I look at the note on the counter, and the tears return.

.   .   .

I WANT you gone by the time I get back. Here's money for a cab. I thought losing Tanya hurt, but it's nothing compared to the damage you've caused me.

MY GOD, I can't take any more. He can keep his fucking money and my heart because neither of them is worth a damn. I walk to the front door, my hand resting on the cold metal, and I turn back around, trying to memorize this space.

"Goodbye, Noah," I croak as a tear slides down my cheek.

I make my way outside with a hole where my heart used to be and walk the four blocks to the closest person who will believe me.

"HELLO?" Erica answers the phone with a sleep-filled voice.

"You need to get that article off the fucking internet. I didn't write that!" I sniff into the phone.

"What do you mean?" she asks.

I don't have the time or the energy to discuss this. I need my friend and I need answers. "Just get the article down, Erica."

"Okay, okay." I hear shuffling around through the line. "I'm taking it down now, but you need to explain why I am. This article was amazing."

The tears fall nonstop as I get closer to my destination. "It wasn't. It was all lies and I never sent it. I don't know what is going on, but take it off, it's done enough damage."

I disconnect the call and head up the stairs. When I reach

the door, I ring the doorbell, now almost hyperventilating from crying so hard.

She doesn't answer so I knock loudly, hoping to wake her.

"What the fuck—" Nicole's eyes open wide, and I fall into her arms. "What happened?"

I start to sob, completely unabashed as I cling to my best friend. "He's gone. He left me."

"Who's gone? Are the kids okay?" I shake my head as she rubs my back. "Kristin, talk to me! What the hell is going on?"

Nicole pulls my shoulders back with her concern etched on her face. I didn't cry like this when Scott and I ended things. It didn't hurt half as much as this does. I see the look in Noah's eyes when he saw the email I never wrote, never sent. The way his voice was full of disappointment thinking I did this to us. His anger as he told me he was leaving anyway.

The stabbing pain in my chest is welcomed. The agony reminds me this is real, and I won't wake up in a few minutes.

"Noah—" I pull in a shaky breath. "The article and . . . oh, Nic, it's so bad. I don't know how this happened, but he's done with me. I'm so stupid for thinking this would work." My voice trembles.

She leads us to the couch and wraps me in a blanket. I curl into a ball with my head in her lap like I did when we were little girls. Nicole looks at me with a sad smile as she plays with my hair.

"Complete sentences, Kris."

"I feel like I'm dying inside."

"I want to understand, honey, but you're not making sense. What happened with the article?"

Nicole listens without saying a word as I explain the events of this morning. I flip between crying and anger when I tell her how I begged him to believe me. Yes, the evidence is damning, but he should've known. Instead, he left me there with a twenty and a note to further break my heart.

When there are no more tears left to cry, I just stare at the ceiling, completely numb.

After I'm silent for a while, Nicole speaks softly. "Would you have believed him?"

"What?"

"If the roles were reversed, would you believe he didn't do it even after seeing it all?"

"Yes." There isn't a pause or a second thought in my answer. I push myself to sit up and wait for what made her ask that.

She sighs, and her gaze shifts to the floor. "I'm saying that it doesn't make sense. How did you send your boss an email that you didn't really send about all the stuff he told you? I know you would never do that, but I've known you since I was twelve. You're not built that way, but even knowing you, I'm sitting here trying to make sense of it. I'm not a celebrity who has basically learned to distrust everyone or believe that people are just using me, but he is. You guys haven't been together all that long, and . . ."

I start to shift, not wanting to hear this, but she grabs my wrist and pulls me back to the couch. "Let me go."

"Not how this works. I *know* you didn't do it, but you've got to see the whole picture."

"Why do you have no problem believing me?" I ask.

"Because for my entire life I've wanted to be like you. I've wanted to be good, honest, loving, and half as pure as you are.

There is no way you're capable of destroying someone like that and living with yourself afterward."

"Oh, Nic, you're all those things."

She pulls me into her arms. "This isn't about me, but right there is what I'm talking about. I tell you something about you, and you turn it into me."

I shake my head, trying to shove down the next wave of hurt. "I can't do this. I can't lose him. I know it seems so crazy, but I love him and I want a life with him. I thought he was my second chance. He was supposed to be . . ."

I can't finish the words. It's all too much. Loving him was easy, losing him is misery.

"I'm so sorry you're hurting. You've had enough shit in your life, I hoped this would be different."

The tears I thought were dried return again. Hurt isn't a strong enough word. Pain, agony, wretchedness, torment . . . those come a little closer, but they still fall short.

"It would be one thing if any of it were true, you know? If I did it, I could accept him leaving and us being over. I have no answers as to how that email was sent. It's there! Sitting in my sent box." I grip my hair with both hands. "How? How did I send something I never wrote?"

"I don't know. None of it makes sense. Whoever did this, clearly doesn't want you to be with Noah. Does he have any crazy exes or anything you can think of? Anyone in his past who would want to hurt him?"

There are so many things about this that don't add up. He told me that he didn't really date and that her family was taken care of, but maybe they changed their minds. Noah and I haven't been photographed together, so it isn't like they would even know we were a thing. Unless he still speaks to them?

"Not that I know of."

"What about Scott?" she asks.

I huff and look out the window as the sun starts to rise. "I would love to make him the villain, Lord knows he plays it well, but how could he? He doesn't know anything about Noah's past. Plus, we've been getting along for the most part. Scott has a new baby on the way and future wife, why would he give a shit about me?"

"Yeah, and he's not that smart," Nicole smirks.

"There's that, too. I wish I could make sense of any of it." I look at her through blurry vision. "As much as I want to think about it, I can't. I want to see him, touch him, hear his voice, but he doesn't want me anymore."

If I had known this was all the time I'd have with him, I would've done everything differently. Looking at it now, I was stupid. Noah was never going to stick around, and I should've seen that. We live in different worlds, and believing this could've worked was reckless.

My phone rings, and I rush to find it. Maybe it's Noah. I hope with all that's inside me that it's him.

However, the name flashing throws me for another loop. Why would my cousin's wife be calling?

"Catherine? Is everything okay?"

"We should talk, babe. I just got off the phone with one of my publicists, and I read the article."

My breath hitches. "The article?"

She clears her throat. "Noah Frazier is represented—"

"By you."

"Yes, my firm handles his PR, and I'm on my way to meet with him, but I have to know . . ."

"I didn't do this, Cat," I say quickly.

"Okay." She hesitates for a second. "When I saw your name, and Noah filled me in, I was shocked to hear you were behind it. Especially when they said you were his girlfriend." Catherine muffles the phone and says something that I can't make out.

I pinch the bridge of my nose, wondering how much worse this can be. My family is involved, my kids are going to have to hear that Noah is gone, and I'm broken.

"I'm sorry," I say as my stomach rolls. There's nothing I hate more than disappointing people. "I made my editor take it down."

She sighs. "I know, but it was already out there, and nothing is ever really gone. I'm doing the best—" She stops, covers the phone, and then comes back. "Sorry, Jackson is flipping out. I'm having to stop him from losing his shit. He's not happy that you're involved."

I wish I weren't. "Tell him I'm sorry, too."

"Let me rephrase that," Catherine says. "He's not happy someone is doing this to you. Listen, we're in Tampa. He's going to drop me off and then come to you. Okay?"

"You don't have to."

"I know, but we're going to."

"I'm at Nicole's. I'll text you the address."

We hang up, and Nicole looks at me with her brow raised.

"Jackson is coming here."

"Your cousin?" she asks, her eyes going wide.

I nod.

"The ridiculously hot one that has abs on his abs?"

"Nicole," I warn.

"Yeah, yeah, he's married . . . I know. Doesn't mean a girl can't drool."

Great. Now my best friend is going to hit on my cousin, and I'm too fucked in the head to care. As if this day couldn't get any worse before nine AM.

CHAPTER THIRTY-TWO

KRISTIN

"HEY, KRIS."

"Hi," I say, and once again, the tears come when I see the pity in Jackson's gaze. I'm like a damn leaky faucet. But Jackson is like a brother to me, and I don't want him to ever see me this way.

His big arms wrap around my shoulders, and he holds me tight. "Don't cry. Don't you know men are stupid when they see tears? We can't seem to say the right things."

I sniff against his chest. "Even big bad Navy SEALs?"

He laughs. "Especially us. Just ask Catherine, it's her best weapon."

"Good to know. I'm assuming you're not here for moral support?"

Jackson looks at me and shakes his head. "No, but I am on your side."

"Right."

"Let's go talk." He jerks his head toward the couch.

As we make our way over there, I pull my shit together. I

need to be strong through whatever is coming. I've had my time to feel sorry for myself, now it's time to woman up. My life has definitely taken some turns, and I've survived them all. It hurts now, but eventually, it will ebb.

"I need you to answer me honestly, and I swear I won't judge or be upset."

I lift my hand to stop him there. I know what he's going to ask, and I'd rather not hear the words again. It's been hard enough. "I didn't write it. I didn't send it. I have no idea who did."

He gives me a sad smile. "I didn't think you did."

"Do you have any idea how this could happen?" I look to him with hope. He owns a security company and has done investigative work. Of course, I have no idea what the hell he can do to help me, but maybe there's someone he knows.

Jackson gets to his feet and grips the back of his neck. "Not yet. I need you to give me anything you can so I can start digging. I told Catherine I was getting involved because if someone is setting you up, I'm not going to sit back and watch."

I want to believe there's a way to get to the bottom of this, but I don't know if it matters. Noah is leaving, so why do I care? He obviously believes I did this. Each minute that passes without a call or text, my faith in us diminishes. I thought we were building a strong foundation. I believed in Noah enough to risk my heart again. Someone took that from me, and I'm not sure how to get it back. Or if I can.

"What the hell can we even do?" I ask him.

"Well, first I'm going to—"

"Jackson!" Nicole squeals from the hallway when she sees him. "It's been forever, you sexy beast of a man!"

Oh, Lord. "Nic," I warn.

"Oh, shut up." She smiles and rushes toward him. "He knows I'm only perusing the goodies."

Jackson gives her a hug, laughing at her antics. "Some people never change, huh?"

"Nope. Why mess with perfection? That's my motto."

I make a gagging noise. "Sorry, I was just choking on my puke."

Nicole slaps my back and then plops beside me. "Anyway, I'm betting you have some master plan to get Kristin's name cleared, don't you, big guy?"

"I need access to your email, phone, and laptop. I'm going to have my guys run a scan and see if we can find anything. You'd be surprised what people can do remotely," Jackson informs me. "Then, if we don't find anything there, we'll dig deeper. All things that are buried find their way to the surface, and I'm one hell of an excavator."

"I bet you are," Nicole practically purrs.

I smack her leg and get to my feet. "I'll give you access to my whole life. I have nothing to hide."

"Good. Let's get going," Jackson urges.

Nicole pulls me into her arms. "It'll be okay. No matter what."

"I'll call you later."

"You better."

We say goodbye to Nicole and head over to Noah's building to pick up Catherine. I tell myself the entire way that he won't want to see me, but that doesn't stop me from wanting to run inside and pound on his door. The distance we had a few minutes ago is closing, and the knots in my stomach grow.

Jackson parks along the curb, and I want to be sick. He's

inside that building. Right through those double glass doors is the only man I've ever truly loved, the only man who made me feel like I was worth something. As he puts the car in park, Catherine exits, for which I'm thankful.

I wouldn't be able to handle sitting here and waiting.

She looks back to me, takes my hand, and squeezes. "I'm doing what I can. Just know that, okay?"

The tone in her voice is a warning, but not in a threatening way. "What does that mean?"

She and Jackson share a look. "It means we need to figure this out quickly."

Realization hits me. Noah is Catherine's priority. She's going to do whatever is necessary to spin the story, and I'm going to be the target. "Noah wants you to take me down, and my dirty laundry is going to be used, isn't it?" I ask without any emotion.

Jackson pulls away from the curb and drives toward my house. Neither answer me. Their silence is all I need. She'll have no choice, and Catherine is very good at her job.

I lean my head back, close my eyes, and allow my mind to shut off. This was how I dealt with Scott's abuse. I learned how to become numb, hear nothing, see nothing, and become nothing. It's been months since I've done this, but here I am, pretending I don't exist and this isn't real. Numbness is a reprieve where nothing can touch me.

"Kristin." Catherine shakes me, bringing me back to the now.

I force my legs to move, and the three of us walk inside.

My breathing becomes labored as my mind replays scenes from the last few months. Noah sitting on the couch with Finn and watching Harry Potter. Noah and Aubrey feeding the animals in her play area. The table where he kissed me before we made our way to the bedroom. The kitchen floor where I tackled him. He's everywhere.

I clutch my stomach and double over, needing this to stop.

Catherine grips my face, forcing me to look at her. "I know this is horrible. I know that you just want him to trust you. Believe me, I wish it were that simple, honey, but we can stop this if we can find out who is behind it. Noah doesn't want to believe it's you. He wants it to be *anyone* else. He's not happy that you're gone. He loves you, he told me, but he's at a loss because everything points to you. Now, are you ready to find a way prove it wasn't?" Her eyes are filled with determination.

I hold her wrists, take three deep breaths, and nod.

Even if Noah is gone, I need to exonerate myself. I did nothing wrong and whoever is behind this needs to feel even an ounce of the pain I'm in. So, yeah, I'm more than ready.

CHAPTER THIRTY-THREE

NOAH

"HELLO, MR. FRAZIER." The brunette flight attendant smiles. "Is there anything I can get you?"

Her hair is the same dark brown color as hers. She has a little more blonde in it, and I much prefer the red in Kristin's.

My throat goes dry as I see her face, hair, body, and voice in every woman I see. None of them compare to her, and none of them have destroyed me the way she has.

"No, I'm fine."

Her red lips turn into a seductive smile. "Okay, if you need anything, I'm happy to be of service. My name is Leighanne."

I smile. "Thanks." There's no service I'll need. All I want is to pass the fuck out and wake up in the future.

It didn't take long for Tristan to get a plan together. He told me the article is down and that they are working on discrediting Kristin. I didn't want to know the details. I can't sit and watch them destroy her. Even though she broke my fucking heart, I hate that I'll be the one doing the same. For all I know, they'll paint her as a desperate ex with a vendetta or a broke single mother needing to make a name for herself.

She's neither of those.

No matter what, I can't turn off how I feel about her.

My phone pings again, and I go to turn it off, but her name flashes.

Opening it is stupid, but I've never claimed to be all that bright.

KRISTIN

> I don't know if you'll read this. I don't know if you care, but I want you to know that I love you with my whole heart. You've given me more in a few months than I got in my lifetime. I would never hurt you that way. You said you were leaving, and I'll miss you more than you can ever understand. I'll tell Aubrey that you asked me to care for her animals, and Finn that you hope to finish the marathon soon. No matter what you think of me, I will cherish every moment we had. I would give anything to see you just one last time, but I know you don't want to see me. I swear that I'll find out who did this.

I sit on the plane, rubbing my forehead as I read the text over and over. The same thoughts continue to circle, leaving me without any answers.

Has the campaign against her started?

Will she hate me and tell the kids that I'm the reason their mother is being attacked?

Will she suffer at my hands?

I picture Aubrey's little blue eyes and big smile falling because my people are making her mother look like a gold digger. Finn will hate me, but not more than I'll hate myself.

I text Tristan.

> Do not destroy Kristin. No matter what, I love her and I don't want this. Find another way.

I power off the phone without waiting for a response.

I hate every part of this, but there's no other explanation I can find. I spent all day going over any possibility as to how this wasn't her, and I came up short. Even though in my heart, I don't see how she could be so manipulative and go to such lengths to sell me on it, my head sees the facts. There's no way to argue with them.

The plane takes off, and I leave behind the woman I love and the life we could've had.

"Noah! Let's go!" The director bangs on my trailer door, and I groan.

My head is pounding, and I have the worst cottonmouth known to man. I've spent the last two days drunk as fuck, courtesy of the minibar in my hotel. It's the only way shit doesn't hurt so much. I've avoided people, sunlight, food, pretty much anything other than vodka.

How the hell I'm going to work today is beyond me. I can barely stand, never mind focus on my lines. I lean back in the chair and close my eyes. If I can just get the spinning to stop, I'll be good.

The door creaks open. "Mr. Frazier?"

"What?" I bark.

God, I'm being such a prick. This isn't me. I don't get

drunk, be late, or treat the crew like shit. I'm the guy who makes everyone laugh, look who's laughing now.

"Sorry to bother you, but Paul is about to lose his mind," the petite blonde informs me.

"You were called to the set thirty minutes ago, and I was told not to leave here without you."

"Shit. Okay, give me two, and I'll be ready." It's an effort to keep my tone even.

She nods and exits but probably doesn't go very far. Time to get it together. I have a job to do, and no one here gives a damn that I'm emotionally spent. All they care about is the movie.

I splash water on my face and chug the coffee sitting on the table.

"Ready?" she asks when I swing the door open.

"Sure." I'm ready for bed, that's about it. "What's your name?"

"Elisa."

I smile the best I can. "Nice to meet you. So, Elisa, what scene are we filming first?"

She sighs, and I can practically read her thoughts . . . *shouldn't you know this?* "It's the scene where your character, Alexander, meets Autumn's character, Kiersten at a party."

My alcohol fog evaporates at the name of my character's love interest.

"Kiersten? The script read her name as Hailey."

Again, Elisa gives me a look, telling me I'm clearly a fucking idiot. "You got a revised script in your hotel the day you arrived. Did you not see all the changes?"

I would've if I read something other than the Surgeon

General's warning on the back of the bottle. "I've had a rough few days. My girlfriend kind of sold me out, I fucked her entire life up by saving my own ass, and I drank enough to forget. I'm clearly not on my game."

Elisa opens her mouth to say something, but I hear someone shouting at me. "Noah!"

My eyes are definitely playing tricks on me. "Tristan?"

Why the hell is my publicist in France?

"Oh, so you do know who I am? Good to know since you refuse to answer your phone." He glares at me.

"Can't answer a phone that's not turned on."

He rolls his eyes and then smiles at Elisa. "Honey, can you give me a few minutes with my *client*?"

Elisa looks at me, and I nod. "Sure. Not like I have a job to do or anything. This will be a new record for people getting fired on set," she grumbles as she walks away.

"I'll make sure she's fine," Tristan says. "I've been calling you nonstop."

Once I landed in France, I felt no need to talk to anyone. My self-restraint isn't strong enough not to call her, text her, or get right back on a plane if I heard her voice, so I chose to shut down.

There's no point in explaining that to him. Tristan doesn't understand any of my apprehension. He's pretty much heartless and thinks I should've went after her the second I had confirmation that Kristin betrayed me.

Funny thing about love, it makes you a fool who can't purposely put the other person in pain. I would rather spend the rest of my life miserable than see her suffer for a single second.

"Why are you here?"

"There's something I need to tell you, and I was instructed that it had to be in person."

My mind spins worse than it was before, I can't handle another bomb dropping. If he's here, this can't be good. "Just handle whatever it is," I say and start to walk away. "I'm not in the mood for bad news."

"Kristin didn't do it," Tristan says, and my feet stop moving.

I clench my fists, trying to keep myself steady. I don't want to hope what I heard is true. There's a possibility that I might still be drunk and be dreaming this conversation. My stomach twists as I turn to face him. "What?"

"She wasn't the one who sent that email, Noah. We had the IP address traced, and it didn't come from her house or yours. It came from someone else."

Please, let this be real. Please, let this be true.

"Who, then? How do you know any of this?"

"I can't say much more than that at this point. I need to have plausible deniability in case this gets out. There's a lot of legalities that she'd prefer me to be in the dark about, but Catherine is one hundred percent sure that it wasn't Kristin. She wouldn't give me more than that before demanding I get on a plane and get to you."

I shake my head while looking at the sky. I want to believe this more than anything. Losing Kristin has been agonizing.

"You're sure?" I press harder.

"Look, Catherine was ready to do what she had to, but she has proof that there was no way Kristin could have sent it."

The guilt I feel crumbles on top of me, making it hard to breathe. I didn't believe her. She told me, begged me to listen to her, and I walked away. Even after I hurt her, she sent a text to tell me she loves me.

I hate myself.

I should've stayed, trusted her, and found a way to prove she didn't write it.

How the hell could I have known, though? All the signs pointed to her, and I just accepted it. Deep down, I never believed it, but I've learned that people you love can do horrible things. People I've trusted have betrayed me, and I didn't want to be a fucking fool again.

Too late for that.

"So I was wrong?"

"Yes, we all were."

No, I was wrong. I'm the person who she needed to trust her. This is on me.

"Goddamn it!" I slam my fist into the wall. "I'm such a fucking idiot. I threw her away so easily."

Tristan places his hand on my shoulder. "What were you supposed to think, man? You had an article with her name on it, on her blog, sent from her email address. It was more than coincidental."

"I fucked up, Tristan. I fucked up, and she's never going to forgive me."

He blows a heavy breath from his nose. "She'll see where you were coming from. It was an impossible situation. You did what anyone would've done."

That doesn't change the fact that I left. I turned my back on her just like people did to me.

"And you think she'll just forget that I gave up on her that quickly?"

He shrugs. "I don't know. I really don't, but in this industry, you did exactly what you needed to. She has to understand that."

"You don't get it. She isn't in this industry like that."

"How not? She's a celebrity blogger, Noah. You do a feature against my recommendation, and fall in love with her, and then, suddenly, something we've managed to keep out of the press is leaked after you confide in her? Come on."

Who cares about the reasons? There's a right and a wrong, and I chose wrong. I abandoned her when she clung to me, begging me not to go. Maybe I did what was best for my career, but not for us, or her, or my damn heart.

I lean against the wall and let my head fall back, making a loud *thump*. "Others believed her." I point out. "Someone else dug deeper."

Tristan leans against the wall next to me, and my self-loathing grows. I could've done whatever necessary to prove she didn't or really did. It isn't as if I don't have the capability, but I saw no other possibilities than it was her.

"Yeah, but you were on the receiving end of the shit-storm. You had to deal with the fallout. I don't know, I think you were in a no-win situation and you did the best you could."

Maybe he's right, but my heart told me she didn't do this. I never thought she was capable of being that deceitful, it was my head that wouldn't get on board. Now, I've lost her, and I have no idea if I can get her back.

I rub my now-throbbing hand. "Tell me you guys didn't do anything to ruin her."

"I was able to discredit the site as fake news, but it's out there. We held off a bit more than I would've, but Kristin is related to Catherine."

"Catherine your boss? The woman who came to my house is part of her family?"

He raises his hands and drops them. "One and the same. She wanted to leave no stone unturned before we did something to Kristin that we couldn't take back. Catherine's husband runs a security company, and . . . well, I was told I don't want to know more than that. They ruled out her sending it about thirty minutes after you sent me the text from the plane."

Jesus Christ. For two days I've been drinking myself stupid while she's been sitting there thinking God knows what.

"Does she know that no one has told me until now?"

"I don't know. We're skating a really blurry line because, typically, we'd never have any contact with her. With Catherine's husband being her cousin, it has made handling this a little different."

None of that matters to me. I told him in the beginning I didn't want to even make a statement. "I care about her, I don't care about the lines."

Tristan chuckles. "I know you don't, but you're our client. I'm paid to fix your messes, and family or not, our loyalty is to you, not anyone else."

"Right." I run my hand down my face. "I want to know who is behind this. I want them destroyed. I don't give a fuck what you have to do, but they framed her . . . I'm not holding back this time."

"Understood," Tristan says with a smug smile. "I wish I could give you more, but you need to talk to Kristin if you want details."

Whoever did this is about to have the wrath of Hell brought down on them. I'm going to destroy their world like they did to ours. However, I'll let Tristan handle that, I have something else that needs to be fixed, and right now, that's all I care about.

"One more thing," I say. "There's about to be another mess you're going to have to clean up."

Tristan chuckles. "Yeah, that's the second reason I'm here. I figured I'd have some work to handle in France."

CHAPTER THIRTY-FOUR

KRISTIN

THREE DAYS.

Seventy-two hours.

Four thousand, three hundred, and twenty-eight minutes without a word from Noah. Now twenty-nine minutes. Not that I'm counting or anything.

I hoped when he heard it wasn't my computer or house it came from, he'd call or text or . . . something. I guess he either didn't believe it or doesn't care.

Broken promises and a broken heart are all I have left of what we shared.

My nerves are shot, I haven't slept, and waiting for Jackson to call with the results from the trace on who sent the email is slowly killing me. I need to know who is behind this. I'm desperate to find out who hates Noah or me enough to set out to ruin both of us.

A knock at the door sends my heart into overdrive. Maybe it's Noah? I leap up from the couch and rush there. What am I doing? I stop short.

He left me without so much as a backward glance. I was completely expendable to him, and he hurt me, worse than Scott ever had.

Another knock.

It's probably not him anyway. I open the door, and sure enough, it isn't. It's Catherine, and she brought a bouquet of flowers.

Seems we're changing the way we handle breakups. Usually, it's ice cream, cake, Four Blocks Down music, and a lot of wine. Flowers is a new one.

"You look like shit," Catherine says, looking at me with her face scrunched in disgust. "Have you showered since I saw you last?"

"Do you have news?" I blurt out, needing to know if that's why she's here.

"These were on your porch without a card," she tells me.

I don't care about the stupid flowers. For all I know, they are from the person who did this to me, and they want to torture me further. I want information about the email. I'm tired of waiting and getting nowhere.

Jackson explained it wasn't as easy as I thought. Since this isn't technically a crime, there isn't a judge in the world who would grant a subpoena to get the IP records. Therefore, he has a friend who has a friend who may or may not have been in the CIA. And then he assured me I should know nothing else.

"Catherine?"

"All I know is Jackson said to meet him over here when I got done working inside Starbucks since I needed to be away from the kids, so I'm here. Go get in the shower, make yourself . . . human, and we'll sort through the info."

"I can't—"

"Go." She points. "I know you're on pins and needles, but he could be another hour. Are the kids with Scott?"

"Yes. I told him I wasn't feeling well and needed him to keep them for a few days."

"Good, go make yourself not look like ass."

Not wanting to argue with her, I head to the bathroom to clean up. I stand under the water, washing away the layer of depression that clings to my skin. There's nothing I can do about my situation. I know I'm not responsible, but it's everyone else I have to convince. Then, I see Noah's face as he walked away. The disappointment, anger, and resolve that we were through.

I close my eyes, leaning my back against the cold tiles, and let the tears fall.

He didn't come back.

He must know it wasn't me, and it didn't change anything.

I'm alone again, only this time there's no relief.

A knock on the door causes me to jump. "Kristin?"

I clear my throat, hoping to cover the ache in my voice. "Yeah?"

"I heard from Jackson, he'll be here in twenty."

"Okay."

Once I'm finished, I get dressed and toss my hair in to a messy bun. Hopefully, the clean-but-still-distraught look is more acceptable than who-cares-if-I-die and dirty. I head into the living room where Catherine is pacing as she talks to someone on the phone.

"I understand. Yes, well, there's not much I can do." She pauses. "Did you tell him I'm doing exactly what I would if she weren't family?" Catherine listens to the other person, and I stay quiet. "He can't do that, Tristan. I don't care that it's already done. He . . . wait, what do you mean . . . done?" She's talking about Noah. I know she is. I shouldn't listen, but I can't stop myself. I have to hear something about him. "Just like that? And you're just telling me now? Why the hell did you wait a *day* to call me?" Catherine groans. "Fine. I'll deal with this here, and you handle the mess there. Let him know he made a big mistake. Big."

My shattered heart falls to the floor, he isn't coming.

I purposely make a noise, not wanting to hear anything else.

Catherine's eyes meet mine, and she smiles. "Okay, I'll call you later." She tosses the phone onto the table, and her eyes are soft. "You look better."

I shrug. Right now, I feel the pain of losing him all over again. It wasn't until then that I realized how much I thought he'd come back. I wanted it so much, and now it's clear there isn't another chance.

"Jackson has news?" I ask and mentally cringe at the sound of my voice.

"Kris." Cat walks over, and I shake my head.

There's a knock at the door, and Catherine touches my cheek. "It's going to be okay, trust me. Jackson will fix it, he always does."

I nod. She walks to the door, and I head to the kitchen for something to help settle my nerves. I have a feeling Jackson's news isn't going to help the knots in my stomach. The pantry door is open, and my lips turn up when I see the package of cookies that Noah and Aubrey shared on the shelf. His face was priceless when I caught them.

There will be no more cookie-faces for them.

Eventually, thinking of him won't hurt. Noah will become a distant memory of a possibility that failed. Time will erase the history, cause the love we shared to fade like an old photo, but today, the vivid colors slice through my soul. There will come a day when I can't remember what his voice sounded like, or the slight variances of green in his eyes. As much as it's killing me right now, I don't want to forget.

I need to stop this. I can't keep doing this to myself. Noah is gone, it's over, and I have to live. On the other side of the door are the answers I need so I can start to move forward.

The door swings open, and I look up right before the cup of water I'm holding falls from my numb fingers.

It isn't Jackson standing in my living room.

I look to Catherine, who just smiles. "I'll go wait for my husband outside," she says before skirting out of the room.

"Kristin." Noah's deep voice fills the air.

This isn't real. He can't be here because I heard her on the phone . . . I'm going insane. I drop to the floor, grabbing the cup, and then his hands appear next to mine.

I close my eyes, hating my head for playing these games. "Stop," I whisper to myself. "Stop this now."

When I open them, he's still here.

"I need to get paper towels," I say on autopilot.

"We have to talk," Noah says, but I can't do this. My breathing is labored, and I shake my head. "Then I'll talk, and you can listen . . . I'm so sorry. I'm so fucking sorry that I didn't listen to you." His voice cracks. "I was wrong, Kristin. There never should've been a doubt in my mind that you didn't do it, but I didn't know what to think."

I don't know what to think. I'm still not completely sure I'm not having a complete mental breakdown. Between the stress of the last few days, and dreaming he would come, I don't trust myself. I lean back onto my heels, staring at the bright green eyes I've longed to look at again.

"You're here?" I ask.

"I came as soon as I heard," Noah answers. "I left the set, and probably my career, but I needed to see you."

I start to believe this is real. Noah is in my living room, and I can't get a grasp on what I'm feeling most. I go from relief, to anger, to hurt, to hate, to love, to disappointment, and then back to relief. The vicious circle swirls like the blades on a helicopter, threatening to cut me with each rotation. No longer caring about the mess on the floor, I get to my feet. I need to feel taller, stronger, and find my courage to get my answers.

"Why?" I breathe the word. "Why now? Why are you here?"

Noah doesn't touch me, but I can feel the warmth of his body. I draw in a deep breath, smelling his cologne, and start to tremble. He's close enough I have to tilt my head to look into his eyes. "Because I love you."

Love doesn't break you in half. If he loved me, he would've seen that I would never want to cause him pain. If he loved me, he would've stayed and fought beside me.

"Love me? You left. You walked out and left the country." I take a step back, reminding myself of all the hurt I've felt. "You can't come here saying you love me when it was so easy for you to leave."

"Easy?" Noah reaches for me, but I move. If he touches me, I'll cave. "Please . . ." He drops his hand and the hurt flashes in his eyes. "There was nothing easy about leaving you, sweetheart. Nothing."

I shake my head, choking back my tears.

"Getting on that plane was the hardest thing I've ever done. I spent two days drinking myself to sleep. I couldn't eat, work, or function. I saw your face in every person. All I wanted to do was come back to you."

"But you didn't," I remind him. "You didn't come for me. You didn't even call."

Noah's face crumples, and he releases a heavy breath. "I fucked up. I knew if I stayed here, I'd never be able to keep away. I was so angry and hurt that I wasn't thinking clearly. You have to believe me, I know I was stupid."

Yes, he did fuck up. "You broke my heart, but more than that, you truly believed I would do that to you."

"What choice did I have, Kristin? It was all there."

"You could've had faith in me!" I cry out. All I wanted was a chance to prove my innocence. He couldn't even give me that.

Noah looks down. "I did, but it wasn't just the fact that every possible explanation was negated, it was everything. I'm not perfect." His eyes meet mine. "I know I have things I need to work through. Trusting someone isn't easy for me. My father left when I was a kid, my girlfriend was my heart and soul but was leaving me for something better, and then almost every person I considered a friend turned their back on me. Not to mention the fact that this industry is a breeding ground for people who will sell you out. Eli is my only friend. Everyone wants something from me, and then I met you . . ."

My heart is in my throat as I listen to his reasons. I can understand and empathize with how difficult trust is for him. I can't say that I wouldn't be jaded, but we were supposed to be different. I've never given him a reason to think I'm like those people.

"I only wanted you, Noah. I didn't want your money, fame,

your story . . . you did that. You were the one who pushed it. I would have never written about you if I had my choice. You hurt me."

He closes his eyes as if he's in pain and nods. "I know, and I hate myself for it. I could tell you all the reasons I had in my head, but it doesn't change anything. The idea that you were behind it was more than I could take. I've never loved a woman the way I love you, Kristin. It was all there in front of me, the timing, the email, the facts that you knew were in black and white. To think that you could betray me was . . . I don't even have words to describe how much it hurt."

I don't need the words because I lived it. The way I felt for him was otherworldly. I loved Noah with every fiber of my being. He was the happy in my ever after. Giving him my heart was the easiest decision I ever made and the hardest thing to take back.

"It took you three days. Three days that we knew it wasn't me, but you didn't even text me. Nothing until now? Why? What changed that made you decide I am worth fighting for?" I find myself inching closer to him.

His hand lifts, brushing against my cheek, leaving a burning streak in its wake. My lungs ache as he stares down at me. Noah has always taken my breath away, but right now, I feel as though I'm frozen. If I move just the slightest bit, I could crack.

"I didn't know until about fourteen hours ago, and I was on a plane within an hour. So, I didn't know." Noah's nose brushes against mine, and I breathe him in. "You're worth everything. I'm a fool who doesn't deserve a second chance, but I'm begging for one. Just this once, forgive me, and I'll never hurt you again."

I close my eyes, and a tear leaks out. Resisting Noah has never been something I've done. From the day I met him, he's had a hold on me, and I don't think I ever really had a choice in falling for him.

"Don't make promises you can't keep," I murmur while moving my hands to his chest. "Just promise you won't walk away."

Noah's hands cup my cheeks. "I promise. I don't think I could survive it."

Our eyes meet, and I see the regret he feels. "I know I can't."

"Forgive me," he pleads. "Forgive me for being so stupid."

"I did the second I saw you."

It's the truth. The instant our eyes met, my forgiveness was his. Noah is the man I love. He's the one I want beside me, and even if he left, he came back, and I can't endure the thought of giving up on a second chance.

Noah pulls me to him as his lips move closer. My fingers slide up his chest and around to the back of his neck. I hold on as our mouths find each other. He kisses me like a dying man who found a cure to save him. For the first time in three days, I'm able to breathe without pain in my chest. His tongue slides against mine, and I could cry.

Our lips break, and he presses his head to mine. "I didn't know if I'd ever get to kiss you again," he admits. "I would've never stopped trying to win you back."

I wrap my arms around his waist, rest my head on his chest, and melt into his embrace. "You wouldn't have had a hard fight."

He rubs his fingers against my spine. "I love you, Kristin."

"I love you," I say, lifting my head to look into his eyes.

"I'm sorry I didn't believe you."

It still stings, and we still don't know who did this, but he came back.

"I can't fully blame you. If I didn't know with absolute certainty I didn't do it, I would have a hard time. This person went to a lot of trouble to make it look like I wrote that article."

Noah brings his lips to mine several times before releasing me. "Do you know who did this yet?"

"No. The only proof we have is that it wasn't any of my devices. There are still a lot of unanswered questions swirling around. Who else knows? How did they find out? And how did they know to use my information because I can't tell if it was to destroy me or you? But Jackson is on his way with those answers, I hope," I tell him.

This person is deeply entwined in both of our lives. There are names I refuse to entertain because I can't fathom they would do something like this, but Noah and I don't know a lot of mutual people.

"What did you tell the kids?" he asks.

"They've been with their father while I tried to pick up the pieces."

Noah rubs his thumb against the top of my hand. "I'll fix what I broke. If it's the last thing I do, I'll make you feel safe with me. You will never have to question how I feel, sweetheart. I love you with every piece of me, and I won't doubt you."

Catherine clears her throat as she opens the door. "You guys okay?"

Such a loaded question. But when I look in Noah's eyes, I don't have to think too hard. He's here. He loves me. And he believes me.

I look back at her with a smile and then nod. "I think we're going to be just fine."

"I was hoping you'd say that." Cat grins.

The door opens the rest of the way, revealing Jackson is standing right behind her. They both come inside, and Jackson doesn't waste a second before asking, "Are you sure you want to know all of this?"

I look to Noah and then back to Jackson. "Not a doubt in my mind."

CHAPTER THIRTY-FIVE

KRISTIN

I'M PHYSICALLY SHAKING.

My hands are trembling so bad that Noah has to drive. Nothing should surprise me anymore, but this seems insane.

We sit outside the address, staring at the red door belonging to the person who Jackson claims his people traced the sender to.

"Are you sure you want to do this?"

"What choice do I have?" I ask, turning to look at Noah.

His eyes find mine, and he gives a sad smile. "We can move on. We can know what we know and be happy together. None of it changes how I feel about you." He takes my hand.

I appreciate that he feels that way. God knows I was in no way prepared for the information Jackson gave me. It still doesn't make sense. How did Scott even find out any of this? I've never breathed a word of Noah's past. I thought the person behind everything was on Noah's side, not mine.

Yet, here I sit, having to confront someone I loved. There's no way I can let this go and pretend it didn't happen.

"Noah, you flew to France because of this. You left me because someone hates us enough to do this. Someone used my name to publish that, and I'm not going to just sit back and let it slide. I want to know why. I want to know *how*. And I want to see his face when I tell him none of it matters because I have you anyway."

He leans over the console and kisses me. "I want to know it, too, but I believe you when you say you didn't tell anyone. I don't need anything else. This can go in our past and stay there."

"I appreciate that, but I need this. I've allowed him to control my life, to try to destroy me, and it ends now. I have to confront him and stand my ground."

I hope he understands what I'm asking. I've spent most of my life cowering, that isn't happening ever again. If I were to sweep this under the rug, he would win. This time, the victory is mine.

His lips touch mine again. "I'll follow your lead, sweetheart."

"I love you."

"I love you."

Noah was incredible through the whole conversation. Jackson explained that we couldn't use the information he obtained—illegally—for anything other than confronting Scott. We had to swear we'd never breathe a word about how he got it, which we don't know the logistics anyway. All he said was he has someone in his office who is very good at getting things without a subpoena. So, really, this is for Noah and me . . . well, me.

"Let's go." I release a heavy sigh and exit the car.

Noah meets me up front and takes my hand. We walk up

the path while my stomach does flips. I'm not sure how I'm going to get through this, but I know I have to. I choke back the bile that rises as I ring the doorbell.

The door opens, and there's no turning back.

"Kristin?" Scott's voice is full of confusion. "What are you doing here? You said you were sick, and I told you I'd bring the kids around six."

"I needed to talk to you, and it couldn't wait." I try to hold back the anger threatening to escape. "Are the kids still with your parents?"

He takes a step outside, pulling the door closed behind him. "Yes, I told you they were twenty minutes ago, why?"

Scott looks to Noah with a scowl and then back to me. "Do you know what an IP address is?" I ask.

"Of course I do." He crosses his arms over his chest. "I work for a technology company. I'm a little surprised you know what it is, though."

Yes, the pathetic housewife who knows nothing learned a lot in a few months. Jackass.

I continue on with my questioning as if his comment didn't happen.

"So, you know they're traceable?"

"No, Kristin, I must've missed that part in my fifteen years with the company." He huffs. "Is this something your new boyfriend taught you? Are you really here when you're supposed to be on your deathbed to ask me about an IP address? If you wanted a few extra days with him—"

"Shut up, Scott."

"I'm in the middle of something. Why don't you tell me what was so urgent you had to run here right this minute so we can move on?"

Noah squeezes my hand when I move forward, but Scott thinking he can talk to me this way makes me want to choke him. I don't need his condescending bullshit. "Don't push me, Scott. I'm doing the best I can not to flip the fuck out."

"Over what?" He drops his arms and spits the words. "You're the one who's acting like a psycho."

"Watch yourself," Noah warns, placing his hands on my shoulders.

"Or what? You come to my house and threaten me? Give me a break with this bullshit." Scott laughs.

Noah has about six inches and thirty pounds of pure muscle on Scott. He'd crush him like a bug. "Talk to her like that again, and you'll find out."

Scott blows him off, but I see the flash of fear in his eyes. He turns back to me and huffs. "Now, tell me what the hell you think I've done so I can get back to my second mistake inside."

The fact that he's going to stand here and try to play stupid and call me names is all I need to go over the edge. I pull out of Noah's grip and move closer to the man I had children with. The man that I loved against my better judgment. I've put up with a lot of shit, but this is the end of the damn road.

"Mistake? I was a mistake? Whatever."

"I have a fucking headache. Could you get on with it?" He grumbles.

He's about to have a much bigger one.

"I *know*, Scott! I know what you did to me! I can't believe you!" I lose it. "If you know that IP addresses are traceable, how did you think you'd get away with it, huh? Did you think Noah and I would sit back and let you try to ruin us?"

"What the fuck are you talking about?" Scott steps toward me. "I don't care about you and your fucking love life. I'm waiting for you to marry your stupid boyfriend so I can stop paying you monthly."

He's so concerned about the money all the time, what does he think will happen when I lose my job? Does he think he'll suddenly pay less? Idiot. "Getting me fired wasn't the smartest move then, was it? How do you think the courts are going to like it when I have no income and they make you increase the checks each month?"

Didn't think about that, did he? I'm not stupid. My lawyer told me we could re-file if he gets a raise or I do. And as far as marrying Noah, I have no plans on that until I bleed Scott for every penny he owes me. I've earned it for all the hell he put me through.

"Fired? Kristin, I don't have a clue what the hell you think I've done, but you're clearly in need of therapy." Scott runs his hand down his face.

"Oh, I need therapy? That's rich. Says the man who spent fourteen years making me feel small in order to make himself feel better."

"Can you control your girlfriend?" Scott says to Noah.

"Don't fucking talk to me," Noah warns. "I assure you, I'm doing just about everything I can not to lay your worthless ass out. It's only because of Kristin and those kids that you aren't already bleeding. But if you touch her, I'll enjoy pummeling you."

Scott laughs. "Right. Lay me out. Whatever you say, dick-head. Why don't you spit out what I did already so we can let your theatrics play out?"

I take a step back and stare at him. I've known him a long time. Scott has a tell when he lies. He rubs his nose and sniffs. It was how I always knew in the back of my mind what was going on, but I never would accept it.

He hasn't done it once.

He's actually confused.

"You really don't know?"

"No, I have no clue what the hell you're doing yelling at me about IP addresses and whatever other bullshit you're accusing me of."

"You didn't do it." I breathe and look back at Noah.

Noah's green eyes fill with concern. "You're sure? We know . . ."

I shake my head.

The last few weeks things have been good between us. Scott and I have been able to speak calmly, do a semi-decent job at co-parenting, and he was nice enough to keep the kids for me.

It's what is confusing me. If he is willing to try to be civil, why he'd do this. And then there was the fact that I couldn't figure out how he found out about Noah's past.

It doesn't make sense.

"Jesus Christ, Kris! I don't even know what—" Scott yells and the door opens.

"What is going on out here? I'd like our neighbors not to think things have gone downhill since I moved in." Jillian puts her hands on her hips.

And then it hits me.

It wasn't Scott.

Scott isn't stupid enough to jeopardize the relationship with his kids and not smart enough to go through the trouble of hiding his tracks. He's too narcissistic to think he'd ever be caught. He always had Jillian handle things for him. She was the mastermind who helped him get around things with me.

This reeks of this bitch.

"I was just telling Scott something, and then it occurred to me that you should probably be here anyway."

Jillian jerks her head back. "Me?"

"You are marrying him, aren't you?"

She smiles and touches her stomach. "I am."

Scott rolls his eyes.

"First, tell me, how did you do it?" I ask her.

Noah's hand tightens minutely on my shoulder.

"Do what?" she asks.

I can't fucking stand her. She's an even bigger idiot than Scott is if she thinks she has this all figured out. If she ever thought I was a bitch before, she's about to see what happens when I no longer care about upsetting Scott.

"How did you manage to get all the information on Noah and send the email to my editor?" I watch her, waiting for the tiniest sign. "Did you somehow hack my laptop? Put some sort of device in my house? Are you that obsessed with me that you had to go through all the trouble to try to hurt me, or are you really in love with Noah and just want what you can't have?"

"Fuck you, Kristin."

I laugh. "No, honey, you fucked yourself. You see, I know what you did, and the sad part is that it's all under Scott's name, so he'll go down for your crime. It's fraud and identity theft to name two," I bluff. There's no crime, but I'm hoping they don't know that.

Scott's head jerks to her and her jaw drops a smidge before she catches herself.

"Excuse me? Scott, you're going to let your *ex-wife* accuse me of this? At our house?"

"What exactly are you talking about, Kristin?" Scott turns back to me. "What information and email?"

I summarize the article and then tell him that someone accessed my email and sent it as though it were me who had written it. Scott's eyes widen when I tell him how Jackson—who he's terrified of—was informed by law enforcement that it was able to be traced back to Scott's home.

"Are you fucking kidding me?" Scott bellows. "Tell me you didn't do this, Jillian! Tell me you didn't—" He clenches his fists.

I give her a small smirk, knowing she has no way out.

It's the straw that broke the bitch's back, too. I can almost see the steam coming out of her ears when Scott reprimands her in front of me.

"You know nothing." Jillian sneers at me. Her hands rise, and in an instant, Noah has me pulled back and he's shielding me. "You think you're so smart! You think you've got it all figured out, huh? All it took was one phone call, and I had every detail I needed."

"Unreal!" Scott throws his hands up.

"You called who?" Noah asks. "How did you even get details?"

She rolls her eyes. "Scott had a monitoring software installed on her phone. It's how we were able to sneak around without you knowing. You sent your little text exchange about Noah's real name and I knew there was something there."

I gasp. "What? You had that installed on my phone?"

He was tracking me? Was there no limit to what he was willing to do? I feel as though I'm living in the Twilight Zone. These people are out of their freaking minds. I'm truly stunned and feel a little stupid. All this time I've been living away from him, but he's been monitoring me?

"This is fucking crazy!" Noah raises his voice. "Let's go, sweetheart. This is illegal, and we're going to my lawyer."

Scott grabs my arm to stop me. "Kristin, please."

"Don't fucking touch her." Noah puts himself in front of me again, almost chest to chest with Scott, who releases me immediately.

"It was what we got for Finn when we gave him a phone. *I* didn't know it was on yours."

Jillian snorts. "Yeah, right. Anyway, I have access. I got his real name and the rest was cake. Your dead girlfriend's parents were all too willing to talk to your new girlfriend." She grins at Noah.

Holy shit. She really is unglued. She called Tanya's parents, said God knows what, and then sent the article. I have never in my entire life wanted to physically harm someone as much as I want to hurt her right now. I wish I had been diabolical enough to record this. Then maybe we could've done something legally against her. But we came here thinking it was Scott. And for better or worse, he's Aubrey and Finn's father, taking him down only hurts them.

But this is a horse of a different crazy . . . the certifiable kind. She needs a straightjacket with her next OBGYN visit.

"Are you *insane*? What the hell is wrong with you?" Scott screams at her.

The list is endless.

"You pushed the wedding back after seeing her with *him* one time!" She yells back in his face while pointing to Noah. "I know you still love her! You love her, and you're going to leave me!"

"So, you go through my text messages and decide to fake an article? Do you even understand how irrational this is? You got *him*! You won, Jillian!" I shake my head. Scott isn't a prize, but she clearly thinks he is. "He's all yours, I've got the man I want, and it is not Scott. But what more do you want? You slept with my husband and got knocked up by him, but yet, you still have to find a way to make my life miserable? Why? What did you think you were going to gain by doing this?"

She rolls her eyes and ignores me.

"Answer me!" I yell.

She turns to Scott and glares. "I didn't wait two years for you to get rid of *her* to be second place!"

Maybe if she went after, oh, I don't know, a single man, she wouldn't have had to wait at all. Instead, she chose a man with a wife and kids. She's a real peach.

Jillian's eyes meet mine, and I clench my fists. "He picks your stupid kids over me. He picks you over me." Her voice is dripping with disdain, and I lose it. It's time for Mama Bear to come out. No one talks about my babies like that.

I move closer to her, keeping my hand in Noah's. I might need him to restrain me. "Don't you *ever* talk about my children. You're a homewrecker that will never be happy in your life. You want what other people have but don't take care of what you do have. You see, I've won and you've lost. Noah is still right here, and now Scott sees you for what you are—a spiteful bitch."

I will never understand someone capable of doing this. I turn to my ex-husband, a forty-one-year-old grown man who is allowing a twenty-four-year-old to ruin his life, and throw out my demands, "She is to be nowhere near my kids. If you want me not to call my lawyer, then you better figure out how to make that happen because I won't allow her to be part of their lives or mine."

"You're not going to have to worry about that. She won't be around anyone for much longer."

There are consequences to every choice we make, some are positive, like leaving Scott and finding Noah. Others are negative, like choosing to be a sneaky, paranoid, whore and ending up with nothing. I'd say I've made some of the better decisions.

Noah is the treasure chest after the shipwreck of my marriage. We may not have had a map leading us to the X that marks the spot, but we have one another as guides.

I look back at him and smile.

"Ready, sweetheart?" Noah grins.

There's nothing else that they can do to me. I'm not the girl I was all those years ago. I don't play games or allow people to run my life. I'm stronger with Noah beside me, but I'm also strong on my own. Standing here, watching these two, makes me realize how much better my life is. My relationship isn't perfect, no one's is, but Noah and I don't want to hurt one another.

Even when we were tested, we found our way through it. He flew thousands of miles just to work it out.

I love him more than I knew I could love another man.

"I'm ready. Everything is behind us now."

He leans in and kisses my lips. "Damn right it is."

CHAPTER THIRTY-SIX

NOAH

"I UNDERSTAND, sir. I promise, I'll be there by the end of the—"

"Day," Paul my director tries to finish my sentence.

Yeah, that's not happening. There's no way in hell I'm leaving tonight. "Week."

Paul groans. "Noah, we've worked together in the past, and this has never been an issue."

"Which is why I'm asking for two days." I push back.

Kristin is passed out on the couch with her feet in my lap. We got home about two hours ago from—hell, I don't even know how to refer to it—her ex's house, I guess, and she practically collapsed.

"Fine. Not an hour more than that, or I'm recasting your role and you can remember why you'll never work in Hollywood again." Paul disconnects the phone.

I sit here, looking at her, wondering how I'm going to leave again. Everything is a fucking mess, and I can't go knowing she isn't taken care of. However, Kristin is resistant to any form of help.

Well, help she knows about.

This is for her own good, but it's also for my peace of mind. I want to care for her. I need to give her back what I took.

I send out a few emails and get things rolling. I have two days to spend as much time with her as I can and get back a little of what we lost.

"Daddy, do you know that kids grow more in the spring?" Aubrey's little voice comes through the walls from outside. I rub Kristin's leg, but she doesn't move. "And that horses sleep standing up? Oh, and did you know that a group of whales are called a pod?" She fires off more. I move Kristin's feet and head to the door.

"Did you know little sisters are the most annoying people ever?" Finn says, and I have to stop myself from laughing.

"Are not!"

"Enough fighting," Scott says as I pull the door open.

"Noah!" Aubrey yells and rushes forward. "Did you feed the animals?"

I chuckle and squat in front of her. "I did. They were hungry."

"I know." She huffs dramatically. "I had to do it myself because you were not here."

Seriously, this kid is the cutest thing that was ever created. I don't think anyone stands a chance against her powers. She's going to be big trouble when she sets her sights on some boy.

"I'll do better next time, I promise."

She sees something behind me and bolts. "Mommy!"

I stand and watch as Aubrey practically belly flops on top

of her mother. "Hi there, Aub." Kristin's voice is hoarse from sleeping and the six-year-old who just knocked the wind out of her.

"What's up, Finn?" I smile, and he fist bumps me.

"S'up."

Scott stands there, and he's the one who looks uncomfortable this time. He's lucky those kids are his. If they weren't, I'd beat the shit out of him. He isn't worth it, though. I will, however, be happy to watch Kristin take his stupid ass back to court if she wants. One slipup is all it will take.

"Scott," I say, extending my hand.

I can feel Finn watching. I'm not ever going to let him see me as less than the man I was raised to be. My father may have been gone, but if my mother ever met someone and he disrespected him, I'd never forget it. A boy, no matter how he acts, wants his father around.

I was able to hide my feelings pretty well as a kid. It didn't stop me from wishing he'd come back on my birthday or writing it on my Christmas list.

Tough kids hurt the deepest at heart.

Scott places his hand in mine. "Noah."

Kristin's hand slides up my arm and comes to rest on my shoulder. It's the most she's touched me in front of the kids. "Thanks for bringing them home. I'll see you in a few days."

I go to shut the door, but he stops it. "She's packing now. Just so you know. I found out she was never pregnant and . . ."

"Okay then." Kristin nods and closes the door with a soft click.

"You okay?" I ask.

"I'm fine. Sorry I fell asleep."

"Don't be," I assure her.

In the car home, she was quiet, but I've learned she needs that time. Kristin spent a lot of her marriage in her head, and bit by bit, I'll get her to come out from there. She doesn't have to be afraid with me. Just the same as I'm going to have to remember she isn't like everyone else.

"How long are you here for?" she asks with sadness in her eyes. "We didn't even talk about that . . ."

"I have two days, sweetheart," I tell her as I touch her cheek.

"Damn."

I feel her pain. The last thing I want to do is leave. However, before I do, I have a lot of shit to take care of. Speaking of which . . .

"Where's your phone?" I ask.

"My phone?"

I raise my brow. "Yes, the phone that got a lot of trouble started."

She grimaces. "That phone."

Kristin walks over to her purse and hands it to me. I don't say anything. I grab my keys to the rental car and head out the door.

"Noah!"

"One minute!" I call back over my shoulder. I place the phone on the road right in front of my tire, climb into my car, and start it up.

Kristin stands on the porch with a confused look on her face. Maybe she missed the fact that I'm going to run the piece of shit over?

I shift into drive and roll forward and backward a few times. Should be good.

"What the hell are you doing?" she asks while descending the steps.

I grab the smashed device from the ground and smile. "You'll have a new one with a new number in a little bit," I inform her as I place the crushed phone in her hand.

"You're insane! That was my phone!"

"It sure was." I wait for the fight.

"You smashed it."

"I did. And I'd do it again."

No one is going to threaten us again. I don't care if I have to run over a hundred phones. Kristin, Finn, and Aubrey will have new, fully paid for, phones within thirty minutes. I'm sure I'm going to get shit for getting Aubrey one, especially since I don't think she currently has one, but . . . I have to keep my status. There's no way I could handle the damn puppy-dog eyes.

"You ran it over." Kristin looks at the remnants in her hand. "We could've just taken the program off my phone or changed my passwords, but . . . Noah!" She smacks my arm. "How the hell am I going to get all my contacts, you moron!"

I didn't even think about that. "The cloud?"

"Such a man! You act first and think second." She starts to walk away mumbling. "Get a new phone now, no job, but sure I can go to the store and say"—Kristin stops walking and yells through her gritted teeth—"my *idiotic,* jealous-for-no-reason boyfriend ran the phone over. I'm sure that's covered under the warranty. Oh, but don't worry, he backed over it again for good measure."

I laugh, which earns me a scathing look, to which I laugh again.

"The new phones are coming. No need to go to the store."

She glares at me, puts the phone on the porch, and grunts. "I can't with you."

I climb the steps two at a time and grab her waist, pulling her flush against me. "You can't without me." My voice is low.

"You think so?" Kristin asks coyly, all the feigned anger melting away as her hands come to a rest on my chest.

I purse my lips and nod. "I do."

"What makes you so sure, Mr. Frazier?"

"Just a hunch."

"Hmm." She plays with the collar of my T-shirt. "Maybe you're right, but how can you be sure?"

"I could kiss you." I tease her. "I could see if you melt in my arms like you usually do when I get all 'flirty,' as you call it. I would be able to tell by the way your body gets tight because you want more, but you can't have it."

"You could." Kristin keeps her tone even, but I see the fire in her eyes.

She has no idea how much control she has over me. If she asked me for anything, I'd find a way. This girl fell into my life, pulled me into the water with her, and I never came back up for air. Even when everything fell to shit, I couldn't convince myself it was over.

I don't see my life without Kristin in it.

"I should," I say as I bring our lips closer together.

Her back arches as my hands glide higher. Just as I finally touch her perfect mouth, I hear a noise.

We both turn our heads to find Finn staring at us.

Shit.

I drop my hands and take a step back.

"Gross," Finn says.

Most of our time together has been just the two of us, so I'm going to need to remember to tone down the PDA around here.

"Oh, give it up," Kristin says with a laugh. "You like Noah, and he gives you street cred."

"Did you seriously say street cred?" I ask her with laughter in my voice.

She shrugs. "What? Isn't that what it's called?"

"Yeah, if you're my age!" Finn corrects her.

"Stop being so jealous of my coolness." Kristin saunters away while flipping her hair back. "I'm like, the leader of the cool people. You all worship at my house of cool."

Finn and I share a look and burst out laughing. "She needs help, Noah. Please"—he drops to his knees and folds his hands—"I'm begging you. Fix her before it's too late."

"I wish I could, but apparently, she has the keys to the house of cool." I shrug and follow her back inside.

I watch her flop onto the couch with her arms stretched, and she takes my breath away. She has her hair pulled up, isn't wearing any makeup, and is rocking a pair of black shorts and a baggy T-shirt. Yet, she's the most beautiful woman I've ever seen.

Kristin tilts her head and gives me a smile that makes me want to take her to the bedroom and wipe it off her face. "What?"

"Nothing."

The corners of her eyes crinkle. "You're thinking something."

I smile and walk to her, place my hands beside her shoulders, and brace myself over her. "I'm thinking I'm a lucky man. Not only did I find you, I made you love me, and I've convinced you that you need me. I'm batting a thousand here."

Kristin rolls her eyes. "Sure, it was all you, stud. I lured you in with my adorable awkwardness, gave you mind-blowing sex, and I have the ultimate weapon."

I chuckle silently. "What's that?"

"Noah!" Aubrey yells from the back of the house. "You forgot one!"

She takes my face in her hands and grins. "Her."

I laugh against her lips and give her a searing kiss. "I love you."

"I love you, too. Now, go feed the animals before I find myself a new man who can keep up."

"I'll give you keep up." I start to lean back toward her, but Aubrey makes her appearance.

"No-ah!" She says each syllable separately. "They could die. They need to eat."

The laughter from the couch doesn't go unnoticed. She's really helping me here. I look to Aubrey, and her eyes go big again, just like with the damn cookies. What is it with little girls? Do they have some kind of magical powers? It's witchcraft or something because here I am, taking her hand and letting her lead me away so I can feed her stuffed animals so they don't die.

"Have fun!" Kristin says as she leans her chin on the top of the couch.

"We will later, sweetheart. Mark my words."

"I'm counting on it." Kristin smiles, and I start to think of anything other than her naked beneath me.

Aubrey looks at me with a huge grin. "I bet the animals would *loooove* some cookies."

I let out a loud laugh and snuggle her. "Do you promise to eat your dinner and not tell your mom?"

She nods.

I'm so going to pay for this.

CHAPTER THIRTY-SEVEN

KRISTIN

~ Eight Months Later ~

"I CAN'T BELIEVE we're packing you *again*," Nicole grumbles as she stacks the box she closed on top of another one.

"And again, you're acting like you've done anything of value," I toss at her.

The construction starts in three days, and I've procrastinated long enough. I can't screw around anymore. Plus, Noah will be home tomorrow and he thinks I've already done it.

Oops.

"Feed me." She lies on the floor. "I'm dying."

She's worse than Aubrey. "Get up or you're going to wish you were dead."

Danielle comes out from the bedroom, looks at Nicole, and drops the box close to her head.

"Bitch!" Nicole snaps. "I almost had a heart attack. One inch over, and you'd be paying for my plastic surgery."

"You got up, mission accomplished," Danni smirks.

"I miss Heather," I say, feeling a little wistful. "She should've come home for this."

She was home last month to sign the deed over to me. I officially own this house . . . with Noah.

We didn't want to move the kids again since they're settled in, and Heather was beyond happy when we approached her. I think she enjoys knowing another family is going to raise their kids in the house that means everything to her.

Or she's just tired of the things that need to be fixed and likes that it's now my problem.

Noah was adamant that if we were staying, we were going to make it ours. So, on one of his long weekends home from France, he did what he does best and hired a freaking crew to dismantle my life.

My phone rings, and my assistant's number flashes. "Hi, Erica," I say with the phone to my shoulder.

"Kristin! It's like a disaster here. I don't know what to do. You were supposed to come in today, and you didn't. I've got four phones ringing and the spread is all wrong. It's just wrong, I need you to fix it. Fix it."

Oh, Erica . . . why did I ever think this was a good idea?

"Take a deep breath. It's going to be fine. I looked over the spread yesterday and made an adjustment. The magazine is going to be perfect," I say in a calm tone.

She's always freaking out. This is our second circulation, and we managed just fine with the first one. You'd think it was her virginal prom night with the way she goes nuts. Now, I get why she had a meditation room, the chick is always needing to do some deep breathing.

"Okay. Sure. Yes. I'll be okay. You'll be okay. I'm going to get my boxed water, have myself a nice bike ride, and pray to the ocean tonight."

I pretend as if she didn't say any of that.

"Sounds fun, honey. I'm sure the ocean will love that you're asking for its help. I'm working now, good luck."

I stand, scratching my head and wondering what I was drinking when I brought her with me to the magazine. I was drunk. I had to be.

And what the hell is boxed water? Boxed? Water comes in a bottle, but this is Erica, and I've learned to ask fewer questions.

"Everything all right?" Danni asks.

There's only one word to describe it. "Erica."

My friends love her in theory. She's been beside me, defending me, and being my biggest champion from the moment we first talked. But even if Noah didn't destroy me personally and professionally—I was done. Catherine explained that she had to discredit the article, which in turn made Celebaholic and me look shoddy.

As much as I'd like to pretend I'm sad about that, I'm not. I hated that job. Now, I own a lifestyle magazine geared to women over thirty. We focus on home, relationships, children, workforce things, and style.

I. Love. My. Company.

As long as I don't say the name.

"Ahhh." She nods. "I McGettit."

Nicole bursts out laughing, and they high five. Assholes.

"You can McGet out of my house."

"And what would we do for entertainment?" Nicole asks.

"I hate you. All of you. Hate."

Erica was in charge of submitting the forms for the corporation. I pre-signed them because I was heading to France for two weeks. She was supposed to fill out the information once I decided on the name, which was Friends in Chic, and submit it. Easy as pie.

She felt our name wasn't trendy enough. So, she named our very prestigious magazine, *Kristin Mc-Gets-it*.

Nicole and Danielle lock arms and giggle. "We accept your hate and raise you a we don't care."

My friends are on my list—with Erica.

Aubrey runs in with a box, stopping our little feud. "Auntie Danielle, can you make sure Aunt Nicole doesn't take this please."

Nicole raises her brows and laughs. "Me? What did I do?"

"You said you were going to eat my animals for lunch." Aubrey pulls the box to the side. "They're not food."

"I was hungry, and you wouldn't let me leave the room."

Aubrey looks at Nicole and shakes her head. These two are a mess separately, but together they're out of control. Aubrey will do things that remind me so much of Nicole it's scary— I'm not excited about it. I love my best friend, but her mother was gray very early in life.

"You're not supposed to eat them, Aunt Nicole!"

Nicole sighs dramatically. "Fine, I won't eat them."

Danielle and I watch with our hands over our mouths as Aubrey extends the box and then pulls it back.

"Aubrey Nicole!" Nic yells. I think she likes using my daughter's middle name as much as she can. Had I known that naming Aubrey after a friend meant she would be like that person, I would've chosen Heather.

Maybe.

Aubrey takes the box and walks off.

"That girl." Danielle laughs. "I can't, she's the best thing ever."

"I happen to agree." Noah's deep voice causes my pulse to spike.

He's here. He's here early.

"You're home!" I break out in a run and leap into his arms.

"Hi, sweetheart." He laughs as he barely catches me.

I kiss his lips over and over, beyond ecstatic that I can. It's been over three weeks since the last time we saw each other. The kids and I video call with him every night, but it isn't the same.

I can't touch his skin, feel his warmth, or smell his cologne. My memory is no substitute for the real thing.

His green eyes are a little lighter and his skin has a bronze tint to it. For the movie he just wrapped filming on, he was playing a spy, and they had him buzz his hair. I thought I would hate it, but he's insanely sexy. If I could've climbed through the computer and have him assault me with his weapon of mass destruction, I would have. However, we don't do anything over the internet. So . . . I had to wait.

I don't have to wait anymore. My tongue delves into his mouth, sliding against his tongue, tasting all that is Noah.

"If you're going to have sex right now, can I watch? I'm all for free porn," Nicole asks from behind us.

Noah breaks the kiss, and I pout. "Go away!" I yell to them.

"Don't worry, there's more of that," Noah promises before kissing my nose.

There better be. I want more now, though. Stupid friends and kids who are keeping us from a little mattress dancing.

"Danni will watch the kids . . ." Nicole offers.

Not a bad idea. I open my mouth, but Noah speaks first. "Good to know."

"I think he thinks I'm kidding." She nudges Danielle.

Danielle snorts. "I think he's afraid you're not."

"Or that I'd join in," Nicole jokes. "I'm game for either."

My legs are wrapped around his waist, and I attach myself like a second layer of clothing. He looks down at me with a mischievous grin. "You planning to interject?"

"She couldn't handle your hotness, baby. Plus, she likes two *men* . . ."

Noah chuckles. "You two have spent too much time together lately." His voice drops low so only I can hear. "Tonight, we'll see what else has rubbed off."

Oh, there will be lots of rubbing tonight. I wiggle my brows and smirk. "I'm counting on that, hot stuff."

"I missed you." Noah twists a little as I continue to hang on him. "You getting down so I can move?"

"Nope."

I'm perfectly content like this. I have three weeks' worth of hugging to make up for. I almost feel bad for him, but then I don't. For the last eight months we've dealt with long flights, time zone issues, his ridiculous filming schedule, press inquiries about our relationship, and me starting my new job. It's been hell.

It's finally over.

I'm clinging to this moment because I've needed it—I've needed him.

"Okay then." He smiles and walks into the living room with me. Noah gets to the couch and drops me on my back with him covering me. "Nicole, you wanted to watch, right? I think someone should entertain the kids—"

"Noah!" I yell and push him off me. "Oh my God, you're such an ass."

"Maybe, but you love me," he challenges.

Damn right I do. But then again who wouldn't? He's freaking perfect.

And hot.

And sweet.

And loves me with his whole heart.

But I do love messing with him and feel it's my duty to keep him humble.

I shrug. "Eh, you're all right."

"I'll give you all right."

Danielle clears her throat. "As fun as it is to watch you two, and by fun, I mean not at all, your contractor will be here soon, and you're not even close to ready."

He gets to his feet and pulls me up with him. I slice my hand across my throat as she talks, but she doesn't take the hint. Damn it.

"Wait?" Noah turns. "Not done?"

I rock back onto my heels and tuck my head down. "I might have exaggerated a little about how much I got done . . ."

Thankfully, my son emerges, saving me from the lecture that was sure to come. "Noah!"

"Hey, man!"

Finn and Noah's relationship has grown even with the distance. It's been great watching them bond. Noah has helped settle everyone without even trying. I'm happier, the kids are happier, and all of us are excited about the changes.

Noah asked Finn's permission to move in, and after that, they were best friends.

"Are you back for good?" Finn asks.

"Yup. I'm here for forever."

His eyes meet mine on the last word, and I melt.

Noah is my forever.

Noah is my always.

EPILOGUE
KRISTIN

~ Eight Years Later ~

"OKAY, we're going to have a detailed plan so we can get through the whole park in one day," Noah tells us while we lean against the car. "I've got the map and times when we'll eat. This is going to be perfect!"

He's out of his mind. I'm not sure why he thought Finn would want to come to a theme park—with his very uncool parents—for his birthday—but here we are. No amount of arguing would sway him. He swears this is the best gift possible.

Not like Finn would much rather have my suggestion of a car.

Finn leans toward me and whispers, "He realizes I'm not a kid anymore, right?"

"Just pretend you are excited, and I'll get you the car," I say conspiratorially.

My son perks up as if he's suddenly very into this. "Yes, a

plan would be great. I am super excited. We should not delay and waste time. Lead us away to our day of jubilee," he says each word with sarcasm.

Jubilee? Really, Finn?

"Sell it better next time, dude." I clap his shoulder.

Noah sighs. "I thought you'd want to see the Harry Potter stuff."

Sometimes he's the most brilliant man in the world, others he's clueless. Finn turned eighteen today, which I cried for a good hour over, and Noah wanted to surprise him. This morning, he woke the kids *at six in the morning* with a box for Finn. There's no way the kid didn't think they had car keys. The box was small and there was a Gryffindor lanyard wrapped around it.

Hell, I thought it was car keys, and I knew it wasn't.

Finn's face was priceless when he opened it.

Aubrey on the other hand blatantly laughed at him. However, the sun shines out of Noah's ass, so she was overly excited just to try to get her way.

I see through her crap. Noah, not so much.

I walk over and touch his cheek. "You tried, honey. It's the thought that counts."

"He used to love this stuff," Noah huffs as we walk behind the kids.

"When he was *ten!*" I laugh.

"I like Harry Potter, and I'm not ten," Noah retorts.

"Yes, but you act like you are."

Noah growls and wraps his arms around my waist, rubbing his scruff against my neck. "I'll give you ten."

"Noah!" I laugh and try to get out of his hold. "Stop! You're tickling me!"

"*Mom!*" Aubrey hisses. "You're embarrassing us. God, sometimes I can't believe I'm related to you people." She huffs and crosses her arms. "I'm almost glad I couldn't bring a friend now."

Oh, the peril of a fourteen-year-old girl. I swear the attitude started at twelve and each year she becomes more pleasantly awful. It doesn't help that her father and Noah spoil the shit out of her. I'm the bad guy.

"Yell at Noah. It's his fault we're here."

She tosses her hand up in the air and keeps walking. "Whatever."

Noah looks at me and we both start laughing. It's a running joke in our home that he can do no wrong. As much as it's annoying, I'm glad my kids love him. He's truly a second father to them, and when he goes on set, we all miss him terribly.

"I love teenagers," I mutter.

We get through the entrance, and a few people snap pictures as we pass. It's easy to forget how famous he is. To us, he's just Noah Frazier, the man who leaves his underwear inside his jeans, doesn't know where the hamper is and likes to fart when it's too quiet. To the world, he's a two-time Academy Award Winning actor who can do no wrong.

Tomorrow, we'll have photos all over social media with hundreds of questions about why we aren't married, if we're really in love, and speculation that the only reason I'm with him is to further my career as an editor.

"Yo!" Finn yells. "Old people, keep up!"

"I'll give him old people," Noah threatens, and I laugh.

"If the shoe fits," I tease him.

Noah still looks almost the same as when I met him. He's

that asshole guy who doesn't have any gray hair, where I have to go to the salon every four weeks to keep myself from looking like I could be his mother. His body is still hard in all the right places, and all his equipment is in working order. Me? I'm lucky I can fit in my leggings without busting a seam.

"You're lucky I love you," he says before swatting my ass and jogging to the kids.

My butt doesn't feel so lucky.

We get back into Harry Potter world, and it's clearly big news that Noah Frazier is here. People flock to meet him, take photos, and well, touch him. I get it. I want to touch him, too. He's pretty freaking hot for an old guy. Plus, he's gotten ten times more famous since we met. The movies he does now are blockbusters, and he's definitely an A-lister now.

He looks at me with the I'm-sorry-I-hate-people face, and I smile back with my I-get-it-you're-kind-of-a-big-deal look. Finn walks over, clearly detesting this aspect of our lives.

"And this is why we can't go anywhere." He huffs and points.

"You know he hates this as much as you do. But it's been almost a decade, time to get over it."

Then I remember at eighteen, your life is really all that matters.

"Finn!" Noah waves him over.

Oh, this should be interesting.

Aubrey is, of course, next to him, soaking up the attention that Noah Frazier is her almost daddy. Yes, she actually calls him that. I have no words for that girl sometimes.

"Oh, my God," a flock of girls start squealing. "You know Noah Frazier?"

Finn turns, and a cocky smile that I've never seen before

spreads across his face. "Yeah, I do. Did you want to meet him?"

"Yes!" They giggle and bounce up and down. "How do you know him?"

"He's practically my stepfather." He lifts his chin with pride.

Dear Lord. I can't believe I'm watching this. "Finn, you should probably save him," I say, reminding him I'm right here.

"Right. I'll save Noah, no problem." He pops his elbows out and smirks. "Ladies, care to join me?"

Oh, for fuck's sake.

My son, the player in training. I should apologize now to the females of his future. I take no credit for that one.

He inherited his stupid from his father. The other bad habits are from Noah. I gave him life, brains, and then they ruined him.

After a few minutes, Finn's groupies get their photo and my—I don't know what to call him anymore—comes over. I loathe calling him my boyfriend. I'm almost fifty, and I feel lame saying it. Not to mention we've been together for a long time and when we say almost ten years, people look at us as if we're mental.

We're married in every way other than on paper. We own our home, own the magazine company, and co-parent with Scott. Noah is as much their father as my ex is. I like Noah. Scott . . . not so much.

"You good?" I ask as he puts his arm around my shoulders.

"I am now. I wanted a normal day out with you and the kids." He sounds dejected.

"This is our normal, Noah. Plus, it looks like Finn has found new friends."

We both turn back, looking at him and his harem of hoochies. "That's my boy." Noah beams with pride.

I'm so on my own.

We walk along through the realistic town that lives in a novel that brought the men I love together. Aubrey is in the shop we're outside of, probably with Noah's American Express Black Card . . . the one I keep confiscating and he keeps giving back.

All in all, even with him overindulging her, she's a great kid and gets straight A's, is in the honor society, and is a member of the student council. Aubrey and Noah share a love of animals, and she volunteers at the ASPCA on the weekends. I may not love her mood swings, but she's a good girl with a good heart.

"Hey." Noah stops me.

"What?"

"Next week is our anniversary," he says, wrapping his arms around my waist as he smiles. I've been with him for a long time, and he still makes my heart race.

"It is." I grin, knowing it is. "Did you get me something good?"

"You'll have to wait to find out."

"Aww." I rub the back of his neck. "You got a refill of Viagra?"

Noah's mouth falls, and he goes expressionless. "You know I don't, and will not ever, need that."

I giggle at the tone he takes. As if I wasn't fully aware. "I know, babe. Your wand works just fine."

"Damn right. I'll Slytherin to your Hufflepuff tonight if you need me to remind you."

I burst out laughing. My arms wrap around my stomach, and I let it go. "Oh my God. Only you!" I continue on. "Only you would make a freaking dirty joke here."

Noah laughs along with me, wrapping his body around mine and walking me as I try to stop my hysterics.

He's ridiculous and irresistible.

We make it over to the side with a lot of stares as Noah guides me and I make a spectacle by being goofy. After we've settled down, he kisses me, and we stay in each other's arms.

I watch his green eyes fill with so much love it becomes hard to breathe.

I love him so much that sometimes I feel like I could burst. Each day with him, I cherish. Sure, he drives me nuts and I make him crazy, but it only makes me appreciate what we have even more.

Most people don't have the baggage we do, but we carry it together.

"When are you finally going to agree to marry me?" Noah asks with his playful grin.

I get this every few months, and the answer is always the same. "Do you love me?"

He smiles. "With my whole heart."

"Are you leaving me?"

"Not going anywhere, sweetheart."

"Do you trust me?" I question him as I stare into his eyes.

Noah's gaze turns serious and his deep voice leaves no room for wonder. "With my life. Do you love me?" he tosses it back.

"In every fiber of my being."

"Are you planning to find yourself a new sexy actor?"

I smile. "There's no one sexier than you, baby."

Noah laughs, kisses me, and then asks the last question in our little skit. "Do I give you everything you need?"

In my peripheral, I see Aubrey and Finn standing there, watching. With the four of us here, I feel complete. For so long, I've said there was no reason to get married, it's just become a thing. I've been happy, blissfully so, and I was getting paid from Scott, so there was that, too. But I see it in Noah's eyes each time I say it.

And right now . . . I don't want to say what I'd normally say.

In this moment, I want to give him back something he's given me.

"Noah," I say softly. "Will you do something for me?"

Confusion sweeps across his face. "Anything."

"Ask me to marry you, just one last time," I say with my heart pounding against my chest.

Noah sucks in a breath, looking for something in my eyes. I don't know if he's worried I'm joking, but I let him see everything in my heart.

I wait, praying he was serious.

"Kristin, will you marry me?" His voice is thick with emotion and there's a shine in his eyes that wasn't there a moment ago.

I take his face in my hands and smile. "Yes, I'll marry you."

Before I can kiss him, two sets of arms are wrapped around us, and tears of happiness stream down my face. I have everything I could ever need . . . and more.

Gah! How amazing is Noah? I mean, swooooon! I hope you loved

*them as I did and you get a lot more of this tribe in Nicole &
Callum's story:*

Read Not Until You Free in Kindle Unlimited

*She's got so much snark and Callum is just the man to take her on!
Just click the title above to see what I mean!*

***

*This book meant the world to me and as always, I couldn't let
them go. So, I write an EXCLUSIVE to my newsletter only bonus
scene! If you'd like to gain access ... keep swiping!*

BONUS SCENE

Dear Reader,

Thank you so much for all your love and support and I hope you enjoyed One Last Time! Do you want more of Noah and Kristin? If so, just sign up with the link below and you'll get an email with the exclusive bonus chapter that you can't get anywhere else!

SIGN UP HERE

BOOKS BY CORINNE MICHAELS

The Salvation Series

Beloved

Beholden

Consolation

Conviction

Defenseless

Evermore: A 1001 Dark Night Novella

Indefinite

Infinite

The Hennington Brothers

Say You'll Stay

Say You Want Me

Say I'm Yours

Say You Won't Let Go: A Return to Me/Masters and Mercenaries
Novella

Second Time Around Series

We Own Tonight

One Last Time

Not Until You

If I Only Knew

The Arrowood Brothers

Come Back for Me

Fight for Me

The One for Me

Stay for Me

Willow Creek Valley Series

Return to Us

Could Have Been Us

A Moment for Us

A Chance for Us

Rose Canyon Series

Help Me Remember

Give Me Love

Keep This Promise

Whitlock Family Series (Coming 2023-2024)

Forbidden Hearts

Broken Dreams

Tempting Promises

Forgotten Desires

Co-Written with Melanie Harlow

Hold You Close

Imperfect Match